KISSING SERENITY

"Chilton," Serenity asked warily, "are you still trying to get me down onto the floor?"

"No need, madam," the marquess responded tightly. "If you will notice, you already are."

"Why, so I am!" Serenity exclaimed. "Goodness, I must get up!"

"No, you must not. And be reasonable, Miss Hoffenduffle," the marquess argued. "You shall perish if you do not stay covered."

"Yet it is not at all proper, Chilton," Serenity sighed, flopping back down upon the piled blankets.

"No one questions that, madam, nor the fact that neither of us wishes to be in this improper situation, but we are. And while in the midst of it, we must endeavor to do what we must to stay alive."

"Very well," Serenity placidly smiled, next passing several moments in which she stared at the ceiling and played with a series of curls.

The marquess chuckled softly. Then, tucking his hand beneath his cheek, he gave in to the compelling need simply to look at the woman lying so close beside him.

"You drive me daft," he at last whispered, his dark gaze bleeding into hers.

"I know," Serenity breathed. "You do the same to me."

"I know that, too," the marquess responded, slowly, ever so slowly, closing the distance between their whispers.

Their lips touched as softly as the touch of fairy wings . . .

Books by Jenna Jones

A MERRY ESCAPADE

A DELICATE DECEPTION

TIA'S VALENTINE

SAVING SERENITY

Published by Zebra Books

Saving Serenity

Jenna Jones

Zebra Books
Kensington Publishing Corp.
http://www.zebrabooks.com

ZEBRA BOOKS are published by

Kensington Publishing Corp.
850 Third Avenue
New York, NY 10022

Zebra and the Z logo Reg. U.S. Pat. & TM Off.

First Printing: February, 1998
10 9 8 7 6 5 4 3 2 1

Printed in the United States of America

For my mother
—Betty VanDyke Gorton Jewel—
a steadfast spirit
1915–1997

Prologue

England—Winter 1824

"Oh, Proppie, I have forgotten my reticule!" Miss Serenity Hoffenduffle exclaimed as their hackney rounded the corner into the dismal prospect of Cannon Street, giving them a view, had they been looking, of the mansion of Edward III. "I vow, I should leave my feet behind if I did not require them to maintain my boots."

"Never mind, darling," her sister, Propriety, replied, calmly smiling as she closed the carriage drapes against the chilly evening's heavy, intrusive fog. "I shall have Bunting bring it to Charity's Hands straightaway upon my return to Uncle's town house."

"Oh, would you? Before I retire I am certain I shall find myself in need of something inside," Serenity stated, her blue eyes still animated with the excitement of yet another of her nightly escapes.

"Undoubtedly," Propriety agreed, a half smile curving one corner of her mouth, "since I am persuaded your bag contains everything that has ever passed through your hands. However, I judge returning to Aldford Street for it would be too hazardous, Rennie. The commotion would surely awake Aunt and Uncle from their after-supper snooze."

"And all would have to be explained then, would it

not? . . ." Serenity nodded, her smile fading somewhat with her slowly drawn breath. "Not only my teaching the children at the charity's school, but more, why I am now living on its premises."

"Uncle would never understand such a risk to your reputation," Propriety affirmed, "no matter that the headmistress's illness left you no choice."

"Nor would Chilton, I fear," Serenity sighed, fingering aside a portion of the curtain so as to ascertain their location, watching as the carriage next headed south to pass by Dick Whittington's house in College Hill before it again turned to the east into Cloak Lane. "He can be such a high stickler at times."

"Ah, yes, Chilton . . ." Propriety sighed, her arched brow aptly expressing her opinion, "your *fiancé*, the marquess . . . my own dear James's brother and, thankfully, his antithesis. What has happened to the curmudgeon of late? I have not seen him about."

"Curmudgeon, indeed," Serenity scolded after breaking into light laughter. "He is not, and you know it. At least not for several years yet. At his present age, however, I should say that he is merely rather . . ."

". . . Irascible?"

"Definite in his opinions," Serenity chuckled as the hackney drew to a halt before a six-storied brick building of grimy exterior and unimpressive design. "Yet I love him more than life. And in answer to your question, you have not seen him because he has been much present at Lords of late. Parliament has once again been trying to deal with Catholic Emancipation, and, as usual, is solidly split on the issue between the Whigs who wish it and the Tories who do not."

"How dreary," Propriety commented disinterestedly, tugging back the curtain to glance up at the school's flaking, black-lettered sign.

"Not a bit of it," Serenity again chided with a patient smile. "And you should be a bit more concerned, Proppie.

It is horrid to deny any British citizen the right to vote or to attend Oxford or Cambridge, not to mention the right to hold municipal office. And this in spite of the fact that many important people in government support it, you know—Sir Robert Peel, Canning . . . even Londonderry before his suicide. Until recently, they had slowly been gaining support, too, for their cause. Unfortunately, word reached Lords not long ago that the Dublin lawyer, Daniel O'Connell, has formed an organization called the Catholic Association and has been collecting what he calls 'Catholic Rent' from others of his faith. He says that he plans to use it only to gain emancipation from Parliament. Members of both houses are suspicious, however, that his intention is perhaps less straightforward than that."

"Serenity, where on earth do you hear such things?" Propriety asked after this lengthy assault upon her feminine sensibilities.

"I read them, of course," Serenity replied, ignoring Bunting's opening of the carriage door and the offer of his hand, "in the *Post*. Now, I am certain you are wondering, Proppie, why Parliament should object to such a move. It is because the rent is being required from the very poor as well as the rich, causing those with very little to have even less. Of no small consideration, too, is the fact that the collection has been amounting to more than two thousand pounds a week, and that, of course, is two thousand pounds that Parliament isn't able to collect. So it is quite a muddle, you see. The Tories are for passing a law restricting such associations; the Whigs against. Chilton has said that the debates are quite heated."

"Which is more than I can say about this carriage," Propriety complained. "Do get out, dearest, so that Bunting might close the door."

"You are impossible, Proppie," Serenity laughed, at last moving to take the footman's hand.

"And you are a bluestocking," Propriety countered with

a grin, "betrothed to the veriest curmudgeon. Do you think that Chilton suspects?"

"That I enjoy intellectual pursuits? Chilton *knows*," Serenity replied, dropping down to the slush-covered ground, "and accepts it, I believe, though he is not much pleased. But if he were to learn about my living here . . ." she added, surveying the facade of the building, setting the thought adrift.

"Yes," Propriety finished much more soberly. "I misdoubt the humble vicar's daughter would not still be a prospective marchioness. Well, we shall just have to see that that does not happen," she added after Bunting had once again closed the door. "Now, dearest, do go inside and lock the door quickly. I am not at all comfortable in this neighborhood even though Bunting rides above."

"Nothing shall happen, Proppie," Serenity insisted as the footman mounted the school's steps to open its door for her. "Taking over the school for Mrs. Burton has proven to be a magnificent scheme."

"Nevertheless, I am quite put out of countenance. It is such an oddly forbidding night, Rennie, is it not? And there is only old Mr. Perkins about to prevent you from being entirely alone in this awful district."

"I shall be fine," Serenity again reassured, kissing her sister through the carriage window. "Good night, Propriety."

"Good night, dearest," Propriety replied.

For long moments Propriety remained, however, watching Serenity quickly cover the short distance to the sturdy oak door, then, before signaling the hackney driver to start for home, listening a moment longer for the heavy snick of the lock assuring that Charity's Hands was secure.

Very early the following morning, a persistent rapping roused Serenity from the cocoon she had fashioned for herself out of the collection of threadbare linens which for years had assisted the headmistress's slumber. The sound invaded a pleasant dream she was reluctant to leave, vexing her slightly, yet not so much as to draw her completely free from its amiable tendrils. Quite without thinking, therefore, she pushed aside her covers, slipped into a woolen robe, and set off across the floor. Even muzzy-headed, she knew Mr. Perkins would not have heard the knocking unless he had by some quirk of chance fallen asleep beside his ear horn.

Arriving on the other side of the insistent pounding, Serenity turned the key in the lock, then opened the door to reveal two men standing before her. Her eyes rounding, she stilled, staring in surprise. Not once did it enter her mind that, as usual, she had forgotten something which might just possibly be important to her. At no time was she sensible of the fine row of bare toes that even now were peeking out from under the delicately embroidered hem of her white woolen night rail.

Suddenly, with not a word and a brusqueness that made her gasp, the two men hefted large grain sacks up from the steps to their shoulders and brushed past her into the school's narrow hall, each gasping slightly as he entered, each bent with the weight of his load. Gathering her skirts, Serenity reeled away from their passage. Fully awake now, she began to call herself every kind of nincompoop. What under heaven had she done? What had she been thinking to open the door? To say that the men she had just allowed entrance into her unprotected presence were unsavory was to say that King George had been merely plump!

"M-May I be of assistance?" she finally forced herself to stammer, turning immediately to touch her candle to those in a nearby sconce, then, owl-eyed, taking a better look.

"Never mind tha'," one of the men growled, his gaze sweeping from her face down over the length of her, then slitting once more as it returned. "Where be th' store-room?"

"The storeroom? You are making a delivery? . . ." Serenity exclaimed, wrapping her arms about her. "Now?"

A harsh bark of laughter rasped against Serenity's nerves.

"When else? . . ." the man sneered. "When the sun be overhead?"

Instantly the second man added, "When charley passes on 'is rounds?"

For no reason that she could think of, Serenity blushed. "I-I am sensible of the fact that donations of food and supplies are often delivered to the school," she informed them, drawing her robe more tightly about her neck, "but you must admit, sirs, given the hour, this is highly unusual."

In response, and quite unaccountably, instead of answering, both men stilled. Moments afterward, their eyes slid sideways to connect over the grain sacks. Then suddenly, disturbingly, they were boring into Serenity again.

"Wot be ye talkin' abou'?" the second man finally asked, slightly shifting his sack. "Wot school?"

"This one, of course," Serenity replied, her attempted smile a tremble. "Charity's Hands."

Again the two visitors glanced at one another.

"Charity's *'Ands?*" the same man squeezed out from between blackened teeth. "You mean this ain't Charity's *Place?* . . . in Garrick Street?"

"No, indeed," Serenity replied, washed with a wave of relief. "This is a school my father, the vicar of St. Mary's in Woodbridge, founded for the education of working-men's children. I certainly do understand your mistake, however. It is quite the coincidence, is it not? . . . Charity's Place in Garrick Street as opposed to Charity's Hands in Cloak Lane? Is your charity also a school?"

Dismissing the question, again the two men looked hard

at one another. Then, foreheads almost touching, they schemed.

"We brought th' goods to a bloody school," the first man muttered to the other.

"Bugger me, Ollie, wot does we do now?" the second man roughly hissed, his eyes like shiny marbles. "The abbess'll 'ave our baubles for this."

"I beg your pardon!" Serenity interjected, stiffening. "I shall have to ask you not to speak with such terms in my presence."

A glance of scorn immediately shattered her objection.

"Got no choice, does we?" the first continued low and awfully, turning his attention back toward the other. "She knows us now."

"On the contrary, sirs . . ." Serenity again attempted, growing even more vexed.

"Aye," the second murmured, nodding. "Best take care of 'er, then."

". . . We have not been introduced," she finished, planting her fists upon her hips.

Slowly, the man called Ollie turned toward her, his eyes barely visible beneath his heavy brow, an odd distortion forming at the edge of his mouth.

"Aye now, missy, an' a shame, too, the mistake we made. Ye does know tha' we've brought this grain to the wrong place, don't ye?" he asked, his voice as oily as the expanse across his nose.

"Yes," Serenity replied, "that much seems obvious."

"Aye, strangers to London Town me'n Ned are," he continued, the odd distortion finally resolving itself into a wide, twisting smile. "An' in need of summat o' help."

"I did assume so," Serenity said, at first fascinated by the formation, afterward backing away from the two a bit.

"Right, then. Ah, ye does seem a right kindly lass, now . . . doesn't she, Ned? Surely she'd come with us an' help us find our proper direction," the man cajoled, closing the distance between them. "We'd be tha' grateful to ye, miss."

"What, now?" Serenity exclaimed, backing away again. "It is the middle of the night, sirs!"

"Nay," the man sighed, slowly shaking his focus down to the polished planks of the floor, "more like th' wee hours of the mornin', to my way o' thinkin', an' comin' on time for them wot's in Garrick Street to break their fast. But wot they're to eat, I doesn't ken . . . them not 'aving this grain, an' all . . ."

"You mean they shall go hungry if you do not get this grain to them?" Serenity breathed.

"Aye, no doubt of it. There'll be nary a mite o' porritch for them little tykes." Suddenly Ollie twisted toward his comrade. "Take 'er arm, then, Ned," he directed, his mouth becoming a thin line again.

Instantly Serenity's elbow was secured. In the next moment, Ned began to usher her forward.

"Really, sirs, this is absurd!" Serenity objected, unsuccessfully digging in her bare heels and toes. "You must see that I cannot go out at this hour. Why, I am still in my robe and night rail! . . . and . . . oh, heaven forfend!" she gasped, glancing down. "Do you see there?" she cried, pointing. "I have even forgotten to put on my slippers. How can I go out into the winter night when my feet are bare?"

"Why, just like this, milady," Ollie said, smiling again. Immediately he turned toward his partner, all pleasantness instantly erased. "Pick 'er up, Ned," he tersely commanded.

The twentieth part of a moment later, Serenity found herself folded over the second man's gnarled shoulder. Worse, before she could even gather the breath to object, she was quite rag-manneredly carried into the street, then spilled onto the strangers' sour-smelling wagonload.

* * *

". . . And another thing," Serenity huffed after Ned had shouldered her off the wagon and dropped her down again on the steps just outside a building identified by gilt letters and decades-old *flambeaux* as Charity's Place, "I shall not hesitate to inform this establishment's headmaster of your treatment of me, I assure you. And more," she continued as Ollie muscled the door open and propelled her into a large sitting room glowing soft gold with gaslight, draped with red velvet and layers of cigar smoke, "if any word of what you have involved me in reaches the ears of my *fiancé*—the Marquess of Chilton, I might add—I shall have him call you out." To herself, Serenity mumbled, "If, that is, I survive the peal he shall ring over me."

Finishing that, for the first time, Serenity looked about. The room was rimmed with people . . . men in black or striped velvet trousers and white lawn, lolling about over chairs and settees; women . . . heaven forfend! in clinging silk pantaloons and delicate chemisettes, lolling about over the men, their hands idly exploring beneath buttons of various and sundry sorts. And all of them staring curiously at her.

Serenity's brows soared. To her credit, it did not take her long to begin to suspect that she had not been brought to a school organized under the auspices of the National Society for Promoting the Education of the Poor in the Principles of the Established Church throughout England and Wales to Spread the Word of God by Teaching People to Read the Bible, as Charity's Hands was.

Suddenly, a woman dressed in a fitted, thinly belted gown, manfully supporting huge beribboned sleeves of gold taffeta upon her shoulders, emerged from the stagnant wisps of smoke to stand before them. Eyeing each in turn, she next raised a cigar to her lips and stated, "*I* provide the girls, gentlemen. You cannot bring your own."

"That's as may be, but ye'll take care of 'er for us, won't

ye, Charity? . . ." Ollie responded, "while Ned an' me fetches them . . . *sacks of grain?*"

At the request, the woman's eyes flared with understanding. Her response shifted accordingly. "Of course," she smoothly replied. "Come along with me, dearie," she coaxed, taking Serenity's elbow and drawing her farther within. "And you two . . . just bring the sacks to the storeroom. All we shall need is there . . . to take care of everything."

Turning away from the men, she began to usher Serenity past several languidly caressing couples, then down a carpeted hall toward a rude flight of descending steps.

"This is not a school, is it?" Serenity whispered as the woman bumped against her, herding her onto the first of the risers.

"On the contrary," the woman chuckled lightly, taffeta rustling with each step, pressing Serenity ever forward. "It is a rather fine school for certain things."

"Then where are the children?" Serenity asked, stumbling slightly when her bare toe connected with a knot in the next step's rough wood.

Deep laughter began to rumble forth from the woman's smoke-filled lungs. "They are upstairs," she finally managed to respond, just as Serenity reached the bottom.

"Sleeping?" Serenity questioned while the woman placed a hand upon her back and directed her down yet another long corridor.

"Why, no, dearie . . . working," the woman responded, husky laughter spilling forth again.

"But that is cruel!" Serenity insisted, as the woman again seized her elbow and pulled her up short before a dimly seen, roughly planked door. "Children should be sleeping at this hour."

"They will be, my dear," the woman assured her, pausing to observe Ollie and Ned appear from out of the dimness behind them carrying their heavy bags. "Happily, so shall you."

Having said that, and in quite the most startling movement, the woman then threw open the door and rudely shoved Serenity forward.

Caught unaware, with a soft cry, Serenity flew into the softly lit room. Unbalanced, she staggered, stepped upon the hem of her night rail, and again pitched forward. Wheeling both her arms, she stumbled and whirled; brown curls bobbed, folds of her woolen robe gaped indecently open. At last, panting, she wrestled tentative control over her topple.

She glanced about.

And then she stilled, too stunned to do anything but stare at what sprawled not three feet away from her own that were still unnervingly unshod.

The twentieth part of a moment later, however, the revelation sent her reeling straight back onto the stacked bags of grain that had just been abandoned by the fleeing Ollie and Ned. Once more thrown completely off-balance, she spilled over straining burlap, upended, then rolled down the opposite side. A ragged ripping punctuated her settling; long moments later, the rush of grain pouring over her tapered into a solemn sigh.

Finally, silence . . . stillness . . . settled over the room.

Slowly Serenity pushed herself up to her elbows. Her robe hung from her shoulders; grain trickled down inside her gaping night rail. On her lap, half-concealed by barley, lay a golden chalice. Ahead, not five feet away, sat the Marquess of Chilton, his visage aghast, his arm still draped around what Serenity now knew was a . . . dear heaven, there was no other way to say it, was there? . . . a woman of questionable character.

Why were there no trumpets sounding? she wondered, beginning to tremble. After all, hadn't the end of the world just come?

One

One year later—

He caught his first glimpse of the overturned carriage when a slight stutter in the wind allowed the swarming cloud of sleet pellets it had been capriciously transforming into a creditable copy of bird shot to ease and regroup, granting him a momentary view of the scene several hundred yards up the road ahead. Frowning, he slowed his matched bays, the bitter blow that had been driving against his hunched form since his departure from the bishop's palace in Ipswich earlier that morning still huffing against his garrick. He was cold and disgruntled, vexed by the unwanted interruption to his inner musings. Too easily, scattered impressions of what he had seen nudged aside his careful consideration of exactly how he would conduct himself in Serenity's presence at James and Propriety's wedding; too readily they rehearsed like flickers of firelight inside his mind.

Still, Randall Torrent, Viscount Wallenford, Earl of Brumleigh, the Earl of Cranmoor, and the Marquess of Chilton, straightened instinctively at the brief glimpse, shivering slightly when his movement allowed tiny beads of ice to craftily invade breaches in his clothing, then trail downward over his spine in frigid trickles. Again his dark brows drew tightly together as his hard stare swept the horizon.

The carriage had been lolling like a jug-bitten *roué*

against a huge, shifting snowdrift by the side of the road, its two left wheels buried in an adjacent ditch filled and obscured by the soft drift. Atop, an exposed front wheel had lain cracked and twisted awkwardly to the side, making way for the carriage pole, still tangled with empty harnesses, to thrust skyward from beneath it like a disjointed limb. Black paint, crazed and powdery with neglect, had been clinging to the exterior.

A vagrant vehicle, he appraised with a *moue* of distaste, daring to call itself a post chaise.

In the distance the sharp wind again gusted violently, scouring a feathery cap of snowflakes from the top of the drift to once more enshroud the carriage, teasing the suspended rear wheel into a slow, rocking spin. The marquess noted the lazy motion, only half-aware of the touches of pathetic yellow that circled in and out of his vision before the wheel was again completely obscured, his total concentration now given over to looking for any signs of what might have caused the accident . . . if that was indeed what had happened.

Exhaling, his jaw compressed. Behind narrowed eyes his senses heightened; his nerves bristled with suspicion.

"Blast that James!" he spat, gritting his teeth against more than the bone-brittling cold. Could his brother possibly be trying something yet again? *Was* this yet another of his and Propriety's schemes to force him into further contact with her sister? In the midst of their wedding preparations could the two of them have managed enough time to stage this? And, deuce take it, had he not yet made it sufficiently clear to the rag-mannered scamp that he not only wanted nothing more to do with Miss Serenity Hoffenduffle but that he never wished to set eyes on the jade again?

Tensing his lips, the marquess huddled into the ungainly folds of the voluminous, unfashionable, sixteen-caped garrick his uncle, the bishop, had insisted he wear as he had climbed into his curricle to take his leave shortly after breakfast that morning and blew an exasperated sigh into the face of the wind.

Serenity.

Wisps of her image sprang unwanted into his mind's eye as they had done with frustrating regularity, in spite of all he had attempted to banish them, since the night when everything had ended between them. It had been almost a year, yet still she blue-deviled him.

He ground his teeth again, the images of her coalescing against his resistance: a cloud of soft brown curls drifting against the arch of her fine, slim neck, defying her efforts to contain them; fair, flawless skin glowing with a blush of health, riding high, rounded cheekbones and a slim, straight nose dusted with—what was it she had called them?—ah, yes, fairy kisses; eyes of a startling color, a royal blue so deep and rich in its clarity that it shamed even the crisp winter sky above Windermere.

And yet she had played him for a fool.

The marquess's lips tightened again with his remembrance. He had been no child in leading strings. And was not the Torrent family motto *"fort comme le chêne"* . . . "strong as the oak?" So how had he, a man trained in intelligence— even then, as now, working undercover with Bow Street to discover the ones responsible for the recent spate of thefts of Anglican church artifacts across the length of England— been so easily taken in? Chiding himself for his stupidity, as he also always did with frustrating regularity, he forced his concentration back upon his surroundings once again, muscling his memories into a deep place inside his mind where they could not bedevil him . . . at least for a time.

The landscape was deserted . . . or so it seemed to the marquess in the instant the snow squall gave him in which to study the scene before the gust he had observed earlier near the carriage closed the distance and swept over him, peppering against the tall beaver he had tied tightly in place with a woolen scarf knotted beneath his chin. Five

of his capes caught the eddy and bounded joyfully into
the air to slap against his reddened cheeks. He ducked his
head against the frigid assault . . . and frowned.

Had he seen shadowed shapes scattered about upon the
ground?

Shoving aside his frolicking clothing, he again strained
to peer through the storm's maddening opacity, certain
that he had seen something. He clutched at the hope that
perhaps the mounds had been the carriage hacks. The
traces had definitely been empty when he had glimpsed
them last and, considering the damage sustained by the
carriage, the poor tits might easily have perished in the
accident . . . if, indeed, it had been an accident and not
one of James and Propriety's crack-brained schemes.

But no, he reconsidered, raising a York tan gloved hand
to brush the snow from his brows and eyelashes as he absently shook his head. He had known that cock wouldn't
fight as soon as he had seen them. The shapes had not
been equine. In the brief glimpse he had been allowed,
he had known of a certainty that the forms had unquestionably been human.

But could his brother be behind this? Uneasily the marquess acknowledged that it was not unusual for James to
put one of his schemes into motion only to have something
go perversely wrong for someone . . . usually him.

A remembrance flared, then, interrupting his thoughts,
reminding him of the first time James and Propriety had
tested their meddling wings. The incident had occurred
not long after the ending of his and Serenity's betrothal.
He and James had been playing on opposing sides in a
cricket match in St. John's Wood—his team out of the
Marylebone Club, James's a motley group gathered from
his fellow students who had been eating in hall as they
awaited their call to the bar by the senior barristers of the
Inns of Court. He recalled that the game had been furious.
Several of the players had broken a number of their fin-

gers. The game had neared its end with the score even; tension had been riding everyone . . . the teams, the crowds. People had long since given up their polite applause in favor of shouted bets, encouragement, and cries of sheer excitement over the game's anticipated outcome.

And then had come his brother's turn to bat. The marquess had readied himself, concentrating as the pitch had tumbled toward James, watching as his brother, too, had prepared, bending slightly in assessment, in expectancy. And then he had swung, connecting with a solid crack. The spectators had roared; all eyes had followed the ball as it had sailed out over the field in a wide arc toward a cluster of shrubs that had been shading several nebulous female spectators in the distance. And the marquess had chased it, his eyes fastened skyward, not knowing where the ball was headed or caring, only running in pursuit of it like a demon after a righteous man; and completely unaware that, like some deuced marionette, he was racing toward the exact spot where Propriety had made sure Serenity would be sitting.

The ball had dropped down from the sky into Serenity's hand.

With the realization, Rand had stumbled to a halt, then had stood awkwardly astonished as Serenity, at last understanding herself who had come in pursuit, had put fingers to her lips and begun to back away in the opposite direction. Not the twentieth part of a moment later, however, and with an unerring aim that would have put Knole's head gardener to shame, she had stopped, cocked her elbow, and fired the ball straight back toward his unsuspecting head.

He still did not know why she had done it. He had been the injured party in the breaking of their betrothal, after all. Blast it all, there ought to be a law! No peer of the realm ought to have to suffer the indignity of being pegged by a crazed female with a cricket ball. Lud, mention of the game in White's parlor still raised eyebrows.

So . . . *was* this another of James's plans? he wondered, his
curricle approaching a slight bend in the road. True, James
and Propriety had grown alarmingly creative in the other
schemes they had plotted since the cricket game, but damme,
it couldn't be! Ahead there were bodies upon the snow!

Unless the bodies in the road were merely pretending,
he reconsidered, tightening his grip on the slippery ribbons and urging his team forward. No, deuce take it!
Where could James have come up with enough of the
blunt to entice a handful of people to pretend injury on
a deserted road during the worst storm England had seen
in recent memory—even if he had not been cut off from
his quarterly allowance months ago? It was impossible.
James was persuasive, but not that persuasive. No, an honest catastrophe had to have happened here, and as near
as he could determine, he was the only human available
for miles around who might be able to help.

Grinding a bulge into his jaw, the marquess again quickened his blood's pace and glanced skyward, monitoring
the storm's strength as he tried to determine what he
might expect next from the punishing wind. Though
ahead the carriage was still obscured, aloft the churning
clouds had begun to thin somewhat, their boiling grayness
lifting slightly and segmenting like cracked scales of mud
rimming a thirsty pond. Under his gaze, they stretched
and flattened, forming and re-forming themselves into bat-
talions of plump, cottony wafers scudding in regimented
place atop the brisk, biting wind. Next, slivers of blue appeared between the clouds like veins on the back of an
ancient hand. Suddenly, a shaft of sunlight poured like
warmed honey from between the clouds to sparkle against
ice crystals remaining stubbornly airborne.

A slight curve tugged at the corners of the marquess's
ruddy lips. The storm appeared to be abating, at least for
a little while. Deciding to take advantage of it, he again
scanned the horizon, searching one last time for help.

It was then that he noticed it . . . another heavy, stagnant cloud mass beginning to rise up in the west from the landscape's napped silhouette of brittle, snow-covered grasses and stark trees. His small pleasure dissipated instantly. Worriedly, he gathered the collar of his garrick closer about his neck and again studied the low, charcoal smudge, watching as it relentlessly bullied the tattered sky behind the arched elms accompanying the road and their modest skirting of sleet-laden hawthorn. He had less time than he thought, it seemed. Vexation flowed over him—at the storm, at the circumstances; more, at his odd reaction.

Why was he even taking the time to explore the situation at all? he wondered on a softly sighed oath. Obviously, there were no survivors, so why did he not just ride on through to the safety of Martlesham, speak to the proper authorities, and let the town's magistrate deal with what had occurred? It was not as if he had nothing else to do, after all. He was on his way to an important family occasion and was expected this very day. He had little time to waste.

A mirthless chuckle then found its escape. What a Banbury tale! If he were honest with himself, he would have to admit that he welcomed the lengthy diversion. He was more than happy to grasp at anything that might delay him from reaching Woodbridge, and James and Propriety's wedding, because, damn it all, *she* would be in attendance, too. And he was not at all certain he could exist in close proximity with her over the span of several days without falling completely apart.

And yet he had to, did he not? He could not in good conscience avoid his own brother's wedding. Such a blatant cut would provide fodder for the *ton's* tabbies for weeks, not to mention the damage it would do to James and his bride's status in the eyes of Society. He could not, of course, allow that. No newlywed couple, not even one including Propriety, should have to bear that kind of notoriety.

And, too, it was important that he talk to James . . . to

try to straighten things out between the two of them and make up for the anger and animosity that had risen up because of his constant interference. But could he tell James the truth? . . . now that his brother was poised to wed Serenity's sister? There was no other choice, was there? James would have to know the whole of Serenity's perfidy if for no other reason than to at last understand why he must end his scheming once and for all. And Rand craved the conclusion. He could not abide much more of the woman's steadfast presence in his mind. He had to convince his brother to give him the chance to purge her from his system and finally get on with his life.

Another romping gust of wind sucked at the snowfall still obscuring the carriage. The marquess watched the eddy drag the opaqueness up and back in the direction from which it had come, gaining him a clear view of the area for the first time. His piercing gaze sought the shapes he had seen before; instantly, he found them. He was close enough now that there could be no mistake. Several human forms lay scattered upon the snow, and none of them was moving. Icy white shrouds already partially entombed them.

A driver and two postillions, the marquess reasoned quickly as his body tensed and grew even more alert . . . no, perhaps one postillion and a postboy. But the other body? It must be the poor soul who had hired the chaise. And yet the hip rose high against the frozen ground. Devil a bit! he thought as alarm surged through his veins. The fourth body had to be that of a woman!

Suddenly, an unexpected movement flickered in the up-turned doorway of the carriage, only to disappear once more. Instantly, Rand's gaze slewed toward the motion and riveted to the darkened aperture. Again a form, bent and cloak-covered, appeared briefly just above the edge of the frame, jerking and rolling against it, jostling the carriage before once more disappearing inside. Almost immediately after, a brown-patched elbow jabbed through the window opening, withdrew, then thrust into the air again at the same time as the huddled back of the other man once again appeared in the door. Muffled sounds began to arrive in bits and pieces on the biting gusts, carrying to him the sounds of struggle.

And then a third man sauntered around the side of the towering snowdrift. Rand twitched involuntarily, then froze, drawing his bloods to a halt unseen behind a clump of tall hawthorn just at the road's bend, observing the man as he continued unhurriedly toward the disabled carriage with six horses in tow.

Highwaymen? the marquess wondered with astonishment. This close to Martlesham? And in this modern day and age? Deuce take it, it had been long years since the likes of Dick Turpin thundered through the night on Black Bess, or Sixteen-string Jack left the warm bed of Lady Lade to take to the High Toby! Since that time the roads had been improved so much that highway robbery had been all but obsolete for the last decade. So why . . . ?

And what the devil was inside the carriage that the blackguards seemed to want so badly? . . . something that the woman lying upon the ground had been transporting? Had she been carrying something valuable and thought that if she did so as inconspicuously as possible she would have a better chance of success? That would explain why she had chosen few outriders and a carriage that bespoke poverty and neglect. And if that were so, her task must have been important. It had, after all, compelled her to leave the warmth and safety of her home to venture out in the midst of an appalling storm. But why? And what bastard's indiscretion had given her plan away? Did he even care that she had paid this terrible price?

Again the marquess turned his thoughts toward the highwaymen, his eyes hardening, assessing. He had counted three of the jackanapes hovering around the carriage, but there were probably four. He had noticed immediately that four of the horses the third man led were sporting riding halters, while the other two, probably the surviving runaway carriage hacks, were being led by ropes.

Three were easily managed, he considered with a half smile of anticipation, rolling his shoulders beneath the huge garrick to ease his gathering tension. Four, as well; while more troublesome, were still not much of a problem. He was, after all, a veteran of the Third Maratha War under Lord Rawdon-Hastings and had handled worse. Then, too, it did not hurt that he carried two primed pistols with him and had the advantage of surprise.

The marquess reached down between his legs, then, his chilled, gloved hands fumbling slightly as they encountered the thin box containing his matched set of pearl-handled pistols. Emitting a grunt of frustration when he could not find purchase, he raised a hand to his lips and bit on the tip of one leather-clad finger, soon freeing his hand from his glove so that he could lift the box to the seat beside him and worry at the latch until it sprang open. In a practiced move, he withdrew one of the weapons from its cradling, velvet-lined groove and hefted its cold, comfortable weight in his palm.

A ride in the park, Rand thought as another smile formed at the edges of his mouth and his gaze grew hard.

And then the Marquess of Chilton yelled like an Irish banshee, chopped his startled bays into a dead run toward the disabled carriage, and put a neat hole in the cloak-covered Cock Robin's arse.

Two

Tucking loose folds of his imposing uncle's cumbersome garrick aside so that he might have at least a slight notion where he was putting his feet, Rand walked among the dead, his teeth clenched against the destruction of innocent life. It made no sense, he thought angrily. Even during the worst of the years when highway robbery was so commonplace that people expected to be accosted, and as a result, carried little of value as a matter of course, it was extremely unusual for anyone actually to get hurt. Yet here, four people had been callously slain. What reason could there have been for it? And was it merely coincidence that it had happened here in Suffolk, where the greatest number of thefts from the parish churches had occurred?

Again glancing down, he came to a slow halt. The bodies would have to be dealt with before he might properly attempt to find the answer. But how? He could in no wise fit them all into his curricle. Burying them immediately was out of the question, too, as the ground was saturated with ice, and he had nothing with which to dig; besides, their families would want to claim them. He was left, therefore, with only one alternative. He would have to find a place of relative safety where he could lay the bodies out until a wagon could be sent from Martlesham.

Once more he scanned the environs. On the opposite side of the road, several towering elms bent in the wind to gather a brood of hawthorn close about their snow-girdled trunks. Rand nodded slightly in recognition of the protected spot. Then, mustering his strength, he knelt beside the woman and lifted her as gently as he could into the cradle of his arms. Afterward, he turned and strode purposefully toward the ice-shrouded copse.

A short time later the marquess settled the postboy beside the others, then straightened and looked about at the several garments that lay scattered over the road as if the robbers had even intended stealing the travelers' clothing in their greed to denude the carriage. Allowing a curl of disgust to mar one corner of his mouth, he quickly moved to gather what lay near; afterward, with care, he covered the driver's face with a tattered redingote, then placed a woolen cap upon the postillion's. He finished by covering the postboy with his sweeping cloak . . . an oversize garment of rude wool, most likely fashioned by the man's wife or daughter. The cloak enshrouded the small man from his head to his short, bowed legs, one of which was still ironclad. The marquess noted it, then tucked the cloak around the man's stubbled, lifeless face. And then he paused, again kneeling, lifting up the corner of the sturdy, utilitarian cloak covering the frozen agony of the woman, once more regarding the face of the mysterious disaster.

She had not, as he had earlier assumed, been of the Quality, he had quickly determined after he had thundered onto the scene and the highwaymen had grabbed what they could and had fled in disarray. He had been surprised at that. Dressed in black bombazine and a frilled, beribboned cap, she was most definitely of the servant class . . . most likely a lady's maid.

So why was she alone here? What errand had she undertaken to put herself in such jeopardy?

Stymied, Rand slipped his pistols into the waist of his pantaloons and gave another quick glance about the horizon, now not only searching for help, but for any further sign of the robbers. In the distance the towering cloud mass seethed, looming larger, seeming to tumble over itself in its approach as if eager to overtake him. He noted the change, frowned in its direction, yet did not concern himself with it. The mystery of the woman and her ill voyage crowded out his apprehensions. How the devil had she come to be here?

There was only one way to find out, of course, he told himself as he again covered her. He would have to search the carriage. Undoubtedly the answer lay there. Something within the disreputable vehicle had certainly attracted the blackguards' interest. Yet perhaps he had arrived too late; perhaps they had already found what they had been searching for and had managed to make off with it when he came on the scene.

The marquess quickly concluded that it really did not matter one way or the other. Even if nothing valuable lay inside, he still had a duty as a gentleman to at least try to find out something about the woman's identity so that he might see her returned to her employers. He admitted that he was loath to insert himself any more than necessary into this strange situation, but she was a woman, after all, and certainly deserved his care. And if, because of doing his duty to her and to these other poor people, he should happen to be delayed in his arrival at James's wedding, well . . .

The marquess could not stop the slight tug of a relieved smile. Lithely, he rose to his feet and strode purposefully toward the upended carriage door.

The blasted chaise was empty.

The marquess's lips twisted with disappointment. Sighing, he scrubbed at his jaw with his gloved hand, then pushed away from the door opening, knowing that it was pointless to spend any more frigid minutes peering into the carriage's cold, dank interior. He had passed far too many already, and still no portmanteaus had suddenly sprung into sight against the ice-covered leathers . . . no mysterious boxes had reshaped themselves out of the worn, faded squabs. Devil take it, there was not even a sign of the woman's reticule!

Rand slammed his hand against the frame of the window, shattering the point of impact into needlelike shards. The highwaymen must have made off with whatever it was they sought after all, he concluded, rubbing his knuckles against his opposite palm.

And then he shook his head, chiding himself for his impatience. The blackguards were not going to disappear off the face of the earth, he thought more reasonably. His chance at them would come again. In the meantime, however, his duty toward the woman still remained, did it not? Again his gaze scanned the dimness. Perhaps there was something that might still identify her. Yet if there were, he decided, it was deucedly well hid.

Given no other choice, the marquess heaved a sigh of vexation, then braced his hands on the doorframe and hoisted himself up and through the opening, squeezing his broad shoulders through the narrow aperture before dropping lightly down to the opposite side. Once there, he crouched in the mixture of snow and straw that had fallen against the lower side of the carriage and again looked about him carefully, using his elbows to support himself against threadbare squabs as he did so, his back settling uncomfortably against the upturned carriage floor.

Again, he could detect nothing out of the ordinary. Faded claret velvet still clung tentatively to the squabs like strands of hair to a balding head. Leather window curtains continued to hang brittle and mottled with snowmelt against the gnawed frames, while a coating of blown sleet encrusted the crazed varnish of the roof and walls in a parody of one of the sugared cakes from Gunter's.

And yet something was there, he acknowledged, biting the inside of his cheek consideringly. He could feel it. For some reason, four highwaymen had viciously attacked this particular carriage and had done the unthinkable . . . they had killed four innocent people traveling on it. But why? And what had they somehow overlooked and left behind? And for the life of him, Rand wondered why the deuce it should matter so much. Yet it did.

He shook his head at his own folly, then, yet remained where he was. It was nothing he could ever explain, he knew, but he had a very strong feeling about what had happened here . . . a feeling that the murders were somehow related to the parish thefts he was still investigating at the urging of his father's brother—the Right Reverend Paul Torrent, Bishop of Ipswich.

It had proved to be an enervating task. For more than a year he had worked with Bow Street on the project, acting as the liaison between the Runners, Liverpool's government, and the Church, as well as coordinating Bow Street's efforts to gather information and to infiltrate the theft ring.

He had come to relish his involvement, and to take great pride in the fact that his role in the investigation had never been discovered. He had quite easily played the part of the bored nobleman wandering about London while he awaited the passing of the holidays and the great migration of his peers back to Town for the opening of Parliament and the Season. In reality, of course, every one of his movements had had relevance. He had learned to attune his eyes and ears to the streets, to the undercurrents of rumor, to the gin-laced mutterings of the criminal classes. And he had embraced it, acknowledging his aptitude for intelligence work, finally finding purpose in his otherwise staid, stultified life.

And then, in the space of seconds, the roof had crumbled quite soundly upon his self-congratulation. It had happened on that one night. His life had collapsed. And for the life of him, he had not been able to recover yet.

Almost a year had passed since. Ben Bradshaw, the Runner who had been working with him in the investigation, had received a tip from one of his informers that the artifacts were being smuggled out of the country in bags of grain, and that the sacks were being stored at a London brothel called Charity's Place until they could be shipped. Ben had immediately set up a raid on the brothel for the time the informer had told him was to be the thieves' next delivery. And then Rand himself had infiltrated the establishment in the early evening, judging it a good idea to verify the information beforehand; even more importantly, wanting to place himself in a position where he might overhear something that would reveal why churches, of all places—even in the poorer parishes—were being singled out for robbery instead of targets that were far more lucrative. Too, it would not be amiss, he thought, to be in position on the inside when the assault on the brothel began.

He could not have imagined that so many things could go so wrong. Not only had he become, well . . . incapacitated . . . but, as if that were not humiliating enough, in the resulting confusion not one of the thieves had been apprehended, nor had a shred of evidence been left behind that would have given them a clue as to where to inquire next. Not even an empty sack had been overlooked whose stamp might have given them an idea from which mill the grain had come.

And, God, Serenity . . .

With a will, Rand quickly forced that particular remembrance back deep inside, muscling thoughts of Ben Bradshaw into its place instead. Why had he heard nothing further from the Runner since that night? He had not been killed or wounded; Rand was certain of that. So why had he not even reported in to Bow Street? Since the thefts had continued unabated, it followed that the thieves must also have found a new place to store the artifacts for shipment . . . but where? And where was Ben? Had he somehow managed to infiltrate the ring? Was it now impossible for him to contact anyone?

The questions swam inside the marquess's mind . . . soft, intriguing shackles. No, of a certainty he could not leave the post chaise just yet. There were too many answers dangling just out of reach, and for some unaccountable reason, he sensed that here, in this dilapidated carriage, he just might be able to begin to stretch out his hands and catch hold of them.

A methodical search was called for, he concluded as he shifted uncomfortably, his gaze again touching upon each surface, studying it. Once more he squirmed in the cramped space, this time his foot accidentally nudging aside one of the curtains obscuring a window on the side of the carriage leaning against the drifted snow. His dark eyes were drawn to the movement, and then they began to widen. His spine uncurled a fraction. The sparkle of packed snow should have been revealed behind the curtain, but it was not. The marquess's lips parted with his growing excitement. Where solid white should have been, instead a vacant, blue-tinted grayness lay beyond the opening.

An eye crinkling smile spread to the edges of Rand's jaw. *Devil a bit!* he thought as he elbowed himself away from the carriage floor. Of a certainty, the maid had known how to think on her feet. Somehow, in the short time she had had before she had been forced from the carriage, the elderly woman had managed to dig a tunnel! Immediately the marquess shoved the curtain fully aside, then slowly leaned forward till his line of vision inched past the lip of snow at the edge of the window. Within his chest, his heart pounded; across his shoulders, thick muscles tensed in expectation.

Suddenly a brilliant flash exploded within the tunnel's deep recess, intensifying the deafening report that immediately followed. At the same instant, a soft lead ball rocketed past the marquess's head, scoured a groove in the flesh just above his temple, then slammed into the squabs behind him, shattering the beleaguered cushion's tentative hold on its stuffing, spraying billowing puffs of it aloft to drift into the air about the stunned man in a soft swirl.

"What the deuce? . . ." the marquess shouted, slapping a gloved hand to his radiant wound, gritting his teeth against rage and pain, pressing his palms against the sides of a cranium that at once seemed to both expand and contract.

Beneath his hands, his hearing pulsed, bruised, thickened into solidity; a tic began a metronome movement at the edge of his left eyelid. He exhaled heavily, gusting vapor from his nostrils into the frigid air, where it coalesced into a cloud of condensed anger. A piece of lank stuffing drifted against his eyelash, snagged upon its midnight tip, and held.

It was the last straw. The outside of enough. He bellowed the most heinous of all his curses. The words made a quaking blancmange of the ancient carriage structure.

The marquess snarled audibly. Batting at the offending fluff, and heedless of the consequences, he stretched out his long, powerful arm and shoved it down into the tunnel, groping wildly about until his fingers sank into something soft. Smiling wickedly, he gave a gentle tug.

To his astonishment, a young woman shot through the window frame to crash headlong into his length, driving him against the carriage floor as she showered him with weeping snow. The woman recovered quickly, gasping her alarm just before she began to fight him with all her strength. Her small fists flailing, she again pitched him back against the carriage floor, knocking his beaver awry and sharply cracking the astounded marquess's skull against the scuffed panels before his nervous system could respond.

Rand's wits did return, however, riding upon a shaft of pain. With a roar of anger, he wrapped his arms tightly about the woman's struggles, easily controlling her by drawing her flush against his body. She protested valiantly, but in a short time was brought to heel nestled sodden, panting, and trembling within the notch of his legs, her woolen skirts and thoroughly soaked blue-wool pelisse sprawling in disarray about her lovely knees, her hands grasping for purchase within his thick hair's dark, lustrous waves. A funnel-shaped bonnet, a confection heavy with yards of snow-soaked ribbon and lace and crowned with a nesting blue bird, bumped against his brow and sprang free. It slid, sagged, and finally drooped against her shoulder like a wilted centerpiece.

God help him, soft femininity draped over him head to toe. A cloud of sweetly scented curls tickled against his face . . . slipping into his mouth on his ragged indrawn breath . . . drifting to snag against his stubbled jaw. His senses reeled, filled with the essence of flowers and warm, woman smell.

Slowly, the woman lifted her head from where it lay cradled beneath his chin.

The marquess watched with rapt expectancy.

Her stunned gaze trailed upward, carefully tracing the planes of his lean face until finally her huge, sapphire eyes rested squarely within the darkness of his.

At the impact, Rand's breath hissed between his teeth.

". . . Chilton?" the woman finally breathed, her eyes widening even more with surprise.

The marquess could not speak. He swallowed thickly; his brow grooved first with shock, then sank quickly into a chasm of condemnation.

In counterpoint, the woman's gaze softened; moistened. Almost hungrily, she stared at him. And then quite suddenly she drew her lower lip between her teeth. Panted breaths grew visible in the icy air, mingling with his. Again she began to struggle against him, jostling parts of him better left to lie in peace.

He arrested her movements easily with a powerful and intimately placed hand, inhaling sharply as she renewed her wriggles after a gasp at his effrontery. Then, closing his eyes against the feel of her, he allowed his head to drop tiredly back against the floor's tilted planks.

"Of course," he uttered with weary resignation, again raising his dark head and opening his eyes wide to regard her. "Why did I doubt it for even the twentieth part of a moment? Who else would dig a tunnel into the snow through a carriage window to escape a robbery and then fire upon her rescuer? Who else would once again appear in my life to plague me like a recurrence of the gout? It could *only* be you, Miss Hoffenduffle."

Three

"Gout! Just what are you implying, sir?" Serenity gasped incredulously, pounding upon his chest a few more times for emphasis. Suddenly, at last becoming sensible of her unorthodox position, much more loudly she added, "And how dare you! I must ask you to kindly remove your hands from my . . . my . . . the afterward of my person!"

"Gladly," the marquess snarled, "if you would kindly take yourself off me. And for heaven's sake, stop wiggling. I am in enough pain."

Serenity's struggles ceased immediately.

"You are?" she questioned as her lovely eyes scanned his face, finally focusing upon his wound. Instantly her gaze blossomed with alarm. "Oh, my, Chilton!" she gasped, sharply drawing up a knee to balance herself less precariously. "You are bleeding!"

Once again she began to squirm above him, pushing against his well-defined musculature with her elbows to loosen his grip on her and to elevate herself, as she did so, soundly rapping the butt of the ancient flintlock she was still gripping in one of her hands against the base of his skull.

The marquess squeezed his eyes closed against his body's urge to fold itself into a very tiny thing. The color leached from his face.

"I believe the occurrence is quite ordinary when one

has been shot, Miss Hoffenduffle," he replied in a thin wheeze squeezed between his teeth. "Now, for the love of . . . put away that cannon and lie still!"

"Oh, dear heavens!" Serenity responded, her eyes rounding. "Never say that I actually hit something!" Obediently, she fumbled her weapon back inside a large, bulging reticule. "Quickly, Chilton, your wound must be attended to," she added, becoming brusque of tone and officious as she tightened the strings. "You are, after all, bleeding quite copiously."

Before Rand could think to stop her she shifted yet again, raising her right arm in a darting movement to press the sleeve of her pelisse against the ragged tissue above his ear, at the same time slipping her other arm behind his shoulders to steady him. The impulsive action removed the support which kept her elevated somewhat above him.

Soft breasts pressed enticingly against his chest.

"Good Lord . . ." the marquess keened in a tone decidedly strangled.

". . . Really, sir," Serenity interjected, wriggling even more in her attempt to stiffen her spine, "I should have hoped for a bit more understanding. I assure you that I am sensible of my small miscalculation and do most sincerely apologize. However . . . well, you see, this has been a rather trying day. I fear I am quite put out of countenance by . . . everything that has been happening of late.

"And who could have known that the gun would actually fire? Goodness, it never has before . . . well, actually I have never even tried to use the thing until today, and would not have had you not frightened me so. But I had no other protection, you see . . ."

Serenity paused then to blow several curls from her forehead. "Oh, stuff, my lord!" she finally asserted. "You must admit that you bear a good deal of the blame."

"*I*, madam?" the marquess queried, his elevated brow somewhat misshapen by the impeding pressure of her sleeve. "How is it that *I* must bear any of the blame for *your* attempt to blow a sizable piece off me?"

"You should have announced yourself, of course," Serenity declared with a nod of her head.

"Announced myself!" the marquess barked in repetition. "Four people are lying dead outside this excuse for a post chaise, Miss Hoffenduffle. Would you have me stroll up whistling and toss my card onto the silver salver?"

The lady stilled.

"Dead?" she finally whispered, her eyes darkening, misting with apprehension. "I heard shots, but . . . Oh, Chilton, was Mary . . . ?"

Vapor billowed into the ensuing silence. A flurry of wind-driven snow swirled into the carriage and settled peacefully over them. Against the marquess's chest, Serenity trembled.

Rand sighed inwardly and cursed his imprudent tongue. She was a jade of the worst kind, of course, but her distress upon hearing of her companion's misfortune was obvious. And he *was* a gentleman, after all, and gentlemen *were* supposed to protect their females as best they could no matter what their sins. Yet there was no way to shield her from this truth. Her companion was dead, and he would have to affirm it. His features softened.

"There was a woman among them."

Serenity's lower lids liquefied.

"Oh, no . . ." she breathed, dropping her gaze to the buttons of his garrick, dampening even more the wet patches of snowmelt upon it with several escaped tears. "Mary was Aunt Mildred's maid. She was traveling with me as my chaperone at my aunt's request. When the men who stopped our coach first demanded that we come outside, she insisted that I remain out of sight and try to find a place to hide. She has given her life to protect me."

Rand felt his biceps tense with the impulse to tighten around Serenity. He resisted with all the power within him.

The lady was far too experienced in wrapping him around her delicate fingers for him to allow himself to succumb to those feelings once again. It was obvious that she was terribly moved by her companion's death, but he could not let that signify. He had only been with her for a short while and already she was shredding his carefully constructed defenses. He had to remember what she had done. As a precaution, he tucked his hands beneath him.

"You have my deepest sympathies," he said more unfeelingly than he had intended.

Serenity flinched slightly, then gathered herself and again raised her gaze to look at him.

"Thank you," she replied quietly.

Rand ground his back teeth. "I have covered her and placed her under the trees at the side of the road," he told her more gently.

"Again, thank you," she repeated, allowing him a soft smile.

Beneath his hard gaze her enchanting eyes warmed.

Rand's body again stirred. Sapphire swam mere inches from his visage; the remembered sweetness of her lips was so tantalizingly close. His fingernails dug into the soft, wet wood of the carriage floor.

"I shall send someone back for the bodies when I reach Martlesham," he murmured, hopelessly lost in her eyes.

"That would be most kind of you," Serenity politely replied.

And then she stiffened slightly on an audible swallow, her manner becoming efficient again. "But we have more pressing problems, do we not? We must bind your wound or you shall not be going anywhere."

Grasping at the return of his senses, Rand seized lungfuls of air.

"It is merely a flesh wound, Miss Hoff . . ."

". . . Do you know, I have several handkerchiefs in my reticule," Serenity interrupted thoughtfully, her eyes brightening somewhat as she began to withdraw her wrist from his temple. "Now that I think of it, I am persuaded that pressing them to your wound might have been the better course, but . . . oh, *dear.*"

The marquess sighed heavily. "A problem, Miss Hoffenduffle?" He knew the answer, of course. It was unfortunate, but he did know the lady all too well.

Sodden gloved fingers began to unconsciously worry one of the capes beneath him, raising gooseflesh along the length of his spine. Rand fought his pleasure, then again shakily sighed.

"I . . . I might perhaps have made another slight miscalculation, Chilton," Serenity finally and softly admitted. "You see, although my handkerchiefs are indeed inside my reticule, my reticule, unfortunately, is looped about my elbow."

The marquess, who had been growing steadily more impatient over the last few moments, and increasingly irritated by the fact that the jade's eyes should be so clear a shade of blue, suggested tartly, "Then why not take it off, Miss Hoffenduffle?"

"Because I cannot get it past my wrist, sir," she hastened to explain.

"And why can you not get it past your wrist, madam?" the marquess asked, drumming his fingertips against a puff of horsehair.

"Because my wrist is pressed to your temple," she explained with an apologetic smile.

Each word of the marquess's response was enunciated quite clearly. "Then simply disengage your wrist, Miss Hoffenduffle."

"I cannot," Serenity regretfully replied.

The marquess stared incredulously into the deep blue of her eyes.

"Why not?" he barked rather loudly.

"That was the miscalculation, Chilton," Serenity responded, briefly lowering her gaze. "Your blood seems to have attached itself quite firmly to the cloth of my pelisse, you see. It is the cold, I imagine. Cold can do the most extraordinary things, you know. Why, my grandfather used to tell of a winter during his youth when the cold in Amsterdam was so severe that the queue snapped right off the back of his periwig! And not just his, either, so he often said. Queues were popping off all over the Lowlands. Quite like dead rats lying about in the snow, I should think. Why, can you imagine . . . ?"

". . . Shall we attempt to stick to the topic at hand, Miss Hoffenduffle?" the marquess suggested awfully.

"Oh. Yes . . . well, you must see, do you not, that if I remove my wrist from your temple, it will tear away the clot that has formed, and you will begin bleeding all over again."

The marquess sucked in his cheeks and bit deeply into both sides as another blast of arctic wind numbed his earlobes.

When the wind had died he commanded, "Kindly do it anyway, Miss Hoffenduffle."

"Oh, no, I could not," she replied quickly, shivering slightly, ducking her head to shake brown curls against his nose and eyelashes before looking at him again.

Rand inhaled slowly, deeply, his eyes piercing hers. "Be reasonable, madam," he implored after taking a moment to regain his composure. "I have no wish to remain attached to you in this position, in this carriage, in this vexing cold, until some time weeks from now when my wound has healed. I shall quite gladly suffer a renewed flow."

The lady pressed so solidly against him grew rigid. "Rest assured, sir, that I have no desire to remain in *your* company any longer than is necessary either," she responded huffily, "and certainly not in this position. And you are the one who is being unreasonable. If you will just cooperate, we shall soon be rid of one another."

"Oh?"

"Yes, indeed." Serenity nodded with assurance. "I have come up with another plan."

The marquess's head dropped back against the tilted floor.

Serenity smiled uncertainly. "It is quite simple really," she said with quickly mustered efficiency. "You must retrieve my reticule."

Rand waited a moment for her convoluted plan's conclusion, but when it was not forthcoming, he again raised his head and looked at her.

"That's it?"

"Yes, certainly," she replied with a brisk nod. "And do stop thumping your head up and down, Chilton. My sleeve shall tear loose."

"Your wondrous plan is that *I* should retrieve your reticule?"

"I have just said so, Chilton. Do pay attention."

The marquess's lips tightened with pique. "That is possibly the most hen-witted scheme I have ever heard escape from your lips, madam, and I have heard a great many of them. Why the deuce do *you* not retrieve it?"

"Because," she explained, tsking softly, "one of my arms is pinned beneath your shoulders and the other is stuck to your head."

The marquess's gaze dulled. "Ah . . . I see," he responded helplessly. He tried again. "Obviously it has not occurred to you that I could raise myself up so that you could free your unoccupied arm."

"Well, of course, it has," Serenity stated indignantly. "Yet I am persuaded that if we jostle one another to that degree, my sleeve might become dislodged. I cannot allow that to happen." Again she stiffened in order to hold him still, and, as a result, sank even more firmly against the length of his body.

Rand's next breath hissed between his teeth. The several

that followed thereafter were deeply drawn, a futile attempt to manhandle his response to the woman into manageable channels. A different tactic was called for. He put one into play as quickly as possible.

"Consider this, then, Miss Hoffenduffle," he was finally able to say. "Suppose one of us does manage to retrieve your reticule and remove your handkerchiefs. Will you not still have to remove your wrist from my wound, and therefore reopen it, if you are to replace the sleeve of your pelisse with them?"

Serenity's head tilted consideringly. Her sapphire eyes narrowed, centering upon his. "I confess I had not thought of that," she murmured, lowering her gaze to study what she could see of his throat.

"Well, then, you see, do you not?" the marquess queried reasonably. "You will have to reopen my wound whether you wish to or not. It is pointless for you to maintain this ridiculous pose."

A brittle spark flared in the depths of Serenity's eyes as her gaze flew to his.

"Ridiculous?" she snapped tartly. "It is hardly ridiculous to come to the aid of one's fellowman, Chilton, and not pointless at all. But I cannot expect a man like you to understand that, can I? Now, hold still, sir! I have come up with yet another plan."

Again Rand slumped back against the floor of the carriage. This time, the thump of his head was really quite jarring. Caught off guard, Serenity surged upward to follow his movement with her wrist, afterward casting a heated scowl toward the vicinity of his chin.

"Here is what we shall do," she told him briskly while carefully shifting her weight so that he might more easily extract his arm from their tangle of clothing when she had finished her explanation.

Elbows ground into his musculature. His body hummed.

"You must take your right arm and raise it over both of mine until you can reach my reticule."

"Sounds like the same deuced plan to me," said the marquess with a sigh, enduring too many waves of pleasure washing over him to move at all.

"It is not," Serenity argued with asperity, "and kindly contain your insensitive remarks. I have quite enough in my dish at the moment as it is."

"Nothing that you, yourself, have not spooned in there, madam," the marquess replied. "You and your maggoty plans . . ."

"And what is wrong with them?" Serenity asked, her tone as brittle as the surrounding ice.

"They are mutton-headed, Miss Hoffenduffle. And you, as usual, are making a cake of yourself."

"A cake of myself! At least I *have* plans, sir," the lady countered.

"Better you than me, madam," Rand threw back quickly, "when it comes to your conception of plans. Tell me, Miss Hoffenduffle, what of the vicar? Is he, too, a man of questionable creativity?"

"My father has only the most noble of ideas!" Serenity defended stiffly. ". . . And if he occasionally sets fire to the altar cloth during his annual sermon on the Eternal Punishments of Hell, well . . . it is only with the best of intentions."

"Hah!" Rand exploded. "I knew it. What's bred in the bone *has* come out in the roast."

Serenity became rigid in the marquess's arms. "I had rather be my father's roast, sir," she vowed righteously, "than mutton got up as lamb like you!"

Rand's aspect dissolved into disbelief. And then he shook his head.

"My congratulations, Miss Hoffenduffle," he finally stated. "*That* is now the most pea-brained statement you have ever made." And then his voice soared. "Are you daft, madam?"

"No, I am hungry!" the lady asserted in return. "And a lot of good that does me, stuck to you like I am."

"Hungry?" the marquess repeated, several vessels roping at his temple.

"Yes, hungry," Serenity affirmed. "It is all that talk of cake and roast and mutton, I suppose."

"Perhaps it has not yet occurred to you, madam," Rand informed her, irritated to discover that the suggestive conversation had rendered him, too, sharp-set, "but dwelling upon food will only make our situation worse. We are in a snowstorm in the middle of nowhere, Miss Hoffenduffle. Talk about anything else, if you wish . . . even your maggoty plans . . . but do *not* talk about food."

"Very well," Serenity agreed. "I shall say nothing more."

"Good."

"About roasts, or cakes, or trifle . . ."

"Miss Hoffenduffle . . ."

". . . Or biscuits," Serenity finished calmly.

"Miss Hoffend . . . !" Rand began. And then he paused. "Biscuits?" he quickly echoed.

"Yes, biscuits," the lady vowed at full volume. "Which I would, of course, have gladly shared with you if you were not such a vile, stubborn, perverted . . ."

"Perverted!" the marquess blasted with narrowed eyes and a mouth that watered. "Whyever? . . . No, never mind," he corrected, grabbing for threads of control over his temper. "You will explain what you are talking about, madam," he stated more moderately. "I thoroughly searched this rolling midden. There is nothing here. From where do you ludicrously think to conjure roast, cakes, or trifle?"

Serenity skewered him with cobalt, and then rolled her eyes. "Where do you think, you overbearing, obnox . . ."

"Enough!" thundered the marquess, now determined

to have any available food simply on the principle of the thing. "From where, madam?"

"From my reticule!"

The marquess's dark head again made solid contact with the carriage floor. From the dim depths, his voice rose in frosty scorn. "You have trifle in your reticule?"

"Certainly not!" Serenity replied hotly. "Think you that I am daft? How should anyone carry a dish of trifle? I carry biscuits, sir—in a lovely tin. Of all the insufferable . . ." she continued in a mumble.

Her voice then soared. ". . . I shall not, I hope you understand, share the rest of my plan with you either. If you think that I wish to endure any more of your pompous ridicule . . ."

". . . Believe me," vowed the marquess, finally yielding at the limit of his restraint, "I have no earthly desire to know what is on your mind, Miss Hoffenduffle. Simply tell me again what I am supposed to do. Give me none of your rambling explanations. Let us just be done with your nod-cock scheme so that we can finally be rid of one another!"

Serenity's jaw slackened daintily. As she stared at him, several thick clouds of vapor exploded from her mouth to pummel the marquess's face, forming tiny crystals of indignation upon his lashes and brows. She struggled, but at last she was able to speak in reasonable tones.

"You are to put your right arm over both of mine until you can grasp my reticule," she responded with clipped words, "and have a care not to jostle my arm while you are about it, if you please."

His glower alive with white-hot flecks, the marquess complied. He moved carefully, bringing his right arm forth from beneath them and stretching it over Serenity's arms until he could grope with tingling, blood-deprived fingers for the string she had said was looped around her right elbow. When he could not readily find it, he began to slide his fingers upward along her sleeve, unknowingly putting pressure upon the conjoining of the pelisse and the wound at his temple.

"Wait! Stop!" cried Serenity, feeling her sleeve begin to draw against the wound. "You cannot put pressure upon my arm, sir. My pelisse will pull loose."

"Then how the devil do you suggest I get my hands on your reticule, Miss Hoffenduffle?" the marquess barked in reply.

"Certainly not with oaths, sir," she rebounded quickly.

"Egad, madam, are you actually taking offense? You?" he all but shouted. "You, who more than likely have heard every vulgarity that was ever invented?"

Serenity wriggled her immobilized wrist just enough to be able to tweak the marquess's hair.

"Ouch, blast it all!"

"My father, sir, is the vicar of St. Mary's as well you know," she cried hotly. "How dare you insinuate that I have open familiarity with the tawdry!"

"Because, Miss Hoffenduffle," Rand bellowed in reply, his scalp still smarting, "as you conveniently seem to have forgotten, it was but a year ago that I saw you in possession of stolen goods . . . in a brothel . . . in, of all things, your bare feet and night rail!"

"What of it!" she returned instantaneously, twisting her arm to tweak his hair again. "If *you* recall, it was also but a year ago that I saw *you* in that same brothel. And *you*, sir, were wearing nothing at all!"

Four

Nose to nose, Rand and Serenity filled the carriage with the opacity of their billowing breath, their hair and brows whitening under the mutual assault of crystalline outrage. Like two cocks at the Westminster Pit the two mentally circled one another, lungs heaving the frigid air to and fro, their eyes thrusting lethal daggers.

The marquess was the first to flinch.

"This is getting us nowhere," he finally mumbled, grinding his teeth against the return of reason, releasing a measure of his tension on a sigh of visible air.

Suddenly cramped, he squirmed uncomfortably against the carriage floor. He was supposed to be a gentleman, deuce take it . . . with a duty to protect the jade, not to plant his fives in her lovely mouth! Slowly, reluctantly, he rolled what he could move of his shoulder muscles and forced the rest of himself to relax, wondering, not for the first time, if he would ever again be free . . . wondering, too, as an idle afterthought, if any man had ever perished from the wounds of a cut-up peace.

Above, Serenity, too, acquiesced, relaxing against him somewhat as she inwardly agreed.

"No, it is not, is it?" she quietly acknowledged. "Besides, we have been over all this ground before."

"Actually . . . we have not," Rand commented, relenting a bit more. "But, considering the extent of what happened that night, there never seemed to be much point, did there?"

"No, I suppose not," she softly nodded, her eyes losing a bit of their warm luster.

"Well, then, let us continue with this scheme of yours," the marquess suggested, his own brow at last releasing its hold upon several deep furrows. "I am persuaded that neither one of us wishes this encounter to last any longer than it must."

As Rand regarded her, a dark cast crept into Serenity's gaze. For long moments she stared into the dark centers of his eyes, then, blinking, she lowered her head until her curls brushed lightly against his mouth.

"No, of course not," she answered in a whisper, her body suddenly seeming heavier atop his. And then she again levered herself to where she could look at him. After a moment, she softly smiled.

"Now, sir, I am persuaded the problem is that my reticule has worked its way up almost to my shoulder since my wrist has been upraised for so long. However, if I carefully slip around toward your side, I believe that my shoulder will be positioned close enough to your hand for you to be able to grasp the loops and move them down."

Saying nothing, the marquess quickly assessed the plan's chances for success. Concentrating, he pictured their required activity. In the back of his mind, hope blossomed; freedom loomed upon the horizon of his soul.

And then his breath caught in his throat. *Devil a bit!* he thought with alarm. *If she does that, she more than likely will . . .*

Confident of her solution, however, Serenity had already begun to move above him.

"Miss Hoffenduffle!" the marquess barked when he realized that she had not waited for his response.

"Really, Chilton, everything shall be fine. Do remain still, if you please," the lady scolded, deftly wriggling away from his stiff-fingered attempt to seize her waist. Slowly, she elevated her hips above the notch of his outspread legs, her elbows again digging into him.

"No, I shall not remain still, Miss Hof . . ."

". . . Lower your right leg . . ."

". . . Deuce take it, Miss Hoffenduffle . . ."

". . . There is no need to bellow, Chilton," Serenity chided softly. "My plan is working wonderfully. Lower your leg a bit more . . . good. Perfect. Now I shall just lift my left leg over your right one and . . . Oh, dear! *Chilton!*"

Her half-boot ensnared within the lace of her petticoat, Serenity dropped like King George's arches. Yet again she came to rest sprawled quite immodestly across the marquess's chest.

Now, however, her legs were straddling his muscular right thigh.

". . . Oh, *my!*" Serenity gasped, swallowing thickly at a series of quite remarkable sensations.

Rand absorbed the feminine heat of her and groaned. Three times his head thumped against the tilted carriage floor.

Serenity felt his muscles surge beneath her. "Oh, my goodness! . . . Dear me!"

Several more thumps resounded in the biting air.

"Really, Chilton," Serenity uttered sheepishly, holding as perfectly still as she could, "this is nothing to get in a pucker about. It was merely a slight miscalculation."

The marquess's eyes rolled to impale her.

"It was a very good plan," Serenity insisted, biting her lower lip in abject mortification.

Five

The marquess slowly raised his right hand, his heated scowl very nearly melting the crust of snow which had settled over them during their incarceration inside the carriage. Wordlessly, his visage fuming, he crossed his arm over both of Serenity's and then fumbled slightly somewhere out of sight. When his seeking fingers came perilously close to portions of her anatomy Propriety had warned her men would always be trying to touch, she flinched slightly.

"Just what are you up to, Chilton?" she asked him rather tremulously.

"From the feel of it, all of twelve inches," the marquess responded in an angry mutter.

"I beg your pardon?"

"Never mind. I am merely proceeding with your plan, Miss Hoffenduffle. Hold very still, if you please. I believe I have located your reticule strings."

"Excellent! Can you take hold of them?" Serenity asked, twisting her head to see beyond her dangling bonnet.

The marquess sighed. "I would have had you not moved," he responded ominously.

"Oh."

He tried again. Several long moments passed during which Serenity's warm breath moistened his Adam's apple.

He tried to ignore the sensation, but was far more success-
ful in relocating the reticule strings.

"Hold still now . . . there. Yes. I have them again," he
informed her with relief.

"Excellent!" Serenity exclaimed, her face suddenly
glowing beneath his. "Now if you will but slide the loops
from my arm, we shall be able to open my reticule and
get what we need from inside."

A thought flickered across Rand's mind, giving him
pause.

"Miss Hoffenduffle . . ."

"Yes, you may have a biscuit or two as well, sir." She
smiled, shaking her head.

"You have my undying gratitude, but, Miss Hoffenduffle . . ."

"It is a simple task, Chilton," she chided gently. "What
are you waiting for?"

"For you to tell me how I am to remove your reticule
from your arm if your wrist is stuck to my head," Rand
informed her dryly.

Serenity sobered almost immediately.

"Oh," she finally responded, drawing her full lower lip
in between her even, white teeth. "Well . . . yes, I can see
that another problem has most certainly presented itself.
A slight . . ."

". . . Miscalculation?" Rand helpfully supplied.

". . . Something like that," she replied, focusing upon
the tip of his nose.

The marquess's mouth drew into a smirk. "Well, I have
no doubt you already know exactly how to extricate us
from this, er, slight miscalculation, madam, since so far
your plans have been absolute pattern cards of tactical bril-
liance. Pray, therefore, do not keep me in suspense any
longer. I beg you, my dear . . . reveal to me your scheme."

Allowing an arrogant smile to whisper across his lips, Rand
settled back against the floor more comfortably and

awaited her response. "Goggle me, Miss Hoffenduffle, with our next course of action."

It did not take her long. After but a moment's thought, the lady's eyes widened. "We shall simply slip the loops over your head," she declared, matching his smile.

"What!" came his lordship's astonished gasp.

Serenity shook her head sadly and wiggled the fingers wedged beneath his garrick in an attempt to pat his back. "It was the report of my weapon, was it not?" she responded soothingly. "I have never before known you to be so hard of hearing, Chilton."

Ignoring her, the marquess thundered, "For the love of . . . ! What is the point of hanging your reticule around my neck!"

Serenity smiled. "In that position," she explained slowly and patiently, "my reticule can lie upon your chest, where you can more easily get into it."

"Where *I* can get into it?" Rand bellowed. "Why the blazes should *I* want to get into your reticule?"

"For the biscuits, of course," Serenity reasoned, "if not your way of escape. And do not forget that you do have the only free hand."

The marquess stared. And then he drew his lips into a tight, white line. When he spoke, the words were squeezed out from between his teeth. "I'll wager there is not, nor has there ever been in the history of England, another peer of the realm who has ever been forced to put a woman's reticule around his neck!" he exploded.

"No man has ever touched the moon, either, Chilton," Serenity said gently. "What of it?"

"I'll feel silly," he grumped.

"No one will know but the two of us, and I have no earthly reason to tell," Serenity countered reasonably.

The marquess hesitated. Gusts of vapor wafted against Serenity's lively curls. "You know perfectly well what will happen when I try to open the deuced thing, don't you?"

he groused. "The loops will grow smaller and I shall be strangled. How am I to explain that, I ask you? . . . the Marquess of Chilton strangled by a reticule."

"You are being ridiculous," Serenity said softly, struggling to hold back a smile. "Put the loops up over your head."

"No."

"And petulant."

"No."

"And you cannot have a biscuit until you do."

". . . Not a word of this to anyone, do you hear me?" he warned from beneath narrowed brows.

"Of course, not," Serenity replied. "Now get on with it, Chilton."

The marquess gave her a look that warmed the temperature inside the carriage by several degrees and did as he was told.

"This is no reticule," groused the marquess after he had looped the bag's strings over his head and maneuvered the oversize, lace-trimmed confection onto the portion of his chest not already covered by Serenity. "It is a portmanteau."

"Never mind," scolded Serenity, casting him a second's worth of glower. "Just open it please. First we must find my sewing scissors, and then we must locate the handkerchiefs."

"You have sewing scissors in your reticule?" Rand questioned in amazement.

"Well, of course," Serenity responded. "One never knows when one will need a pair of scissors. Now, if you please, Chilton, begin your search for the necessary items. My arm is becoming quite numb and extremely cold."

"My apologies," the marquess uttered sarcastically, his eyes glittering with ill humor.

"The scissors and the handkerchiefs, if you please," Serenity urged, another shiver skittering over her.

"The biscuits," countered Rand, his glance daring her to contradict him.

"Of course," she wisely agreed, quickly ducking her head to hide a grin. "I believe there might be a bit of chocolate, too."

"Chocolate?" repeated the marquess hopefully.

"Just a bit," Serenity qualified.

An embryo of suspicion suddenly arose within Rand's mind to drift idly through his thoughts. Schooled by his months working with Bow Street, he nurtured it.

"You seem to be quite well prepared for this crisis, madam," he commented guardedly as the seed planted itself and sent down roots.

"Because of a bit of chocolate?" Serenity replied, smiling unsuspectingly.

"That . . . and other things," the marquess stated.

He turned slightly, his gaze piercing her as his suspicion blossomed forth into full-blown doubt. Of course. It had to be. The conclusion was inescapable. Had she not been secretly involved in the theft ring before, during the time they had been engaged to be married? Had he not caught her at it red-handed? What else was he to make of the fact that here she was again, well armed, stocked with what a woman would consider provisions, and most tellingly, the only one still alive after a bizarre attack against her carriage in the one county in all England suffering the most under the thieves! No other conclusion seemed possible. It could only be that the jade was in league with the men who attacked the carriage . . . still involved in the theft of church treasures!

Yet in his inner being, Rand recoiled from the notion. No, deuce take it! People had been murdered here. She could not have fallen so far! It was impossible. Yet swiftly on the heels of that denial came another thought: if she were indeed innocent of all this, why then did she not shoot at the highwaymen when they were inside the carriage with her?

Why did she instead blast away at him with her flintlock?

Again Rand's gaze slid toward Serenity's and connected. She smiled at him questioningly.

"The reticule, Chilton?" she prompted gently.

The marquess continued to stare into her eyes, searching for, expecting to find, confirmation of his suspicions. What he discovered was curiosity held captive in deep, royal blue. His certainty crumbled into confusion.

He gathered himself. "So . . . it is usual for you to carry a weapon?" he continued, determined to uncover the lie.

"Dear me, no." She chuckled. "As I told you, I have merely felt the need for a bit of protection of late. The pistol is on loan to me from my uncle Hans."

Again the marquess studied her. Nothing in her face, in her eyes, revealed what he knew should be there . . . signs of her perfidy. She was that good, he acknowledged, as an emptiness opened in the pit of his stomach . . . good enough to fool St. Peter himself with her innocent act.

The need suddenly overwhelmed Rand to find the deuced scissors and to put the whole of England between himself and the jade as quickly as he could. The very air she breathed condemned him as a fool. He had to get away. Casting her one last penetrating gaze, he seized the gathers of the reticule, determinedly using his free hand to spread it open until the loops tightened about his neck. Then he thrust his hand inside.

"What the devil have you got in here, anyway?" he spat out distractedly after he had been rooting around inside the bag for several unproductive seconds.

"The usual, I suppose . . ." Serenity responded guardedly, having finally grown aware of the waxing of the marquess's usual irascible behavior. "A woman's necessities.

Perhaps if you take out some of the larger items first, you shall find the ones we need underneath."

Rand needed no second prompting. From within the reticule he first withdrew two volumes, Mingleforth's *Rules of Polite Decorum,* and Mrs. Bruton's *Self Control.*

His brow, the one still free to move at will, arose.

"They are wedding gifts for Propriety," Serenity justified softly.

"Good choices," Rand muttered, as Serenity elbowed the volumes into a precarious balance against his shoulder.

". . . I suppose my sister does lack a certain restraint," Serenity cautiously agreed, "but she has a good heart."

"She has a good right jab," the marquess countered.

Serenity's gaze dropped. "Yes, Propriety told me she had gone to see you the day after you decided to end our engagement. I did try to apologize though . . . when she and James locked us together in that building . . ."

"Yes, well . . . those things are best forgotten," Rand mumbled, again reaching into the reticule. "What are these? Slippers?"

"Yes, I . . . if you must know, Chilton, after that night, I felt it was rather important that I always carry a pair with me," Serenity explained uncomfortably.

Rand stared at her. "Having your feet bare was hardly significant compared to everything else that was happening that night, Miss Hoffenduffle. Have you forgotten? A great deal occurred that was far worse!"

"I . . . I am aware of that," Serenity stammered, becoming flushed with embarrassment. "It was most improper to be seen in my night rail . . ."

"Night rail!" the marquess barked. "Is that all you . . . ?"

"No, it is not!" Serenity snapped, her temper finally getting the better of her discomfiture. "I have not forgotten *your* part in that evening, my lord Chilton. To have discovered you in that storeroom . . ."

"I had a perfectly good reason for being in that storeroom!" he bellowed.

"Well I know it!" Serenity countered at full volume. "You were happily cavorting with a . . . a woman of questionable character!"

"There was a reason, I told you . . . Blast it all, madam," Rand exploded, "this gets us nowhere. It is history, Miss Hoffenduffle. It serves no purpose to dish it all up again."

"Then why do you insist upon doing so?" Serenity returned hotly. "Believe me, sir, at this point all I want is to be free of this thoroughly improper situation . . . and you! Kindly give less of your attention to recalling a past neither one of us wishes to remember, and more of it to finding my scissors!"

Scowling fiercely, Rand complied. In a jabbing motion, he again dug his hand into the reticule, withdrawing this time four roundish, earth-colored, encrusted masses which, upon closer study, caused his lips to turn downward in a look of wholehearted distaste.

"Good Lord, what are these things?" he muttered. "It appears you attended a gelding and brought home souvenirs."

"Really, Chilton, I must ask you to remember I am not one of your stable hands," Serenity scolded. "And do not lose them, sir."

"Do not lose them?" the marquess uttered contemptuously. "Madam, they should either be given the last rites or be pickled."

"Don't be absurd," Serenity chided. "They are part of Propriety's present and shall be most welcome by her. They arrived not two days ago from relatives of ours who still reside in Amsterdam, and since you have just revealed yourself to be quite shamefully in ignorance of one of life's more pleasant endeavors, I shall tell you that they are bulbs, sir, of a most beautiful variety of ruffled daffodil."

"Bulbs," Rand repeated. "You carry garden bulbs in

your reticule. Along with a pair of slippers and two books. And who knows what else. The necessities."

"Yes indeed," Serenity stated firmly. "Growing bulbs is Propriety's greatest delight, as it has been for generations of Hoffenduffles since before my ancestors ever came to these shores. Had you ever visited the manse in Woodbridge when we were . . . well, you would have seen her garden. It is all that is lovely."

"She has bulbs in her reticule," murmured the marquess as he began to dig around in the bag again.

"Only because they are a present," Serenity defended tartly. "Of course I do not carry bulbs in my reticule as a matter of course."

"I cannot tell you how relieved that makes me," commented the marquess as he laid two whip points, a bottle of attar of roses, and a parched, gnawed apple core upon his chest. His brow again soared.

"My father shares Propriety's love of bulbs," Serenity continued contentedly, her smile soft, "as did his father before him. In fact, it was Papa's interest that piqued hers. Papa often says that bulbs are the perfect picture of life. You see, deep inside, each bulb contains a miniature replica of the beautiful plant it will become. Given the right conditions . . . good soil, sunshine, water . . . the tiny flower will begin to grow, soon revealing itself in all the splendor God intended for it. But if something is not right, if the conditions are poor, the tender plant will either die or grow stunted and misshapen, never achieving its full potential. I am certain you can see the parallel. Is it not a perfect picture?"

"Perfect," commented the marquess, still rummaging. Onto his chest came a kit of powder and balls for the pistol, the gun itself, a three-inch length of green-velvet ribbon, and a small wedge of cake, flattened and dried into the texture of stucco inside an oiled paper fold. On his next foray, quite suddenly, he barked, "Ouch! Devil a bit!"

"What is it?" Serenity inquired, leaning closer to his nose to get a better view as he withdrew his hand from her reticule.

"I have been pierced!" Rand growled.

"Whatever? . . . oh, it is my hatpin!" she cried, her face transforming with delight. "I misplaced that pin months ago. How kind in you to recover it, Chilton."

"It is not kind at all, madam," he growled in disagreement. "It is painful. Kindly remove it from my palm."

"But I have no hands," she reminded him.

"Use your teeth," the marquess ground out in suggestion.

Serenity shook her head in a tiny scold. "Really, Chilton, you are quite demanding. Here, turn your hand toward my mouth."

The marquess did as he was told. Serenity then bent her head and maneuvered close to his open palm. As she seized the pin, Rand's cupped fingers unavoidably ensnared themselves in her mass of curls. The sweet thicket was all softness and warmth. To his chagrin, his fingers shaped themselves to her skull. Their eyes met; soft breathing stuttered.

Smiling nervously, Serenity carefully pulled her hatpin from his hand, then lowered it to his chest. The marquess exhaled heavily and slowly withdrew.

"Soil preparation is very important," Serenity suddenly blurted as a wild gust rattled against the carriage.

The marquess shot her an incredulous glance, then tucked his neck deeper into the garrick and began removing more articles from the reticule.

"It must have just the right mixture of sand and loam," the lady explained uncomfortably into the silence as he withdrew a bottle of *sal volatile,* the three handkerchiefs, and a small painted tin. "Ah, at last you have found the handkerchiefs and the biscuits," she then commented with a hopeful smile.

"Indeed," Rand responded flatly, giving her only a cursory glance. Balancing the tin on one of the garrick's straps, he then levered the lid off with his thumb, withdrew one of the buttery wafers, and poked it into his mouth.

Serenity subsided, regarding him as he followed the first with two others.

"Fertilizer is important, too," she said after a time. "Father and Propriety prefer to add a good measure of manure to their soil mix, but I believe that it is somewhat strong for plants which do so well in the wilds of nature. I prefer a compost of leaves and other plant life for my fertilizer. Which do you prefer, sir?"

"I prefer to eat my biscuits, madam, without having to think of fertilizer," Rand stated quellingly.

"Oh."

"I don't suppose you wanted one of these things, too," he inquired after a longer stretch of heavy silence in which he munched through half the tin's contents.

Serenity brightened. "If you please. I have become quite sharp-set, too, I fear."

"Very well," the marquess said, taking a biscuit from the tin. "Hold still and open your mouth . . . there."

Soft, warm lips closed over the tips of his fingers. He shuddered.

"Thnmph-mm," Serenity said politely, unintentionally firing a round of dry biscuit crumbs toward Rand's chin.

Instantly, the marquess's jaw began to jut and squirm. Moments later it rolled to a halt long enough for him to complain, "Congratulations, Miss Hoffenduffle. You have managed to get crumbs down my collar!"

Serenity swallowed again. "I do beg your pardon, sir," she choked in reply.

"Do you know how uncomfortable it can be for a man to have crumbs down inside his shirt?" he inquired.

"I am sure it is most irritating," she consoled.

"It is. And I am already irritated past being rational.

Now where are those blasted scissors?" Again the marquess poked and prodded inside the reticule, withdrawing a wax jack, a limp tuzzy-muzzy, and a chipped saucer painted with clumps of narcissus, before at last coming out with a miniature pair of scissors fashioned with tiny stork handles. Amazed, he held them in the air before his eyes.

"Tell me these are not your sewing scissors," he commanded softly.

"Of course they are," Serenity replied with a smile. "I assure you, they are quite adequate for snipping threads."

"And you intend to rescue us with them?" he asked again.

"No, indeed," the lady said quite soberly.

Rand's gaze slewed to hers. "No?" he barked unpleasantly.

"No," Serenity replied, her countenance serene. And then she reminded him, "After all, I have no hands."

The marquess rolled his eyes. "I take it, then, that *I* intend to rescue us with them," he concluded wearily.

"You do," the lady confirmed.

"Madam, my fingers do not even fit into the holes," he groused.

"You haven't even tried them," she countered.

"Because I know I shall get stuck in them," the marquess objected.

"You shall not," she chided. "Proceed, Chilton."

"The picture is getting more and more ugly," he muttered. "I can see the headline of *The Morning Post* now: The Marquess of Chilton Found Dead in an Overturned Carriage . . . Cause of Death: Mortification from Stork Scissors Stuck on his Fingers. Possible Strangulation by Reticule."

Serenity bit back another smile. "There are worse things to be stuck in," she comforted.

"Yes," he snapped angrily. "This carriage, with you."

Serenity's smile faded.

"Well, that is almost over for both of us, is it not?" she said after a time.

The marquess sighed. He had hurt her. He had not intended to do so, but he had hurt her just the same. The comment had slipped out before he had thought to stop it. Yet perhaps, after all, it was for the best. A distance now stood between them again. And any distance, no matter from what source, was more than pleasant . . . it was a necessity.

"Yes, it is," he finally, unapologetically, replied. "What do you wish me to do?"

Serenity spoke quietly. "It is quite simple. You must cut the sleeve of my pelisse close to where it is attached to your head."

"The deuce, you say!" the marquess responded with raised brows. "I shall poke out my eye!"

"Don't be such a baby," the lady replied.

"My apologies," Rand sneered sarcastically. "How foolish of me to be concerned over the fact that I will be able to see nothing of what I am doing while I am doing this impossible chore. Tell me, Miss Hoffenduffle, do you also have a pair of pliers in that carpetbag of yours? Perhaps I should extract a molar that has been bothering me of late while I am about it."

"I shall guide you, Chilton," Serenity said calmly, ignoring his pique. "Now get on with it, if you please. I am becoming quite chilled."

Rand felt the tiny tremor that coursed through her as she spoke and rested his gaze upon her. Chewing on his inner cheek, he chided himself for his thoughtlessness. How had he not seen it? Concealed within the snowbank as she had been, of course she would have been quite thoroughly soaked as a result and would be nearly frozen by now! Studying her more closely, he noticed for the first time that not only had the color faded from her complexion, but the thin outline of her lips had taken on a grayish hue. His brows gathered. Was there to be no end to his constant torment? Deuce take it, the jade continually rendered him addlepated! Worse, he supposed that he would have to try to warm her somehow.

Resigning himself to his fate, he at last slipped his fingers as far as they would go into the tiny scissor holes, then carefully moved them toward his wound. At the same time, he curved his other arm up around Serenity's shoulders, reluctantly drawing her closer to his body's heat.

"Tell me in which direction to move my hand," he commanded tightly.

"What are you doing?" she questioned warily.

"Attempting to get directions out of you, madam," he responded through his teeth, not at all pleased with how pleasant her form felt against him.

"No . . . I meant with your other hand," Serenity corrected.

"Trying to keep you from freezing," he muttered testily.

"Oh. I see," the lady breathed. "Th . . . That is most kind in you, Chilton. Yet I hardly think it necessary for you to . . ."

". . . To what?" the marquess queried impatiently, angling the scissor points toward his wound.

"T-To stroke . . ."

". . . What?"

"It . . . It cannot be proper . . ."

Awareness dawned. Rand jerked his arm away.

"Since when have you concerned yourself with propriety, madam?" he questioned angrily. "Nothing about this situation is proper, so tell me where I must place my hand so that we can both make good our escape!"

"There is no need to continually shout at me, Chilton. I am only inches from your face, you will notice, and nothing is wrong with my hearing. Besides, it will be better if I guide you." Catching the marquess completely by surprise, Serenity closed her teeth gently around the outside edge of his palm, then steered his hand toward her sleeve. "There," she said, releasing him after the tiny points had touched against the hem. "Open the scissors and advance them just a bit . . . yes, that's it. You have it, Chilton. Now just cut in a straight line."

The marquess concentrated and squeezed his throbbing thumb and finger together. It took several minutes before the tiny blades began to gnaw through the thick wool of Serenity's pelisse and make forward progress; several more before the marquess was able to maneuver them around the entire area where the fabric was attached to his wound. But in the end, and much to their mutual relief, his head at last dropped back against the floor and Serenity's wrist sprang free.

"Goodness, that certainly feels better," she exclaimed as she reared up upon both pointed elbows and began to rub a bit of circulation back into her leaden arm. "You owe me an apology, Chilton."

"An apology?" the marquess echoed, wincing at the sudden sharp pain that stabbed into his musculature while he was gingerly touching his fingers to his wound.

"Yes, indeed," the lady told him smugly. "Admit it, sir. My plan worked perfectly."

"Your plan left me with a piece of blue wool stuck to my head," the marquess denied in a growl.

"A mere detail," she responded tartly, again trembling against him. "I am persuaded that you are quite as relieved as I am that you are at last free of me."

"I am not free of you, madam," Rand corrected. "I am not yet even free of this carriage. Kindly repack this 'ridicule' of yours, if you please. I shall be relieved only when I am out from under you, out of this carriage, and driving my curricle away."

"Then I shall do my best not to delay you any longer!" Serenity responded huffily, perilously tightening the loops still wrapped around his neck as she began to jam her assorted possessions back between the drawstrings.

"Good!" the marquess asserted, sliding a finger between his neck and the constriction to again loosen it. Drawing his lips into a thin line, he then elevated his head to an awkward angle and carefully affixed his beaver and scarf back upon his head.

"I cannot tell you how delighted I am that my agreement pleases you," Serenity returned bitingly, her sapphire eyes glowering as she placed the last of the articles into her reticule and drew the strings tight.

"Your delight, or lack of it, madam, does not signify," the marquess responded cuttingly. "And if you have *anything* to tell me before I rid myself of you once and for all and put this whole ridiculous episode in the past, let it at long last be the truth."

Serenity's eyes widened. "What do you mean, sir? What truth?" she questioned softly as her head tilted to the side.

The marquess's gaze suddenly pierced her. "The truth about why the deuce you are out here in the first place, Miss Hoffenduffle," he snarled, reaching out to seize her shoulders in a powerful grip.

Serenity's body went rigid. "I . . . I was on my way to the wedding, of course," she stammered, alarm raising as much goose flesh upon her arms as did the cold. "Surely you cannot question that?"

"You and I both know that is just a cover," the marquess ground out, his eyes brittle with disdain as they stared into hers. "You forget how well I know you, madam. I will know your real purpose, if you please."

"My real purpose? I have no idea what you are speaking of," she asserted warmly. "My purpose is exactly as I have said."

"Then you lie," Rand accused harshly. "What did you steal that you were bringing to those murderers, Miss Hoffenduffle?"

"What? Nothing! Merciful heavens, Chilton," Serenity breathed in astonishment. "What are you accusing me of?"

"Collusion, madam," Chilton replied coldly. "Of all the travelers accompanying this carriage, you are, after all, the only one still unharmed. I find that fact most telling."

"Only because I was able to hide from them for a time!" Serenity defended.

"Is that so? Then perhaps you would care to explain why, when I first noticed that two of the scoundrels were in here struggling with something, and obviously you had to be in here with them, not once did you fire your pistol at them as you quite readily did at me."

"I . . ."

". . . None of your carefully concocted alibis, if you please," he snapped. "What was in this carriage that was so valuable that everyone on it had to die?"

Serenity responded by trembling violently. Then, in a startling movement, she suddenly reared up and away from the marquess's body, breaking his hold upon her shoulders just before rolling off him and flattening herself against the squabs.

"I don't know!" she gasped, squeezing herself against the frayed fabric, her eyes pooling with tears as her rapid breathing filled the space.

"Yes you do, damn it!" the marquess bellowed. "Tell me!"

Tears spilled over Serenity's lashes to trickle down her cold, pale cheeks, her sapphire eyes bleeding fear as she gazed at him imploringly. When she spoke, her voice was a thready whisper.

"I am afraid . . . I-I can only assume, sir, that it was I."

Stiffening, the Marquess of Chilton bit into his cheek.

Six

"You." It was a statement voiced in tones dulled by disbelief.

"Yes, me."

"Madam, you continually amaze me."

"You are entirely mistaken, Chilton," Serenity informed him after a shaky swallow. "About whatever it is you think."

The marquess surged to life. "Blast it all, Miss Hoffenduffle, stop lying!" he shouted, hauling himself to his feet and propelling himself out through the door opening to drop upon the thickly layered snow concealing the road. "Do you think me such a fool?"

"I think you an idiot, sir!" Serenity countered heatedly, brushing away her tears, rising up to poke her head through the same aperture before bracing her upper arms against the frame. Empowered by her fresh surge of anger, she then began to push against the panels with her elbows, struggling with all her might to lift her weight up past the body of the carriage so that she might join him to continue their discussion outside.

"I was . . . merely trying . . . to explain," she gasped, again levering her arms against the ancient wood, panting and straining as she concentrated upon her task. "And, by the saints, Chilton, if you insist upon asking me questions, cease . . . shouting at me when I respond."

The marquess watched her efforts with growing irritation, his fists planted upon his hips.

"Oh, for the love of . . ." he finally muttered, striding back between the carriage wheels to seize Serenity beneath her arms and yank her free of the doorframe, afterward lowering her to the ground with all the delicacy of a rock-sledging railroad navvy, embedding her legs like two fence posts in the trailing edge of the snowdrift. Giving her a frigid glower until she had steadied herself, he then turned away again toward his curricle without a word, covering the distance to where it stood waiting in long, purposeful strides. Granting her no further notice, he began brushing accumulated snow from his horses' flanks.

Serenity regarded him, shivering again as the deep drift melted against her stockinged legs and cascaded in wet chunks and dribbles over the tops of her boots to sink slowly inside. Even more readily, her temper soared. Through narrowed eyes, she sank darts of animosity into the marquess's retreating back.

"And I am not lying!" she shouted at a point between his shoulder blades, beginning to plow a path over to intersect his so that she could more easily follow him. "They *were* struggling," she continued breathlessly, quickly closing the distance between them, "but they were struggling with me."

"Hah!" Rand cried, abruptly interrupting his inspection of the traces to whirl around and scowl at Serenity, forcing her to collide quite solidly with his broad chest. "Why did you not shoot then?"

"Because," the lady responded, leaping back, "I was still in the process of digging myself out of the carriage through the window at the time. When those villains entered and found me, the only thing I could face them with was my . . . the afterward of my person. Oh, stuff, Chilton! I was pointed the wrong way. I could not have fired at them even if I had been able to reach the gun in my reticule . . . which I was not," she added, holding up her hand to arrest his show of scorn. "At the time, my reticule was trapped beneath me."

"You managed quite handily to shoot at me," Rand countered witheringly.

"Certainly I did. By the time you had entered the carriage, I had managed to turn myself about," she explained, propping her gloved fists upon her hips as he turned dismissively back toward his team, "and to extricate my pistol, too, of course."

"Of course," Rand repeated, tightening the traces, running a final, knowledgeable hand over his lead bay's steaming mane. Again he turned to face her. "And you shot at me, therefore, because you thought I was one of them."

"Yes, that is it exactly!" Serenity cried with relief. "You must see that there was no way I could have known who you were, Chilton. And, of course, I was rather overset at the time."

"Assuredly," the marquess commented. "And you have made everything in your elucidation seem quite plausible, Miss Hoffenduffle . . . except for one small thing."

"What is that?" Serenity queried, again dropping her hands to her side.

The marquess slowly shook his head. "You have not explained why four highwaymen would want you in the first place, madam," he stated meticulously, "nor why they should find you so valuable that they would murder four other people to get to you."

Serenity's countenance sobered. Her gaze fell to the shine on Rand's snow-speckled Blüchers.

"Nothing to say, have you?" the marquess observed after a moment in which he skewered her with cold disdain.

When she still gave him no answer, he shook his head in disgust and left his horse's side to bound lithely up to his curricle's leather-clad seat, putting away his pistols and settling himself comfortably upon the tufted squabs before taking the ribbons into his gloved hands.

Serenity stood motionless throughout his preparations, raising only her gaze to follow his progress, refusing to give in to tears. Then, angrily, she caught at the edges of her bonnet, righted it, and forced it back upon her curls, the tiny blue bird bobbing drunkenly in its limp, beribboned nest.

"I assure you they did not find me valuable, Chilton," she snapped at last as she reached to recapture the bonnet's wind-capering blue ribbons in order to retie them under her chin. "No one places value on that which they wish to destroy."

Taken aback, Rand's gaze slewed toward her. An immediate silence thickened around them while his spine lost all its curve.

Serenity did not notice. Unable to hide her burgeoning tears any longer, she quickly presented her back to his astonishment and strode purposefully toward the four snow-burdened mounds lying still and silent beside the road, stopping only for a moment to dab at her eyes with the ragged flap of her pelisse sleeve before coming to a halt by their side.

It had become Rand's turn to stare after her.

"You've done something again, haven't you?" he called out as she dropped to her knees beside her companion.

Serenity, for her part, ignored him.

"Answer me, deuce take it!" he shouted.

Serenity sniffed once, but remained silent.

The marquess bore her disregard as long as he could, then huffed soundlessly. Again he impatiently tied off the ribbons and jumped down from the carriage. Long, stalking strides brought him back to the opposite side of the road, where he stood towering over her, his garrick whipping about his body, his hands fisted at his sides. His mouth opened, drawing breath for an awesome tirade.

"Please, Chilton, I am praying for Mary and her family," Serenity said softly, efficiently corking his opportunity as she reached out to rest her hand gently upon the woman's form. "Besides, I have no idea what you are talking about."

It took a moment for the marquess to recover.

"Then allow me to inform you," he finally stated beneath a narrowed, knowing gaze. "You've stolen from those highwaymen as well, haven't you?"

"I haven't stolen from anyone," Serenity stated sadly.

"You've made enemies of your own cohorts, and now they want revenge, isn't that right?" he expanded disgustedly.

Serenity's shoulders drooped the tiniest fraction from their proper posture. She sighed softly, then, using the heels of her hands, rubbed at a new freshet of tears that had formed silvery trails over her cold-blushed skin. When she had finished, she pushed against the ground, sinking up to her elbows in soft snow as she steadied her legs beneath her, finally rising to her feet. Turning, she brought her gaze to rest upon the marquess, wrapping her arms about herself as she did so. She perused his face for long moments, her eyes glistening softly, and let her focus slide to a distant point somewhere beyond his shoulder.

"Go away," she said quietly.

"What?" Rand hissed, again jamming his fists against his hips.

"Just go away," Serenity repeated, squeezing herself against a visible tremor. "Please."

More minutes passed as Rand stood staring down at her in outrage, his chest rising and falling with his effort to restrain his vexation. Then, spinning about angrily, he again strode over to where his curricle stood waiting. "Gladly!" he finally bit out. "The last thing I wish is to be caught up in another of your perfidious schemes." In one swift movement, he mounted the carriage and again sank

into its squabs, his fist once more closing about the ribbons.

"Once was quite enough for me, madam," he continued
as he touched his whip to his leader's shoulder. Instantly,
the restless horses surged into motion, plowing powerfully
through the drifted snow, propelling the marquess easily
past Serenity and several yards beyond.

"It has, as usual, been a joy passing the afternoon with
you, Miss Hoffenduffle," he called back, touching the brim
of his beaver as the curricle moved away. "I wish you a
long and profitable life!"

Serenity followed him with her deep blue gaze.

Suddenly, the carriage drew up to a halt. More silent
moments passed in which neither moved.

And then Serenity heard a word bitten out from between
the marquess's teeth that she had never heard before. She
had no idea of its meaning, yet still her cheeks grew pink.

"What are you going to do?" he finally, brusquely, called
back to her, not turning around.

"You needn't worry, Chilton," she returned with an ab-
sence of emotion, her eyes now downcast. "I shall stay with
Mary until the help you send arrives."

More silence stretched between them as Rand touched
his tongue to the rawness on the inside of his cheek and
decided that he really should not chew on it anymore.

"You cannot do that," he at last countered in vexed
tones. "You will freeze to death."

"Perhaps!" Serenity spat back at him, again shivering.
"Or perhaps my 'cohorts' will return to finish the job they
first set out to do. What does it signify?"

"It does not!" he shouted back. "Except . . ."

". . . Except what?" she demanded angrily.

"Except that I have this deuced conscience," he yelled.
"I, madam, am a gentleman!" he bellowed louder "I cannot just ride away and leave you."

Serenity quieted, then, heaving a great sigh as she nodded her acceptance of the fact. "Even without a conscience you could not leave me, Chilton," she told him softly.

"The deuce you say!" Rand countered. "I would already be in Martlesham by this time if it were not for my gentleman's duty."

"No, you would not," responded Serenity, her disagreement causing her little blue bird to dart back and forth in its nest like a reluctant sparring partner. Elevating her nose, she next clasped her hands before her waist like a woman long on the shelf. "You might try to leave, but you are no thief, sir."

"On that we are agreed, madam," Rand stated icily. "But how can that possibly signify?"

"Because," Serenity replied, nodding seriously.

The marquess waited for her to continue. More moments passed. At last his mouth twisted with vexation. "Blast it all, madam, will you just once cease stretching out your ridiculous explanations and come to the point?"

"And will you for once stop shouting at me while I am going about it?" Serenity countered heatedly. "It signifies because it is the very reason why you would have to come back!"

"That is the most knuckleheaded logic I have ever heard!" cried the marquess. "Why would my disdain of larceny compel me to return to you once I had had the good fortune to escape?"

Serenity's fists balled. "Because, you arrogant, unctuous . . . Corinthian! . . ."

". . . If you please! Just answer the question, madam," the marquess interrupted.

Serenity clamped her arms beneath her breasts. "Obviously, it is because you would in no wise wish to be guilty of stealing my reticule, sir, and my reticule is still hanging around your neck," she responded, and then she began to drum her fingers upon her biceps.

The marquess's gaze widened, dropped to his chest, and then closed against a deeply felt sigh.

"There is no help for it, is there?" he muttered wearily. "It is always the same. All I need do is come within ten miles of you and my life unravels with astonishing speed. Come here, then, Miss Hoffenduffle, and kindly remove your property."

"This situation is hardly my fault, Chilton," Serenity replied, beginning to wade toward him through the piled snow covering the road. "You act as if I had planned for you to happen by."

"This 'situation' as you call it is indeed your fault, madam," Rand argued. "However, I do not think I was meant to become involved. That would be too great a risk even for you to take, would it not? I may have kept silent for your sake once before, but you could have no assurance that I would do so again."

"You speak in riddles, sir," Serenity stated, coming up beside him. "What have you felt the need to keep silent about?"

Rand's gaze grew astounded. "The past, of course," he spat at her. "That night . . . in Charity's Place."

The lady stiffened. "And well you might wish to keep that occasion secret, sir," she said indignantly, "but not for my sake. *I* was not the one rolling around on a store-room floor with a woman of questionable character in a state of . . . of complete *déshabillé!*"

"Madam, I was not rolling around . . . well, perhaps I was . . . but there was a reason for it, deuce take it!"

"I am not interested in your reasons," Serenity stated calmly.

"Nor I in giving them," shouted the marquess.

"Nor I in receiving them," Serenity asserted with a newly elevated nose.

"Excellent!" Rand replied, somewhat comforted that he

had at least wrested the last word from the lady, albeit failing altogether to dazzle her with his eloquence.

Suddenly, a shadow touched and enveloped them. Their argument withered; died of neglect. They quieted, both of them, glancing toward one another before turning to seek the shadow's origin.

Seven

Awe trickled through Rand's veins. Above, the great, restless cloud mass that he had noted less than an hour before now hovered like a foretelling only a few miles distant, completely blanketing the western sky. Even as he and Serenity watched, the storm drifted closer, spreading low and wide atop the roadside march of elms as it did so; at times seeming to snag upon their thrusting branches, pausing briefly; at other times stretching into gelatinous tendrils in the places where the trees resisted the onrush. A flock of ravens rose in muted cacophony from distant hawthorns to run from the wind, crying out their cowardice. Encouraged, the clouds surged forward once again, at last consuming even the struggling sun with an advance of slow-scudding, seeking filaments.

Then, suddenly, from beneath the gathering a huge bubble of white sank from the clouds to touch upon the fields below it, forming what appeared to be a solid wall of snow that quickly obliterated the horizon. With Rand and Serenity still looking on, the strange snow curtain seemed to hesitate momentarily, then almost languidly begin to flow forward over the landscape like spilled cream. The marquess sucked in his breath at the sight, letting the ribbons go slack as he scanned the development with new urgency. Beside him, Serenity trembled and drew in a very slow breath.

As if mocking her trepidation, the huge snow squall began to pick up speed.

The marquess's lips thinned and blanched. "Devil a bit!" he murmured as his gaze widened. "It does not much please me that whatever that phenomenon, it happens to be heading directly toward us."

Serenity's own lips parted with awe. "Good heavens!" she breathed, unconsciously tugging the damp collar of her pelisse more tightly about her neck. "I have never seen the like before, Chilton. What can it be?"

"A great deal of trouble, I'd wager," the marquess responded absently, his assessing attention still fastened entirely upon the storm's headlong progress. Suddenly, his gaze slewed toward Serenity. "Get into the carriage, Miss Hoffenduffle," he ordered brusquely. "We must find shelter immediately."

Serenity did not hesitate to comply. Gathering her skirts about her, she accepted the marquess's offer of a hand and stumbled quickly into the seat beside him, wrapping her still-sodden pelisse even more tightly about her in an attempt to conserve some of her body's heat against the increasingly brisk gusts now rising ahead of the onslaught. Cold seeped past the wet wool's weave to touch against her skin, pebbling it. She closed her hands around her elbows as a wrenching tremor shook her. In spite of a tightly clenched jaw, her teeth began an unnerving chatter.

Rand glanced at her in vexation. "You are going to perish before I can get you to safety, aren't you?" he grumbled. "Probably out of sheer spite. Did you bring no extra clothing?"

"Of c-course I did," Serenity told him, shaking now, "but none of my valises s-seem to be about."

The marquess recalled, then, the highwaymen's laden arms as they had ridden away in hasty retreat from his attack. Obviously they had managed to purloin a good deal more than just what was of value inside the carriage. Blast!

he again thought irritably. Once more where the jade was concerned, he was to be left no choice. He was going to have to be noble once more. The knowledge chafed. He knew his duty, but at times it was very vexing being a gentleman.

"You had better come here, then," he said, thoroughly nettled to have been forced into the offer.

"Wh-What?" Serenity stammered, peering at him from underneath her wind-buffeted bonnet.

"Come here," Rand repeated, beginning to unfasten his garrick.

Serenity's eyes rounded. "I *am* here, sir," she told him, staring at him as if he had escaped from Bedlam.

"Not *there* here, Miss Hoffenduffle . . ." Rand clipped out in explanation, pointing to her side of the seat, ". . . *here* here," he finished, pointing to his lap.

Serenity's jaw dropped prettily. "You mean . . . ? You c-cannot . . . ! But . . . but I just got off of you!" she cried.

"Get back on," the marquess commanded.

"I will not!" Serenity asserted.

"You will," Rand countered coldly.

"On the contrary, sir! I shall never . . . mmph!" Serenity objected under the surprise of a strong arm cast about her shoulders, followed by an unyielding hand clamped over her lips.

Mere seconds later, she was wedged between the marquess's outspread legs, jostled into a more comfortable position, then completely enclosed within the huge garrick. Warm, wonderful heat began to flow between them, seeping quickly into Serenity's damp clothing. Unwillingly, mind you, she wilted against him in relief.

"Ouch, blast it all!" the marquess swore.

Serenity sat bolt upright. "Whatever . . . ?"

"No, do not turn around, Miss Hoffenduffle," Rand insisted. "Your bird has already pecked its pound of flesh from my face. I have no wish to be gouged in the eye by your hatpin."

Serenity huffed softly in exasperation. "Might I point out, Chilton, that if you had but heeded my objections to your scheme and not arbitrarily dragged me into this completely improper traveling position in the first place, your features would still be intact. Still, as my bonnet was at fault, I recognize my obligation to beg your pardon . . ."

"Do not!" the marquess demanded in vexation. "Do not do anything except take the blasted thing off. Not only is it vicious, but I can no longer see past that ridiculous froth of lace."

"This is my newest bonnet, Chilton," Serenity defended, stiffening against his chest.

"Indeed," the marquess commented, staring down at her from above a loftily upraised nasal passage.

"Yes, it is," she said, twisting to eye him stubbornly, as she did so clipping him quite soundly upon the nose with her brim.

Rand seized his opportunity. Taking hold of the streamers visible just under the bow beneath her chin, with a deft movement he dragged the bonnet from her curls and flung the frilled confection in a high arc toward the storm. Ribbons, lace, and lolling blue bird were easily caught by the blustering wind.

"Not anymore," he judged after the two of them watched the bonnet tip end over end, caper across the road, and come to rest amid the thick undergrowth of hawthorn.

"How dare you, you arrogant, overbearing . . . !" she sputtered.

"Easily," he told her, again planting his hand atop her head, settling her against him, and gently tucking her soft curls beneath his chin. After she was situated to his liking, he snapped his whip above his bays' heads and once more started his team down the road toward Martlesham.

The curricle had traveled no more than a few yards, however, when, from around a shallow curve in the road several hundred yards distant, two riders suddenly appeared and began to gallop toward them. Rand quickly drew his team to a halt once again. Then, his cheek aside Serenity's, he leaned forward into her resistance, his muscles tightening, growing ready; once more his thoughts prickly with suspicion.

"Is it help, do you think?" Serenity asked hopefully, struggling to free a hand from the garrick neck opening so that she might restore some order to her coiffure.

"Help, madam, arrived less than an hour ago," the marquess reminded her absently, scrubbing with the rough points of his teeth at the puncture her restless head had put in his tongue, at the same time putting an end to her aggravating wriggles by clamping an arm about her and using his larger hand to poke her smaller one back into the garrick's warmth.

"So it did," Serenity replied, reluctantly subsiding back against him, "however grudging."

"There was nothing grudging about it, Miss Hoffenduffle, until I discovered you."

"Indeed?" she replied archly. "May I remind you, sir, that if anyone has cause to begrudge anyone else's unwelcome presence, it is I who have the perfect right to feel so toward you!"

"Is that so?" Rand growled, still trying to assess the nature of the approaching riders through each newly lofted layer of wind-borne ice. "I assume that once again we are speaking of that night."

"Yes, we are," Serenity insisted, again clacking against his chin. "You keep forgetting, sir, that it was not I who was engaged in rollicking upon the floor with a . . . a woman of questionable character."

"No, you were not, were you?" the marquess growled.

"Yet what I was doing was not the least bit improper by the standards of the *ton*, Miss Hoffenduffle."

"Yet it most definitely was, sir, by the standards of the Bible."

"To which requirements of behavior you, of course, are so devoted," the marquess witheringly noted. "Cease pretending innocence, and admit it, Miss Hoffenduffle. What you were doing that night was unconscionable."

"I will admit no such thing, as what *you* were doing that night," countered Serenity, "was obscene."

"Poppycock," the marquess remarked, his focus still intent upon the nearing visitors, his gaze narrowed appraisingly over the top of her curls. "You know very well that, if for none other than reasons of health, what I was doing was quite acceptable for a single man."

"As opposed to what I was doing, I misdoubt you wish to imply," Serenity huffed, clutching angrily at her upper arms beneath the voluminous garrick.

"Just so," the marquess replied.

Serenity bit her lower lip. "Very well, I can be honest about this, Chilton. I do admit to a shocking breach of propriety," she confessed as the riders' features began to become discernible through the swirling snow.

"Breach of propriety?" Rand repeated, glancing down at her, his jaw agape. "Madam, you were engaged in a hanging offense!"

"Because I was from home in my night rail?" Serenity gasped, straining against the garrick to return his glower.

"Will you stop rattling on about your blasted night rail?" Rand cried, again giving his attention to the road ahead. "What you were engaged in was treason!"

"Treason!" Serenity breathed in even greater astonishment. "Whatever can you mean?"

The muscles of the marquess's jaw began working in exasperation. "You know very well what I mean!" he finally exploded.

"I do not!" Serenity insisted, continuing to peer up at him, again bumping against his chin with her disavowal.

Suddenly, against her back, the marquess stiffened.

"Then perhaps you would care to consult your friends," he stated, staring ahead, great mounds of muscle forming just beneath his sideburns even as he began to unconsciously, protectively, curl around her smaller form.

"Wh-What? Who?" Serenity asked, still stunned by the marquess's accusations.

"Those two," he told her, pointing toward the fast-approaching riders with his chin. "You might give special notice to the one on the right," he added, indicating the rider following awkwardly and slightly to the rear of the other. "From the look of him, the poor fellow is not too comfortable making contact with his saddle."

"Are you indeed daft, sir?" the lady asked, totally at sea. "Undoubtedly we are about to be offered shelter. This is no time to critique our rescuer's seat!"

"Oh, I heartily disagree," Rand countered, "since, unless I miss my guess, madam, that particular gentleman is carrying one of my pistol rounds in his ars . . ."

". . . the afterward of his person," Serenity interrupted absent-mindedly, slewing about, her attention now riveted completely upon the approaching riders.

"His arse," Rand finished firmly, securing his grip upon the ribbons. "And it does appear that you are correct, Miss Hoffenduffle. One of us is indeed about to be rescued—you, by your partners, unless I miss my guess. Assuredly not I."

Serenity's whole being stilled, stiffened, trembled.

"Dear heaven," she whispered tightly. "Are they the highwaymen, then? Chilton, you must turn immediately and go the other way!"

"Never say that you would not be welcome among them, Miss Hoffenduffle," Rand commented smugly.

"I would not!" Serenity insisted, gripping his thigh. "Chilton, please!"

"So it is true, then," the marquess stated flatly. "You have fallen out with your ring of thieves."

"I have not!" the lady insisted. "This entire conversation is absurd!"

"Well, then, if you have not fallen out with them," the marquess summarized, "you must still be a part of them as I originally thought. And that, of course, leaves me with no other conclusion than that your partners have obviously returned to join you in plucking a bigger goose."

Serenity's eyes grew huge. "You *are* daft!" she stated breathlessly. "I told you before, you are not the target. Those scoundrels bearing down upon us are set to put a period to *me!*"

"Blast it all, madam, can you not for even the twentieth part of a moment cease your flummery? There is no further need on your part for this show of timidity. You and I both know that since, by your own admission, the jackanapes are still partners of yours, it follows that they must have come back for me."

"What nonsense!" Serenity cried, again twisting toward him as she dug her fingers into his thighs. "Why should they want to return for you? And I admitted no such thing!"

"You did," he responded roughly, "and yes, their target could be none other than me. Any others who could identify you and your cohorts are dead, are they not? Of course they are after me."

"Now you are accusing me of complicity in your attempted murder! What idiocy!" Serenity angrily snapped. "There is simply no reasoning with you, is there?"

"There is all the reasoning in the world," the marquess stated smugly. "There is just no lying to me."

"Is that so?" Serenity queried hotly, insensible of the

building whistle of the wind through the hedgerows and the counterpoint rhythm of approaching hoofbeats.

"Yes, that is most certainly so!" the marquess told her, awash with the virtue of his point.

"Then attend to this, sir," Serenity said, leaning away from him and twisting around inside the garrick until she could peer up challengingly into his dark eyes. "I, Serenity Hoffenduffle, do solemnly swear that I am top over tails in love with you, Randall Torrent. So tell me, my fine, arrogant lord . . . do I lie?"

A great length of throbbing silence passed after Serenity's declaration.

And then the Marquess of Chilton's muscles turned to water.

Rand had little more time than a twitch to absorb the rush of emotion that washed over him following Serenity's astounding challenge before a lead ball quite suddenly tore through the curricle's hood near his right shoulder, then disappeared behind him into the approaching squall.

Eight

"Get down!" the marquess shouted instantly as a second ball, more poorly charged than the first, thumped against the tufted squabs and dropped down onto the seat beside him. Instinctively he crushed Serenity against his body, crouching even farther over her.

So the scoundrels actually did think to put a period to him, did they? he assessed, feeling his muscles' flaccidity again congeal under this new, and wholly welcome, distraction. Well, let them do their damnedest, he vowed, his eyes glittering with sparks from anticipation's forge. Happily, this attack was no wayward jade's thunderous revelation slamming into his skull like a skittish colt's iron-shod hoof, leaving him addlepated and gasping for air. *This* he could understand, he nodded, grinding a bulge into his jaw. *This* was something he knew how to handle.

Tensing his body, the marquess surged into action. Squeezing the ribbons in his fist, he pulled hard upon them, wheeling his bloods abruptly about on the narrow road with a finely feathered turn that even he was forced to modestly acknowledge put to shame the skin-pebbling pivot Algernon Peck, the current president of the Four-In-Hand, had accomplished four months ago around Woden's Wrinkle in the wilds of Northumberland. A smile of exhilaration notched his cheeks beneath the wind's blast, and he noted with vast satisfaction the frantic clutch of Serenity's fingers into his thighs for balance as the carriage abruptly reversed direction.

Confidence surged through his veins. Loudly cracking his whip above his leader's head, he toweled his team into a ground-eating pace back toward Ipswich, only just arresting a bark of laughter. With highwaymen on his heels, he no longer had to try to wade through the morass that his mind had now become thanks to the appalling hoyden tucked securely between his legs.

As the curricle once more sped past the wrecked post chaise and another ball buried itself in leather and horse-hair, he acknowledged that he had never felt quite so relieved. Someone, for some reason, was trying to put a period to him. Ah, yes, this was much to be preferred. For the nonce, in the place of cork-brained female idiocy he could deal with a few of the simpler things of life instead . . . murder, for instance. Perhaps, if he were lucky, even a little pleasant mayhem.

Again a ball ripped through the carriage hood, slicing off a bit of the marquess's beaver brim before dropping like a pebble against the lead gelding's flank, its force spent. Rand turned abruptly to peer through the hole; just as quickly, he slewed back around to his place again. Excitement glowed in his eyes; vengeance throbbed in the intensity of his softly bitten oath.

"Your friends appear to be gaining on us, Miss Hoffenduffle," he sneered between the curl of his lips. "It also appears that they know how to load and fire while doing so."

"What do you intend to do?" Serenity asked from her comfortable position wedged within the notch between the marquess's shoulder and neck.

"Return fire, of course," he responded, maneuvering his galloping bays across a low-arched limestone bridge.

"Oh, excellent, sir!" Serenity exclaimed, abruptly

brightening as she warmed to the notion. "Where have you put your pistols?"

"In their box. Naturally, I returned them there when I took my seat," Rand told her, quickly countering a skid caused by the curricle's heady career over a washboard series of frozen ruts. "You will have to reach down and get them for me. I cannot risk losing control of my team."

"Of course," the lady readily agreed. "Wait but one moment. I shall have them for you in a trice."

Immediately Serenity stretched her arm down inside the voluminous garrick, snuggling the damp fabric of her traveling gown and pelisse close to her inner thighs so that she might reach between her legs to take hold of the wooden box. She bent no farther than a few inches, however, before, in mid-reach, the neckline of the garrick cut quite cruelly across her sensitive throat. Vexed, she turned a bit to the side and tried again. Once more the garrick's tight fastenings arrested her. Reluctantly, she straightened and twisted toward the marquess.

"You shall need to unfasten the top strap, sir," she ordered. "I fear I shall have to be completely inside this garrick if I am to retrieve the pistols."

"And how am I to do that?" Rand asked in annoyance, skillfully guiding his surging bloods over a dangerous patch of ice. "I cannot let go of the ribbons at this headlong pace."

"And I cannot reach the pistols if you do not!" Serenity cried after another insufficient charge sent a second ball thumping harmlessly against the curve of the curricle hood.

Almost immediately after, another report rang out into the wind-whistling expanse. Serenity gasped slightly as she heard the shot fly directly over her curls, then felt the man pressed tightly against her back jolt sharply at the impact.

"Blast it all to . . . !"

". . . Chilton, have you been hit?" Serenity exclaimed,

clinging to his thighs against the jostling shift of the curricle, twisting about to peer up at him, her blue gaze filled with concern.

"No, madam, I would not give you that much pleasure. The scoundrels have merely done violence to my beaver," Rand muttered above her ear. "Punched a hole right through it, wouldn't you know. Positively drafty now."

"Then they are continuing to gain on us, are they not?" Serenity queried, still worried.

The marquess's response came beneath a forming frown. "It would seem so. See here, Miss Hoffenduffle, there seems to be no other choice but for *you* to take the ribbons," he declared after a short moment's thought.

"What, me?" Serenity gasped, her eyes growing round.

"Who else, Miss Hoffenduffle?" asked Rand, his tone not the least bit solicitous. "You *can* drive a team, can you not?"

"Well, yes . . . of a sort," she responded, her voice fading into a mumble.

"Here then," the marquess responded. "Take them. Keep the tits steady on between the hedgerows and don't let them get too close to the ditches or drifts."

Gathering her resources, Serenity raised her hands inside the garrick. And then she paused.

"Chilton?" she asked, her brow furrowing.

"What now?" he snapped as another round clattered against the curricle spokes.

"How am I to take the ribbons through the front of this garment unless you unfasten what you vow you cannot?"

"Easily, Miss Hoffenduffle," he explained, his brow revealing the thinning of his patience. "You insert your arms into the sleeves, of course."

Serenity twisted to gaze up at his chin. "But *your* arms are within the sleeves," she replied, her eyes the size of his library's ceiling medallions.

"So? This garrick could hold the Horse Guards, Miss

Hoffenduffle," Rand countered impatiently, glancing down at her above a facial expression Serenity thought he most likely reserved for foul smells. "Put your arms in the sleeves alongside mine, and after you have taken the ribbons, I shall withdraw and get the pistols myself."

Countered by the marquess's unassailable logic, Serenity sighed. Afterward, with her second thought, she had to admit she could see no harm in the idea. It was improper, of course, to touch so much of the extent of one's arm to a gentleman's, but then there was nothing at all proper in her being crushed against that gentleman's entire length either, and she had so far managed to weather that indecency without too much pother.

Dear heavens! she thought with sinking spirits. How was she to explain any of the day's happenstance to her father and Propriety after the whole bumblebroth finally resolved itself? She could not imagine. Of course, at the moment, she was again forced to admit, the matter was hardly of consequence. As there seemed to be an increasingly good chance that they would neither of them survive their scandalous situation to once again become notorious, what could another breach of etiquette signify? Nodding in acquiescence, she shrugged slightly. Afterward, pointing her fingers, she thrust her hands down alongside the marquess's muscular arms.

"Ah, decided to comply, have we?" Rand chided, expertly navigating a collecting drift. "Take the ribbons then, if you please, Miss Hoffenduffle. In all this indecision we have wasted quite enough of our advantage."

Chastened, Serenity stretched out her right hand. "Very well," she replied, seizing hold of the gathered leathers just below the glove of the marquess.

"No, with your left, madam," the marquess impatiently corrected. "Ribbons are always held in the left hand."

"What difference does it make, sir," Serenity objected,

"to two people who are being chased by highwaymen and are trying to outrun a storm?"

The marquess's nose arose. "If a thing is worth doing, Miss Hoffenduffle, it is worth doing well."

Fuming, Serenity shifted the ribbons into her left hand.

"Very good," Rand congratulated. "Now if you'll but . . . no, madam, one cannot manage a team with everything in one hand. Take the whip into your right. I thought you said you knew how to drive."

"I—I have driven before," Serenity responded defensively, juggling assorted strands of leather.

"Good. Then kindly do so."

Vexed, Serenity glared at the team with such heat that, had she continued, she might have curled a good number of the hairs on their tails. As it was, though, she held her patience, calmly sorting out the ribbons and whip after securing her gloves with tiny tugs, then bidding the marquess to, for heaven's sake, stop annoying her and turn the bloods over to her control.

Pricked almost beyond endurance, he did.

And in the next moment, Serenity was wrenched forward and flattened against the heavy wool of the garrick by the bays' powerful pulls.

Gasping, she immediately counterbalanced, rearing backward as she worked her feet to the fore to brace her boots against the curricle's kickboard. After taking a deep breath, she pushed against it with all her strength. She might just as well have been trying to force a piece of straw through a stone.

Behind her, the marquess tsked in her ear and shook his head.

Serenity's cheeks burned. She gritted her teeth, then grew rigid as he easily drew her back against him and forced her into a more useful position between his legs. At last, after huffing another warm, moist blast against her curls, he again placed the ribbons into her proper hand and withdrew his arms from the voluminous sleeves.

Immediately after, Serenity felt the marquess begin his search for the box of pistols, fumbling about inside the garrick, twisting his limbs this way and that, shoving aside clothing as he tried to locate his weapons. She would have liked to have given him the set-down he richly deserved, but, after taking a deep breath, she decided to pay him no heed. Considering their circumstances, after all, it mattered little that the man was a pompous, obnoxious libertine. They were both now in deadly peril, perhaps from the highwaymen, certainly from the storm.

And she had been given a duty to perform, an important task to which her total concentration was due. She had been charged to keep the curricle ahead of their pursuers so that they might escape to safety while the marquess returned fire. Escape! she thought as her eyes rolled. Escaping the highwaymen would be the easy part. Much more difficult for her, she knew, would be simply keeping the dratted vehicle on the road.

She was not sure how she was to make this happen. She knew all too well that her experience with driving was not exactly as she had allowed the marquess to believe, but, of course, it was far too late for her to correct that mistaken impression now. Yet she still had the obligation to rise to the occasion and prevail. Both their lives depended upon her success in this endeavor. But more importantly, she had no doubt that if by some horrible misjudgment she were accidentally to drive his lordship's lithe, racing curricle into a ditch or, heaven forfend, to wrap its polished veneers around a sturdy tree, to the end of what life remained in her body as she lay sprawled upon the road, broken beyond recognition, she knew she would never hear the end of his rag-mannered peal.

She decided to experiment. Hesitantly, she tugged upon the ribbons, first this way, and then that. Huge, muscular flanks surged and sank before her widened eyes, responding to the merest touch of her fingertips. Surprised, she tried clucking to the horses, urging them to run faster. They stretched out their necks and complied. A fallen hawthorn loomed across part of the road ahead. She narrowed her gaze, accepting its audacious challenge, then pulled upon the ribbons. The bays swerved as if one with her, sweeping past the obstruction with thundering accord, not once slackening their pace. Serenity smiled broadly, inordinately pleased, suddenly heady with the power she now controlled, power that responded instantly—more, only to her command.

And then a fat, wet snowflake splashed against her eyelid, startling her quite indelicately back from heading into Ascot's final stretch.

With awareness came the rather unexpected realization that the clumsy poking and probing which had been going on beneath the garrick had suddenly stilled. Curious, she glanced back toward the marquess as best she could, her brows narrowing the distance between themselves.

The marquess's eyes were closed.

Disconcerted, Serenity tipped her head and turned about even farther.

She did so just in time to receive the Marquess of Chilton's heavy exhalation of breath into the soft shell of her ear and to ripple with the ensuing gooseflesh before she next felt him settle one large, shaky hand upon her lap, then, most extraordinarily, begin to slowly slide bare fingers down the length of her gently curved thigh.

Nine

"Good heavens, Chilton, w-what are you doing?" Serenity breathed, straightening quickly when his cold, bare fingers reached the soft, sensitive place behind her well-formed knee.

The marquess's next inhalation was oddly deep and ragged beside Serenity's neck. His fingers stopped their downward progress.

"Trying to find my way past your clothing to the floor," he husked, losing the battle to prevent his fingers from stroking gently back and forth across the tender cleft.

A volley of sleet tapped against the carriage hood along with two rounds from the highwaymen's pistols, and Serenity gasped—not, however, from the sharp, percussive sounds. That she had ceased attending moments ago. Instead, and quite beyond her control, her complete attention had coiled around the astonishing sensations the marquess's gentle touch had begun eliciting. For that reason, it was even longer before she abruptly realized that those same exquisite feelings were springing from a knee which, along with the marquess's fingers, was also quite mortifyingly bare.

It came as quite a shock to her. She could only guess at how that might have happened. Had she uncovered it herself in her own search for the pistols? . . . or had her skirts gotten tangled when the marquess had dragged her over so unceremoniously onto his lap? Perhaps it had happened during all his fumbling about while he searched for his weapons. She had no idea.

Of one thing she was certain, however. She could not in good conscience cut up stiff with him. If her limb had become exposed, it had most definitely been an accident— oh, yes, of that she was most positively convinced. Given his recent behavior toward her, Serenity knew that there was no way under heaven the Marquess of Chilton would ever have bared her limb or touched her in any manner on purpose, given the choice. Quite generously, therefore, she allowed the marquess to have the benefit of the doubt.

"Is it absolutely necessary that you m-make contact with my l-lower extremity?" she finally managed to utter as the most unusual sensations continued to skitter over her.

"Unfortunately, it is a bit crowded down there," Rand groaned, his fingers suddenly embedding themselves in her soft skin. "I could not locate the deuced box, Miss Hoffenduffle. To my everlasting regret, I judged following your leg to be the most efficient path."

"Oh. I see. Well . . . d-do hurry, Chilton," Serenity breathed unsteadily. "Those villains are coming quickly."

"Lud, so am I," Rand breathed.

"Whatever . . . ?"

"Never mind," he interjected after a series of pants, at last mustering the willpower to slide his hand the rest of the way down her leg. After more moments of groping over her well-rounded calf and slim ankle, he again settled. "I have located the box now, Miss Hoffenduffle. Just hold everything steady while I load and prepare to fire."

Again the marquess groaned. This was hardly the time for a double *entendre*. With a will, he struggled to ignore the painful discomfort of Serenity's compliance, which caused her to straighten officiously and conscientiously brace herself even more firmly into the notch of his legs.

"You need have no fear, Chilton," Serenity told him with

a delighted smile, her blue eyes once more sparkling with purpose as she again turned her full attention upon the team. "I shall drive this bang-up set-out of blood and bone to an inch. I shall chop the tits with feathered turns that shall rival any nonesuch among whips. Why, I shall . . ."

"Do you think, Miss Hoffenduffle," Rand growled against Serenity's curls, "that you could manage merely sitting still?"

Serenity subsided, her lips ribbed with chagrin. "Well, of course, if that is what you wish . . . though it is hardly the most thrilling of occupations," she groused.

"We are being pursued by murderers, madam!" Rand spat out as he deposited the box upon her lap and began to fumble with the latch. "We are being shot at . . . not to mention the fact that we are on the verge of being swallowed whole by that approaching storm. Is that not thrilling enough for you? Or do you need the theft and smuggling of irreplaceable treasures to enliven your blood?" Irritatedly, he took the pistols from their case and tossed the box to the carriage floor.

Serenity wheeled about to the limit her several restrictions allowed her to successfully wheel.

"For the last time, sir, whatever are you talking about?" she inquired hotly.

"You know very well," Rand responded, inserting powder and ball into his pistol beneath the garrick by feel, a skill he had learned on the smoke-obscured battlefield.

"The only thing I know very well, my lord, is that you are daft," she countered. Again she spun about to face the team.

It was then she discovered that the speeding curricle was only seconds away from punching a rather large hole in the highway's bordering hedgerow. Less than an instant later, a scream caught behind the pudding that had suddenly welled up within her throat. The twentieth part of a moment later, her mouth formed a horrified "O."

"Chilton! Oh, my goodness! *Chilton!*" she at last managed to cry out, sawing back upon the ribbons with all her strength.

"The deuce!" Rand shouted, instantly looking up from his loading.

Desperate now, Serenity did not wait for directions. Bracing herself even more tightly against him, she again performed a cow-handed correction, feathering another tight turn which, happily, once more sent the flying curricle toward the center of the rutted road. The carriage's spindly wheels, however, did not fare so well. Losing their traction upon the uneven ice, they shimmied, jumped airborne upon the ruts, and then began to slide.

"Pull left, Miss Hoffenduffle, left!" Rand blasted into the increasing shriek of the wind, still struggling to untangle his arms from the garrick's enveloping wool. "You must compensate for the slide!"

Instantly, Serenity responded. The twentieth part of a moment later, however, the curricle made grinding contact with the roadside hedgerow, shivered, bounced three times sideways, then, as Rand braced her even more closely against his legs' notch, spanked the brittle bushes once more before again swerving away.

With the curricle bouncing off in an entirely new direction across another section of rutted macadam, unable to withstand any more, Serenity squeezed her eyes closed and ducked beneath the topmost of the flapping garrick capes.

"You may as well come out again," the marquess uttered awfully after what seemed an interminable time.

Deep within the garrick, Serenity considered the suggestion, rejected it, then finally pushed her curls back up into the blustery air.

"Are we alive?" she asked, the gathering storm driving against her question as she raised one cautious eyelid.

"Judge for yourself," the marquess responded after a

round from the highwaymen's pistols flattened against the curricle's springs and twanged into the mounting storm.

Summoning all her daring, Serenity opened her other eye.

To her astonishment, the curricle had somehow managed to center itself and was now dashing quite smartly down the narrow country road behind the marquess's powerfully pounding bays. Even more wondrous, the ribbons were still clutched tightly in her gloved hands. How had such a miracle happened? She hadn't the least idea, but there could be no other conclusion drawn than that she had accomplished it, could there? Smiling proudly, straightening all the way out into the weather again, she decided then and there that surely there could not. Drawing in a deep breath of satisfaction, she next glanced back the way they had come.

Receding into the distance, several holes now gaped in the brittle hedgerow, standing ready, like a bumpkin's toothy smile, to greet the next passersby.

At once, Serenity sighed, her shoulders deflating like Propriety's last attempt at popovers. There was no help for it now, she knew. As surely as the sun would always rise and fall over the British Empire, she was certain it was only a matter of time before Chilton would begin a monstrous peal. Again her shoulders heaved. She deserved it, she supposed, though she dared not look to see. Goodness, if she had done that much damage to a sturdy row of shrubs in her effort to bring the carriage under control, what must she have done to the curricle?

Behind her, two more shots rang out into the strengthening shriek of the wind. Rand drew in a deep, steadying breath. "You have no idea how to drive a curricle and four, do you?" he began awfully, removing his arms from around her and again adjusting the pistols in each hand.

". . . I have driven," Serenity returned rather meekly.

"Madam, I would wager my life that the only thing you have driven is me to Bedlam."

"It so happens, sir, that I have upon several occasions driven . . . a dogcart," Serenity admitted, her tone airily aloft.

Silence sat heavily upon the curricle, to the degree it was possible alongside the percussion of shots being fired and the rush of an oncoming storm.

"A dogcart?" the marquess at last exploded. "Do you mean to say that I have given over the safety of my carefully bred, spirited bloods to a female whose only experience is driving about her father's parish in a dogcart?"

"Far worse!" Serenity shouted, too vexed and embarrassed to think better of such an unladylike outburst. "I have not driven it about my father's parish. I have only driven it back and forth between the manse and Papa's service."

Rand's brow elevated in spite of himself. His jaw worked.

"But there can only be a few yards between the manse and St. Mary's," he finally exclaimed in astonishment.

Serenity caught back her next retort. Suddenly she bit her lower lip, colored, and returned her attention to the road.

"I am aware of that," she at last replied.

"Yet you hitch up . . . a dogcart," the marquess continued.

"Well . . . yes."

"And you all climb aboard."

". . . Yes."

"For a trip of fifty yards or so."

"I have said so, Chilton," Serenity responded, again finding her spirit in vexation.

"And *you* drive"

"Yes, I do!" Serenity replied.

Rand sighed powerfully. "I hesitate to ask this question, Miss Hoffenduffle, but curiosity is consuming me completely."

"What question is that, sir?" Serenity asked with mustered politeness.

"A simple one, madam," he responded. "Why?"

". . . Because," Serenity answered rather softly.

"Because?" Rand encouraged.

"Yes. Because," Serenity stated more emphatically.

And then she fell silent.

Behind her, Rand waited. And waited. And then stiffened with ire.

". . . Because why, blast it all?" he finally bellowed. "Lud, madam, why can you not just once come quickly to the point?"

Serenity sagged noticeably beneath the marquess's chin, almost disappearing again beneath the garrick's wide topmost cape. At last, from the folds of wool came a mumbled response.

Rand's frustration grew. "What did you say?" he questioned, bending lower over her curls.

Missing his words, Serenity once more surged upward, at the same time twisting so that she might look at him.

"Well?" he queried again impatiently.

Serenity sank once more.

"Because . . ." she bit out reluctantly.

"Because why?" the marquess shouted again, at the end of his very short store of patience.

". . . If you must know, it is because my mother dislikes strolls," Serenity sniffed, and then she loftily spun about to again face the road.

"Lud," Rand mumbled, wondering how the deuce he had ever managed to get himself involved with a family as maggoty as the Hoffenduffles.

Shaking his head, he drew Serenity back in place against him, gently tucked her beneath his chin, then began sucking the blood from the new wound she had battered into the edge of his tongue while he finished the loading of the second of his pistols.

Ten

Another shot tore into the buckram padding lining the garrick's shoulder. Startled, Rand bit into his tongue again.

"Blast," he muttered, staring at the frayed wool not far from his ear. He turned, then, to peer out one of the holes now scattered across the carriage hood, quickly locating the rider who had just shot at him. "Give me but one clear shot at that bounder . . ."

". . . Ah, now there's the rub, in my opinion," Serenity interrupted, momentarily ducking her head away from the sting of a new peppering of sleet.

Rand's eyebrow soared. "Indeed. And is it my resolve you question, madam, or just my ability to point my weapon and fire?"

"Neither, of course, Chilton," Serenity responded. "I merely . . ."

". . . For your information, Miss Hoffenduffle, I am quite capable of putting a period to anyone who threatens me. Have you forgotten who drove these blackguards from your post chaise in the first place?"

"No, of course not. I merely wished . . ."

". . . I am a Torrent, Miss Hoffenduffle. My family motto is *fort comme le chêne!* . . . 'strong as the oak.' There is a reason for that, you know. We Torrents have always . . ."

". . . I am certain you have, Chilton," Serenity inter-rupted. "Still, you must admit that even you, a stalwart

Torrent, cannot fire upon our pursuers when your pistols are trapped within this garrick."

The marquess paused.

"Well, of course not. I was aware of that," he stated after a time.

"I was certain of it," Serenity affirmed with a nod, snapping the whip quite dashingly aside the leader's shoulder. "However, you need give the matter no further thought, Chilton. I know just what to do. I have come up with a plan."

"God save us," muttered the marquess as he sank back against the squabs. "How is it, Miss Hoffenduffle, that the very concept makes me wish to turn my pistols on myself instead?"

"What nonsense!" Serenity chided warmly. "Now listen carefully to what you must do. First, place your weapons upon your lap."

"I have no lap, madam," Rand countered testily. "What lap I had has for quite some time now been straddling your a . . ."

". . . The afterward of my person!" Serenity corrected loudly, throwing her head back to arrest his very improper word with a mouthful of curls. "Chilton, I must insist that you refrain from speaking like a costermonger in my presence. Gracious, why I ever thought to marry you . . . !

"Oh, stuff, that is quite beside the point. Now, sir, I am certain that there is a bit of room back there somewhere. Simply insert your pistols between your person and my, er . . . well . . . my aforementioned part. I assure you they will only have to remain there for a short time."

"And I, of course, put great faith in your assurances," replied the marquess.

Still, he complied. Pointing the two pistols inward, he shoved them between their two bodies, balancing them against his abdomen and atop his tensed thighs.

"Good heavens!" Serenity gasped as the hard barrels nestled against her. "Oh, my!"

"Complaints, madam?" Rand queried smugly.

"Why . . . no," she stammered, arching her back slightly. "No, of course not."

"Excellent. Continue with your plan."

"Well . . . let me see. Oh, yes. Next you must take hold of the ribbons . . . and do so quickly please. We are, after all, being pursued. Chilton, must you rest the barrel tips at exactly that spot?"

The marquess grinned wickedly. "This is your plan. Now why do *I* have to take the team?"

"We are in a dire situation here, Chilton," Serenity reminded him. "There is no time for explanations. Just do what you are told."

"*Do* what I am *told*, madam?" he bellowed as he hastily shoved his hands back down into the garrick sleeves.

"Yes, certainly," Serenity replied. "I am, as you yourself acknowledged, the one with the plan. Now, I shall just remove my arms once again from the sleeves . . ." she added, handing him the ribbons and whip. "There now. Next I shall turn like this . . ."

"Have a care, madam!" Rand urged sharply. "You have the most damnably daggerlike elbows."

"Ah . . . *'fort comme le chêne,'* eh?" Serenity commented, heartlessly squirming about even further. "Indeed. Well, bear it for but a moment longer, Chilton. I shall just place my left arm down inside your right sleeve, and then . . ."

Suddenly Serenity gave a mighty twist within the spread of the marquess's legs.

"Oof! Miss Hoffenduffle, what the . . . ?"

". . . and then I shall put my right arm down inside your left sleeve. There, now, do you see?" she said brightly, a charming smile curving the corners of her mouth though her arms were now awkwardly extended behind her. Letting the smile grow, she looked up at Rand, settling comfortably against him once again. "I told you I had come up with a plan."

Rand looked down into her deep blue eyes. He had no choice. God help him, he had no will left to battle the compulsion at all. The impossible jade was now facing him, pressing firmly against him . . . nose to nose, mouth to mouth, and, Good Lord, breast to soft, sweetly alluring breast. Pure, unrefined lust suddenly jolted through him. He closed his eyes against it and released a low and heart-felt moan. With all his heart he prayed for the accuracy of the highwaymen's next round.

"I truly hesitate to ask, Miss Hoffenduffle," he managed to weakly rasp, "but, as you and I are now facing each other and neither of us can see past the other's head to drive skillfully or return fire, what is the advantage of your shatterbrained, cockleheaded scheme?"

"None as yet, of course," Serenity replied, drawing back a bit at the set-down. "It should be obvious to you, sir, that I am not yet through!"

"The thought gives me no end of relief, madam," Rand commented dryly. "Well, what is to be the next step, then? Will you have us climb onto the hood and stand on our heads?"

"Of course not!" Serenity chided. "If you will but control your sarcasm, you can see quite easily what I am about. The problem we had before, you see, was that you needed to be facing in the opposite direction from me so that you might return fire. I have now solved that dilemma quite nicely, I believe."

"And how the devil have you arrived at that conclusion?" Rand asked her with carefully spaced words.

"It is obvious. You are now facing the rear, and . . . oh. You are not exactly, are you?"

"Not even close," the marquess agreed.

"I believe I might have made just the slightest . . ."

". . . Miscalculation," Rand finished.

"But never fear!" Serenity suddenly cried, her smile blazing. "The solution is at hand. You must simply pick me up and turn the both of us around!"

Rand's eyes rolled. "Miss Hoffenduffle . . ." he began, as another pistol ball rang out against the curricle wheel's metal rim.

". . . Chilton, please! Do not waste any more of our time!"

"Miss Hoffenduffle . . ."

"Goodness, sir, have you no care for our safety? Just let me take the ribbons in my left hand . . . yes. Now, Chilton, turn us around."

Rand saw that there was no way in which to divert the woman from her course. It had been his experience that there never was. The maneuver would not help, of course . . . but then it would not hurt them, either. He complied.

The curricle bobbed and wove with the force of the shift, but in a short time Serenity was facing forward again with her arms in the sleeves and the ribbons in her hand. The marquess, on the other hand, was exactly where she had been before, his arms stretched awkwardly backward into the sleeves, his body pressed intimately between her warm thighs. In fairness, though, it had to be said that, just as the lady had planned, he was now facing to the rear. It also had to be said that he certainly wished it to be otherwise. Situated as he was, the scent of her femininity arose like a Siren's temptation in a warm, inviting current that drifted straight to his keenly expectant senses.

"There, it is just as I told you, Chilton," Serenity stated with satisfaction. "I am now facing front to drive, and you are now in a fine position to return our pursuers' fire. And you might wish to begin doing so as soon as possible, Chilton. I vow I can hear the breathing of those dastards' mounts just behind." With a complacent smile, Serenity leaned forward to look past the marquess's head, her cheek softly brushing against his as she deftly maneuvered the bays past a building drift.

"Good Lord." Rand shakily sighed, removing his arms from the sleeves so that he might better balance himself from inside the garrick against the tufted leather. "You think I am in a fine position, do you?"

"Yes, obviously," Serenity responded with not the least bit of hesitation.

"Then I should have no trouble now firing my pistols at will?"

"No trouble at all," the lady replied, snicking to the team for more speed.

"How, madam? If you will notice, I am still trapped inside this overcoat."

Serenity's cold cheek bumped his as she drew back to look at him. "I beg your pardon?" she questioned, her blue eyes wide.

"I will grant that you have managed to get us facing in the proper directions, Miss Hoffenduffle," Rand generously allowed. "Unfortunately, the opening of the garrick is still at my back."

Serenity quickly peered once again over the marquess's shoulder, and then down. "Oh, dear," she said at last.

"Hardly conducive to an excellent aim," the marquess added.

"Yes, I . . . can, of course, see that," Serenity breathed.

"Alas, another slight miscalculation," Rand knuckled into her discomposure, enjoying every moment of plucking the crow. "Getting to be quite a long string of them, is it not? Odd, though. I am almost becoming accustomed to your little disasters, Miss Hoffenduffle. It is quite entertaining to see how you escape from them."

"I would be more pleased to escape from you, sir," she replied tartly, quite put out of countenance by his teasing.

"And I from you, madam," Rand told her mildly, elevating his brow. "Perhaps you would care to tell me how?"

"You will just have to slide behind me," she responded.

"Ah, but the garrick opening will still be in front of you," he countered.

"Then we must switch the whole garment around," she stated with no hesitation. "Do it, Chilton."

"Do it?" he barked in renewed affront, sensing every male leaf on the Torrent family tree begin to tremble.

Serenity raised her chin from his shoulder and glared at him. "Well, who else?" she shouted into his ear. "Do it, Chilton."

Rand's countenance grew thunderous. Jabbing a hand back into one of the sleeves, he wrested the ribbons from Serenity, then turned himself around so that he was kneeling in front of her, their positions now exactly reversed from when they originally started out near the ruined post chaise.

"Turn around," he commanded tersely as gusts of vapor shot in a furious rhythm from his mouth and nose.

Serenity wasted no time in squirming about upon the seat. She wavered with the carriage's unsteady motion, almost toppled; but managed to again balance herself with her knees resting stably upon the seat and her feet tucked into the space on either side of the marquess's trim waist.

And then she gasped. "Oh, my goodness!"

Chilton's strong, firm posterior was pressing quite warmly, and in the most unseemly fashion, against the, er . . . well . . . her oft-aforementioned afterward part.

Rand gritted his teeth against the corresponding sensation. Wanting only to get the whole deuced maneuver over with, he quickly gathered a huge handful of the wool fabric into his free hand.

"Now move around to the front as I move to the rear," he ordered, noting the hoofbeats that were beginning to assert themselves in a soft patter above the moan of the wind. "Yes, that's it. Now we must remain just as we are, madam . . . back-to-back."

"Are . . . are you certain that is absolutely necessary?" Serenity asked a bit breathlessly.

"Deuce take it, Miss Hoffenduffle . . . !" Rand shouted, almost at the end of his tether.

". . . There is no need for you to shout, Chilton," Serenity interjected. "If that is what you wish, I shall of course comply."

The repositioning took surprisingly little effort. After a mighty tug, the garrick spun about and the marquess found himself facing the rear with his arms extended out through several unfastened straps, while his pistols and powder lay on the seat nearby. Behind him, Serenity again faced the team, her arms swathed in the garrick sleeves, her breasts pressed into the garment's back, her gloved hands once again inexpertly controlling the sleek matched bays.

The marquess steadied his knees on the seat and quickly cocked his pistols. Then, with sure movements, he unfastened latches on either side of the carriage and lowered the curricle hood, afterward tying it down so that it would not fly open again to spoil the damage he intended to inflict upon their pursuers.

"Well, I must admit, Chilton," Serenity conceded brightly, "that scheme worked brilliantly."

"Only because part of it was mine," he stated as he brought his pistol up to take aim.

Just at that moment, however, the curricle collided with a small squall which had suddenly dropped down onto the road ahead from the edge of the approaching cloud mass. For the next several seconds, the turbulence worried at the carriage appointments like a ratter pup with a newly discovered mouse, soaring and sucking, ruffling the tattered hood and tugging the harnesses into a wild dance before, growing bored, it pounced one last time upon the garrick's capes, then, picking up its playful wind, moved away to find more objects to torment.

Vexed by the interference, Rand brushed the snow from his lashes, then absently glanced upward after the squall's retreat. Instantly, he froze.

"Bloody h . . ." he breathed, at last comprehending the extent of what was fast bearing down upon them.

". . . What?" Serenity shouted above the wind.

"Never mind!" he suddenly responded. "Never mind anything. Just drive, Miss Hoffenduffle. Now. As fast as you can!"

"Whyever . . . ?" asked Serenity, twisting around.

"Do not waste time looking, madam!" the marquess bellowed, his eyes fixed on the maelstrom hurtling toward them. "Devil a bit! . . . I have never seen the like. Get us out of here, Miss Hoffenduffle. Now."

"My goodness!" Serenity breathed, her own jaw dropping as she disobeyed. "Chilton, we must be away!"

"What do you think I have been trying to tell you, madam!" he cried as a bit of flame spurted from the pistol of one of the pursuers closing in on them. "Deuce take it, Miss Hoffenduffle, chop the team!"

Serenity instantly complied, whirling about to crack her whip above the leader's shoulder, instantly sensing the curricle's powerful responding surge. Several seconds later a report reached her, exploding in counterpoint to the building shriek of the wind. A ball nipped again at the garrick sleeve. Serenity heard the marquess cock his pistol; heard the explosion of his return fire. Thirty yards behind, a highwayman clutched at his arm and howled with pain. This time she did not turn around to see; instead, she again snapped the ribbons atop the lunging bays' flanks, braced her back even more firmly against the marquess's, and rode out the new swell of speed.

The carriage hurled them toward Ipswich; Serenity hung on for dear life, all sixteen of the garrick's capes flapping beneath her chin in the storm-swept gusts like spirited semaphores while the marquess fired and rapidly reloaded to fire again.

And then, some distance ahead two new riders suddenly appeared, spurring their mounts out onto the road from behind the cover of several huge, ancient oaks, afterward beginning to whip them into a punishing gallop straight toward the onrushing curricle. Serenity started as she caught sight of them, then wiped her eyes against the wool of the garrick sleeves to clear the thick accumulation of snow from her lashes as well as what she was persuaded must have been foolish imaginings.

She looked again; suddenly, pistols flashed pewter against the dull winterscape. Could it be help? Serenity wondered, a tickle of hope dulling a bit of her discomfiture. Were they finally to find a way out of their predicament? Had someone heard the shots of pursuit and ridden to their aid?

The answer came quickly when, within moments, Serenity saw the riders direct their pistols not at the highwaymen behind them, but straight toward her own brown curls. A single fluttering thump later, her heart made jarring contact with her half-boots' soles.

"Chilton!" she at last managed above the increasing scream of the wind.

"Not now, Miss Hoffenduffle!" Rand thundered in return, firing off two more rounds before pressing even more intimately against her as he stooped to reload.

"Chilton, I must tell you . . ."

". . . Madam, as you can see, I am rather occupied," he interrupted before straightening and firing again.

"But . . ."

"Not now!"

"Yes, now!" Serenity exclaimed, using her elbow to jab the marquess quite smartly in the, er . . . well, you know. "Turn around, sir, at this exact moment!"

The marquess whirled about. "Madam, whatever it is," he snarled, "you shall have to take care of it."

"With what, good intentions?" she responded tartly, jabbing him again. "Hardly an antidote to the other two highwaymen, Chilton."

"The other two?" Rand exclaimed. "Where?"

"There," Serenity indicated, pointing with the whip.

"Why did I doubt it for a moment?" the marquess bit from between his teeth.

Quickly thrusting his pistols into each of his redingote's side pockets, he began to struggle to turn about inside the tangled garrick so as to meet the new frontal attack. He did not manage it before the tumbling wall of the storm swept over them at last.

Eleven

"Chilton, what am I to do?" Serenity cried as the icy advance rolled over the curricle. "I can see nothing ahead now!" Willing away her panic, she rubbed her eyes. The storm was a generous confectioner; fiercely driven snow began to frost her in a growing layer of heavy wetness.

"Bring the bays up to a walk," Rand shouted in return. Hanging on to the seat back, he renewed his struggle to turn around, jamming his lengthy appendages into the impossibly small spaces left within the twisted garrick while yanking on the sturdy fabric in an effort to make more. "Remember that if you can see no more than a few feet in front of you, Miss Hoffenduffle, neither can the highwaymen. And what they cannot see, they cannot fire upon."

"Being shot is the least of my concerns, sir," Serenity objected loudly, sawing back upon the ribbons. "Have you forgotten that the horses shall reach any dangerous obstacle far before my limited vision does? Good heavens, I shall run us into a ditch! . . . or a fence! . . . or the point of a gun! And, mercy, Chilton, do have a care for where you are thrusting your foot!"

"My apologies. I suggest you watch for glimpses of trees at the road's edge, madam," Rand offered as the garrick bulged and bubbled around his movements. "They are large and you should be able to make them out occasionally. Try to steer between them. And keep an eye out for posts that might mark a crossroads. If we can manage to find a hole in this trap through which to make our escape, with any luck those bounders will run into one another and put periods to themselves."

"If I only knew why they were doing this!" Serenity cried, methodically wiping the quickly accumulating snow from her eyes with the back of her glove, peering studiously ahead.

"We have had this discussion before, Miss Hoffenduffle," Rand asserted, finding a place for his knee beside the shapely flare of Serenity's hip. "I see no reason to go over it again."

"Oh, surely, Chilton, you do not still hold to your maggoty notion that these scoundrels are after you?" the lady questioned, quite properly recoiling from the pressure of the marquess's limb.

"I do . . . and hold still, madam," he commanded. "If I am to face forward, I must get my leg uncocked. If you will allow me . . . no, do not move any further, Miss Hoffenduffle . . . Miss Hoffenduffle!"

The curricle rocked with the marquess's unbalance as his knee, accompanied by his dignity, slipped from the narrow seat and plunged toward the floor. Cursing roundly, he sank and rolled, flailing wildly in his attempt to catch himself; quickly, and quite ignominiously, settling with his knees upon the floor, his Blüchers hooked over the kickboard, and his hands embedded in Serenity's firm flesh.

Of its own accord his body went limp. It simply was not fair, he thought as his head sagged forward to nestle quite comfortably within the deep valley between the jade's softly scented breasts. There was never any escape. He inhaled the scent of her and sighed in a hopeless wheeze.

"Good Lord," Rand whispered into the blue wool pelisse. "Devil a bit."

Serenity's entire body mortified.

"S-Sir!" she gasped into the ear directly beneath her

chin. "I insist that you remove your person from my p-personal protrusions."

"I am trying," Rand shakily husked. "I have spent the last year trying, madam."

Slowly, tremblingly, he tensed his arms, then pushed away from Serenity's tempting warmth. In the same motion, he lifted her, still curved into a sitting position, slid his body beneath her, and settled her once more between his outspread legs, this time with considerably more discomfort.

Serenity, reassured that once again a modicum of propriety had been restored, snuggled back against the wondrous heat the marquess had so generously offered.

Rand groaned again, disheartened, discomposed, and once more thoroughly aroused. He had to be losing his mind, he thought as he absorbed the nearness of her. There was no other explanation. Why did his body keep reacting to the jade so intensely . . . worse, why would the nodcock notion have butted into his thoughts that she was back where she belonged, else?

Below his chin, Serenity sighed.

"I know," she murmured into the scream of the wind, confident that he could not hear her above the storm's buffeting frenzy. "So have I."

Inexplicably, the marquess's chin came to a gentle rest upon her snow-encrusted curls.

And then he slipped his gloved hands down the length of the garrick sleeves and took the whip and ribbons from her hands.

"There should be a lane somewhere close by that leads southeast toward Waldringfield," he stated, his lips brushing her ear. "If we can make our way onto it without the highwaymen knowing, no doubt we shall find help there."

"I know the place," Serenity replied. "I shall watch for the posts, Chilton, but everything looks so different in the storm."

"Nevertheless we must try to locate the turn, Miss Hoffenduffle. It might also be a good idea not to speak further," Rand suggested. "Sound carries oddly in this wind. I have no wish to be discovered before we make good our escape."

"Nor do we wish to miss any sounds that might give away their location, I should think," Serenity added.

"Just so," the marquess allowed, glancing down at her in slight surprise. And then he snicked to his bays, increasing their speed. "Very well, Miss Hoffenduffle, let us proceed with our plan."

"As you say, sir," Serenity replied, officiously straightening so that she might improve her forward view. "But, Chilton, I do ask that you put away your pistols."

Rand's brows inverted. "My pistols?" he questioned, noting the feel of their solid weight within the outer pockets of his redingote.

"Yes, your pistols," Serenity enunciated clearly. "At least the one that you have on your lap. It is jabbing the, er . . . well, it is jabbing me quite uncomfortably."

It took no more than the twentieth part of a moment's consideration of Serenity's odd statement before Rand squeezed his eyelids into tiny threads.

"Chilton, if you please," Serenity reiterated, her gaze scanning the road.

The marquess's eyes opened. His lips thinned with chagrin. He stared doggedly ahead.

"No," he finally, firmly, replied.

"No?" Serenity queried, digging her fingers into his thighs while squirming about to look at him. "But I insist. Move it, sir. It is most distracting."

Rand gritted his teeth as she wriggled back into place.

"My sympathies, madam," he responded, "but, no."

"You refuse?"

"I do."

Serenity again shifted her hips. Her eyes were cobalt with vexation and affront at his rag-mannered treatment of her simple request. She prepared an appropriate set-down.

"If you were truly a gentleman, Chilton," she leveled awfully, turning to face forward again, "you would remove your pistol."

The marquess drew in a pitiful breath. "There is no earthly way I can remove it, Miss Hoffenduffle." He moaned as the breath escaped. "And, for God's sake, madam, sit still!"

Twelve

Storm swells rode the howl of the wind to batter against Rand and Serenity—growling beasts that harried the curricle as it crept toward Ipswich, sapping the waning warmth of the garrick with damp, clenching cold. The carriage fought for safe passage, its high, spindly wheels slipping from side to side over the shifting drifts as the gusts teased them. Ahead, the bays shuddered against the stinging wetness, dropping their heads so low in the face of the onslaught that their noses plowed steaming paths through the mounting snow. Serenity dug deeper into the curve of Rand's warmth, eking out the comfort his nearness offered. A deep trembling began to unravel within her core.

"Here," Rand spoke into her ear, "unfasten my redingote and tuck your shoulders and arms into it."

"I c-cannot get inside your coat!" Serenity hissed back. "It would be most unseemly . . ."

". . . Blast it all, Miss Hoffenduffle," the marquess countered, "you are freezing! Obviously I cannot release the ribbons to force you, so for once in our unfortunate acquaintance, madam, will you cease your constant quibbling and simply do as I tell you?"

After a moment in which Serenity delivered the best of her glowers, she twisted about and began to unbutton his impeccably tailored fawn-wool frock coat.

"You keep a most unusual silence, sir, I must say," she

finally parried testily. "*I* must not speak a syllable, but *you* may shout your petty displeasure to all the world."

Separating the garment, she turned toward the front again and shrugged her arms and shoulders inside. The marquess's warmth flowed through her damp clothing to enfold her. It was magnificent. Heavenly. Serenity almost smiled along with her lengthy sigh.

"My petty displeasure!" Rand muttered in as close to a shout as he dared. "Oh, for the love of . . ."

Serenity suddenly tensed against him.

"There is nothing petty . . ."

". . . Hush, Chilton!"

"Hush?" he bleated, stung. "Madam, I . . ."

"Chilton, please! I hear something."

The marquess fell instantly silent. He bent forward slightly, his head cocked to the side, listening raptly. One cheek touched gently against Serenity's. As one, their heads slowly slewed about within the collar of the wrong-way-around garrick, searching, sensing. Then, from somewhere just ahead, a soft thump carried to them on the wild wind. They strained against the collar, leaning toward the sound as they listened again. More thumps sounded; a rhythm formed.

"Approaching horses!" Rand whispered moistly into Serenity's ear. "Do not make a sound!"

Serenity nodded, her eyes huge. Unconsciously, she pressed herself ever more securely against Rand as he brought his team to a slow, easy halt, murmuring to them in soothing tones before settling the creaking harnesses. Silently, one strong arm slowly wound about her. Spooned one within the other, the two waited, hardly daring to draw breath.

The storm pounded against the curricle, masking the murderers' approach as it hurled frozen fury over the landscape from every direction. Serenity's raw cheeks stung from the force of it. When she could stand it no longer, she winced and shuddered violently, then turned to tuck her face against the marquess's wilted cravat.

In unconscious response, Rand drew her even nearer, then protectively curved a gloved hand over the exposed skin of her face and neck. At the same time, he lowered his head slightly, positioning the brim of his beaver where it might deflect some of the wind away from her. Serenity sighed with relief. Again a watchful silence settled over them; the scattered, muted hoofbeats intensified, beginning to reach them with greater frequency as the highwaymen slowly closed the meager distance between them. Rand peered expectantly in the direction of the oncoming sounds; Serenity trembled again, acknowledging the fear now augmenting the chills racing to and fro across her skin. Within the frock coat, she slipped a tentative arm around Rand's waist. He answered with his own arm's tightening. And still they waited, cupped together, unmoving and silent.

And then, quite suddenly, two blurred, gray shadows began to coalesce out of the frenzied sweep of white. Rand straightened; Serenity arose along with him. Slow clops of horses' hooves, storm-muffled, separated themselves from the steady whine of the wind and began to grow even more defined. Serenity peeked out from the security of Rand's neck to watch the shapes' approach, thought better of it, then sharply twisted about again once more to bury her face deep in the neckcloth's layered loops. Beneath her cheek and fingertips, she felt Rand's muscles tense.

Suddenly, he released her and began to fumble about inside the garrick's pockets. Serenity pushed slightly away from him, curious; more, embarrassingly bereft without his familiar warmth. Yet before she could wonder at her reaction, his movements became quite purposeful. After a short time, an unmistakable metallic click sounded softly within the folds of the garment.

The pistols! Serenity almost gasped, sagging with relief.

Chilton had kept his weapons at the ready and was again armed. Never had she been so glad that the scoundrel had refused her simple request to remove them and put them away. Why, just imagine the trouble they would have had retrieving them from the box this time!

And then she paused, dropping her gaze slightly, her forehead brushing against the marquess's stubble-roughened chin. Odd. The weapons had not been retrieved from his lap inside the garrick, she realized, but, she was certain, from the redingote pockets located altogether without. But that could only mean . . .

Goodness, if the pistols had been in those pockets all this time, what had been poking . . . ?

Perplexed, Serenity once more lifted her cheek slightly away from his frills, slipped her hand from around his waist, then began to slide it hesitantly, experimentally, toward the front.

Rand's breathing stumbled.

In the next moment, however, she suddenly relaxed.

La, what can I be thinking? she scolded herself as she again burrowed against his warmth. What does it matter where the pistols were to be found? They must deal with the highwaymen now. Besides, there would be time enough to figure out that particular mystery later, she reasoned. Time enough, that is, if they managed to avoid the inconvenience of being killed.

Above her curls, once again air spilled into the marquess's lungs.

Ahead, the gray shadows finally resolved into the shapes of the murderers.

Wrapped within Rand, Serenity watched them approach, their shoulders hunched against the slash of sleet and wind as they swung back and forth upon their saddles in narrow arcs, ever nearing; steadily, relentlessly, searching. Seeing one of them seem to gaze straight into her eyes, she caught at a gasp and froze. Still closer they came;

even closer. Serenity dug her fingers into the marquess's thighs.

Yet beneath her cheek, Rand remained completely still, his breathing unnoticeable, his body expectant, cocked and primed. Serenity felt his fingers flex involuntarily against his pistols' pearl handles and relaxed somewhat. Drawing upon his strength, she stilled even her inner shuddering. Within her boots, however, her heart still thrummed against her toes.

Suddenly, a fierce downdraft of stinging sleet once again obliterated everything within sight of the curricle. Rand reacted instantly, folding Serenity into his body's curve as ice drops and fat, wet flakes of snow lashed his beaver and drummed against the garrick with the wet violence of a New Delhi monsoon. The twentieth part of a moment later, however, as quickly as it had come, the squall faded.

Slowly Rand uncoiled his length and looked about. The carriage—the whole world, it seemed—stood shrouded within a heavy, crystalline cocoon. Serenity, whose head still shared the garrick's collar, moved synchronously. As one, their heads swiveled over the path of their observations as if attached to the same spine.

It became immediately apparent that the road stood empty where the shadowed riders had once been.

Serenity placed a tiny bit of distance between herself and the marquess. "Chilton?" she questioned softly as wet snow dropped down into the cleft.

In answer, next to her ear, Rand began to chuckle.

"Chilton? Why in heaven's name are you laughing, sir?" she asked again. "What is it?"

"A stroke of good fortune, I think," he responded, drawing her with him as he relaxed back against the encrusted squabs and deeply inhaled. "Amazing for me to encounter such a thing, is it not, Miss Hoffenduffle? . . . considering the company?"

Serenity's lips drew into a chiding line.

"Chilton, what has happened to the highwaymen? Only a moment ago we were on the brink of attack."

"They seem to have passed us by," he told her, his voice holding a bit of wonder and a smile.

"But how? I am persuaded that one of the blackguards was staring directly at me. How could they have missed what was right before their eyes?"

"I am inclined to think that it was Providence, madam," Chilton replied. "I, too, was certain that we were on the point of discovery. Yet that last snowfall hid us completely."

"Then we are safe!" Serenity assessed brightly, her head popping up to rap against his cheek.

"Hardly," the marquess responded readily. "Those criminals are still in the vicinity, Miss Hoffenduffle. It is only a matter of time before they join the other two, and we shall have all four after us. Come now, madam, face forward and release your death grip on my thighs. It is still imperative that we find that road leading to Waldringfield."

Nodding her compliance, Serenity once again squirmed around inside the garrick.

Rand clucked softly to his bays. As the curricle resumed its cautious pace, Serenity began to studiously scan their environs, alert for each brief glimpse of the landscape that appeared through rents in the heavy storm curtain.

"Turn, Chilton!" she hissed, suddenly beginning to pound upon his left thigh. "There is a low wall on the right!"

"As it happens, I see it," he muttered, correcting their course just as another downdraft of snow obliterated all sign of it. "You may now stop pummeling my leg."

"I am not pummeling, sir. I am tapping," Serenity replied, her gaze still searching. "I believe it to be the quickest way to let you know in which direction you must steer your team. It is an excellent idea, do you not agree?"

"I would, were I a masochist," Rand grumbled in re-

sponse. "I must have a dozen holes in my tongue thanks
entirely to your battering ram of a brow, madam, and now
you think to beat bruises into my leg."

"Nothing of the kind," Serenity tsked. "And do keep
your voice down, Chilton. As you noted, those four scoundrels must still be close by. If we again find ourselves in
peril, it shall not be me who has given away our position.
It shall be you and your groundless complaints."

The stark shadow of an elm suddenly materialized out
of the thick whiteness directly in their path. Serenity
gasped. The twentieth part of a moment later, she threw
herself quite solidly back against the marquess's broad
chest.

Rand grunted at the impact. "Egad, madam!" he cried,
even as he heaved them both upward so that he might
scrabble after the whip that had been suddenly knocked
from his grasp to be driven like a lance by the wind into
the depths of a distant drift.

Watching it disappear, the marquess's jaw worked under
nostrils that steamed. Once more clamping his arm about
Serenity, he again sank down upon the seat.

Serenity heard his next epithet with mortifying clarity.
Her cheeks stung like a fresh abrasion; clinging snow began to slide over her skin's radiant heat.

"Miss Hoffenduffle! . . ." Rand next squeezed out while
the curricle deftly swerved away from the tree.

". . . You know, Chilton," Serenity offered, "I am seeing
a side of you I have never before seen."

Taken somewhat aback, the marquess paused. "What
side?" he grumbled over the new spanking of sleet strum-
ming a staccato rhythm against his beaver's pitiful wounds.

"This one," Serenity answered, staring ahead. "This rag-
mannered, wholly unacceptable side which thinks nothing
of employing words no gentleman would ever use in the
presence of a lady."

"Precisely why you have not seen it before, madam,"

Rand stated evenly, transferring the ribbons into one hand and, with a few twists of his body, easily raising what remained of the tattered curricle hood with the other. "Before, I thought you *were* a lady."

Serenity grew taut. "And now?" she questioned, her voice airy.

"Now, we both know what you are."

"I have not changed," she replied softly. "I am still the same as when we were betrothed."

"I am painfully aware of that, madam," Rand said coldly. "How refreshing to hear you admit it."

"Whatever can you mean? What are you aware of?" Serenity cried, twisting around to face him. "What is it I have done?"

"Kindly have done with your charade, Miss Hoffenduffle," Rand ordered as he suddenly caught sight of something somewhere beyond the top of Serenity's head.

"There is no charade," the lady insisted, insensible of his avid concentration.

"A Cheltenham tragedy then," he suggested, next drawing the curricle to a slow halt. "And, I assure you, there is no need for you to continue it in my presence. After all, I am one of the few in all England who know the truth about you."

"The truth?"

"Yes, madam, a truth which gives you no right to expect further consideration from me."

Serenity's spirit bruised.

Gathering herself, she rallied. "If these last few hours are your idea of consideration, Chilton . . ."

". . . I have done my duty, Miss Hoffenduffle," Rand interrupted, "just as I did a year ago when I did what I could to keep you from justice for the sake of your father and the duty I owed you as my betrothed, but you are not my betrothed now. Be grateful that you are still free to *act* the lady in the presence of others, madam, and push me no farther."

"Be grateful!" Serenity repeated, rearing back within the confines of the collar to look squarely at him. "If I am grateful for anything, sir, it is that we did not speak our vows before I discovered your penchant for . . . for base activities with women of questionable character!"

Glancing down, Rand gritted his teeth . . . in anger, frustration, and in reaction to the power her blue eyes still could so easily wield.

"Indeed . . ." he slowly answered, working the ribbons to control his team. "And are you not at least a little grateful for *that,* Miss Hoffenduffle . . . ?" he asked, again lifting his gaze, this time motioning with his chin toward the scene ahead, ". . . for the fact that it might easily be you hanging in that poor devil's place?"

"What . . . ?" Serenity mouthed, turning at his gesture, following the direction of his gaze.

And then her whole being clutched, too stunned by the sight before her even to tremble at the snow that had begun to catch at the newly exposed surfaces of her neck. She had wondered why the marquess had stopped the carriage, and now she knew. And the knowledge almost overwhelmed her sensibilities.

Just ahead, only sketchily visible through the blowing snowfall, stood the crossroads they had been searching for. Marking it, a tall gibbet rose at the far corner like a gaunt, shadowed specter. As Serenity watched, a buffeting gust lifted the snow for several moments, letting her see the gibbet clearly. Cringing, she wished it had not. From the crossbar hung a man in chains, his flesh bloated with the beginnings of corruption, his body looking wrenchingly animate as it swung and curvetted in the capricious wind. Serenity turned aside on a surging wash of revulsion, then, unaccountably, looked again.

Suddenly, the wind sucked at the man's clothing, forcing

its way inside to catch within his great coat, billowing it outward and sending the body spinning. Dangling, dancing, it finally slowed. This time, however, it twisted toward her on its chains.

For the first time, Serenity was allowed a glimpse of the outlaw's face.

Behind her, Rand finally stirred to slap the ribbons upon the backs of his bays and start the team moving again onto the narrower, snow-clogged lane heading toward the southeast.

Serenity was aware of the motion of the curricle, yet still her gaze clung to the man. Bound by fear, she could not speak; nor could she look away. She could not break the riveting hold the ghastly form held over her. Her heart stuttered beneath her breast.

How had the man come to be here? she wondered as a chill coursed through her. Was it a warning of some kind? What did his presence on a gibbet, at this particular crossroads, mean?

She had to tell the marquess, she impulsively decided.

And then she paused. How could she? Given what she had learned of Chilton's regard for her in the hours since he had first come upon her in the post chaise, how in heaven's name could she tell him that the man on the gibbet was one of the two who that night had forced her to accompany them on that fateful ride to Charity's Place? How could she tell him anything that the dratted man would believe?

Thirteen

Another shiver shook Serenity's shoulders as the curricle distanced itself from the gibbet and rounded the first bend in the road, taking the gruesome scene from her view. At last straightening, she relaxed back against the marquess's warmth, letting her gaze settle upon the rolling rhythm of the horses' flanks before, after a time, focusing upon the caked snow coating the garrick's button fastenings. From beneath, she began idly to tap at the woolen fabric with her fingernail. Clumps of crusty ice jumped from the cloth to catch in the vigorous wind. Still she stared unseeing; memories rolled in storm-tossed waves across a sea of turbulent musings.

She had never meant for things to happen as they had. She had tried to be so careful . . . of her own reputation and that of her aunt and uncle, the Earl and Countess of Swinburne . . . assuredly of what her wonderful—and, she had once thought, charmingly irascible—betrothed believed of her. And in truth, had she been fully awake on that night, she would never have answered the knock herself. She would unquestionably have summoned Mr. Perkins to take care of the matter at that late hour.

Of course, startling the poor dear in such a fashion would most likely have effected another of his bouts with the shaking palsy, so perhaps . . .

Oh, stuff! Serenity countered along with her shoulders'

sag. The time had long since passed for such an excuse. The fact remained that she had not been fully alert at the time else she would never have given the strangers entrance. At the very least she would—she *should*—have asked for the identities of the two who had so rudely dragged her off to that . . . that wholly unacceptable address!

Yet, truth be told, she had always impulsively dashed about her duties, had she not?—much to her father's exasperation—and, as a result, had often forgotten things of importance. No, she could not deny that uncomfortable flaw. After all, because of it, had she not found herself carted off that night to a brothel? And then, dressed only in her robe and night rail?

She remembered the shame of it even now . . . the discovery of just where she had been taken, the dawning realization that if only a breath of it should ever become bruited about the *ton*, her father surely would close the charity immediately and whisk her back to Woodbridge never again to see Town . . . the flush of mortification in finding her betrothed in that—that *woman of questionable character's* arms. It had been a horrid bumblebroth, Serenity remembered with a shake of her brown curls. Indeed, at the time it had put her quite out of countenance.

But it was worse now. One of the two men who had taken her now hung on the gibbet at that crossroads. Serenity shivered again . . . a trembling from the cold, yes, but also from the growing conviction that she was only just now beginning to glimpse the true extent of her peril owing to the scandal in which she had become involved.

Once more she remembered the man's face, as it was now, lifeless and bloated; as it had been that night when questioning glances had passed between the two upon their discovery that they had delivered the sacks of grain to the wrong building. It had been naive, she supposed, to discount the oddness of the delivery, but, in truth, she had at first. It was not at all unusual, after all, to receive donations or deliveries at odd times during the day. She could, in fact, count upon being interrupted from her classes or her ledgers time after time, and was glad of it. After all, charities could not survive apart from others' generosity.

Yet none of that signified, did it? Nothing changed the fact that she had opened the door late that night to two perfect strangers, and with that impulse had risked her family's reputation, as well as set off the past year's unbelievable events.

And she had lost the marquess. That had been the worst humiliation, she remembered against the squeeze of her lids. Of all that she had unleashed from Pandora's box that night, that had cut the deepest slash.

"Still sulking, Miss Hoffenduffle?" Rand broke into her contemplations.

"I am not sulking, sir," Serenity responded quietly, drawing herself back to the present.

"Hah! You lack even as much life as that poor devil back at the crossroads, madam," Rand countered. "You are sulking."

"I am not s-sulking," she repeated, beginning to look about her again.

Ahead, and unexpectedly, she thought, the terrain was changing. On either side of the lane the trees had thinned considerably. She searched farther between the snow swirls, scanning curiously. It was true. Beyond the trees, large stretches of tall, brittle grass spread out toward the horizon, the land growing flatter in the distance as if sighing over its fate before sinking to sea level. She straightened.

"If you must know, I am wondering," she concluded softly.

"Wondering what?" Rand asked, one hand shooting upward to steady his tilting beaver as a strong gust rocked the curricle.

"Why we have s-seen no sign for Waldringfield," Serenity responded, not very effectively stilling the shudder that claimed her teeth.

"Yes," Rand commented after a downward glance raised a crease between his brows. "I have been wondering the same. The land does not look right, does it? Blast this storm! I grew up in these parts, yet in the face of this wind, nothing looks familiar to me."

"Be careful, Ch-Chilton," Serenity thinly warned. "The storm that you now curse is the same one hiding us from those villains."

"Point taken," the marquess replied, his concern increasing as again he observed her.

"Could we have taken the marsh road by mistake?" she asked. "Look how the land falls away when you can s-see into the distance."

"That is seeming more and more likely. Deuce take it, I have no idea where this road leads, do you?"

"I am afraid n-not. I do not believe anyone lives this way, though. At least, to my knowledge, Papa has n-never paid a visit out this far."

Rand thought for a moment. "Yet there was a way, was there not, of traveling through the marsh between Waldringfield and Brightwell? I am certain I remember going that way as a lad when I was staying in Ipswich at my uncle's palace. A friend and I decided to explore what we could of the marsh on a lark, but it was so deuced many years ago!"

"I have no idea, truly," Serenity told him. "But, given the l-location of the villages, if there were such a road, it would have to c-cross this one I should think."

"Yes, I agree," Rand replied, straightening considerably, dragging Serenity along with his body's motion. "And that means that most likely somewhere ahead lies another way into Waldringfield." Once again his eyes gleamed with purpose. Tucking Serenity more firmly against him, his spirits greatly improved. "All that remains is to find it, Miss Hoffenduffle. Although you realize, do you not, that in this storm we are likely to miss it."

"That certainly is a p-possibility," Serenity agreed. "It is also a possibility, it seems to me, that by the time we get to the village, so also might the highwaymen."

Rand's brow soared. "Why, Miss Hoffenduffle! A flicker of intelligence? You are correct, of course. Yet, as I see it, we have no choice. We can neither of us remain out in this storm for much longer." Again he glanced at Serenity. Snow clung to her face and hair. Roughly, he brushed it aside. "We must find the nearest shelter, and, hopefully, a few pistols to join with mine. The nearest of both, madam, is in the village."

"Then we must by all means l-locate the crossroads, sir," Serenity said as more chills coursed through her. "Let us be away."

The marquess slipped off one of his gloves and touched his fingers to Serenity's cheek. Her flesh was beyond cold, it seemed to him. His pulse quickened with worry. Biting back a word he knew he'd only receive a scolding for, he put his glove back on and drew the garrick more firmly about her legs, then tucked the ends of his scarf over her exposed ears and cheeks. That accomplished, he set his team surging forward at a somewhat faster pace.

He had been correct when he had told her that they could not remain out in the cold much longer. Devil take it, the jade was almost frozen solid! He had been able to keep her warm enough up to this point because of his own body's heat, but now they were both losing even that. They had to find shelter soon. For both of them, but mostly for Serenity, it was quickly becoming critical.

Slowly, steadily, the curricle forged a way past the last copse of elm and began to struggle out onto the open marsh land. Away from the sheltering trees, the wind strengthened, roaring across the vast sea of grass to drive the onslaught against the carriage in a punishing horizontal line.

Rand and Serenity turned from the face of it, looking about them when they could, blinking repeatedly to clear their vision as they strained to see farther into the barrenness, searching for some sign of the crossroads they only hoped lay somewhere ahead. Wet snow spattered against them and stuck, piling up into a building layer over their huddled forms, coating the carriage, lading the horses with an ever-increasing burden. Rand did not try to sweep it away. It did not take long for him to realize that the packed snow served as an effective windbreak, and he was desperate for it. Serenity could no longer control her shaking now. Over her objections, he tucked her fully inside the garrick and his frock coat, nestling her against what warmth remained in his body as he continued to scrub the snow from his eyes and strive to catch sight of the elusive crossroads.

Suddenly, an updraft parted the heavy snowfall and gave him an instant's view of the narrow track ahead. Not far distant, an object stood its ground against the turbulence, straining to keep a part of itself above the rising drifts. Rand blinked, clearing his eyes of snow, unsure of what he had seen or had imagined, then peered ahead again. The object was still there, bracing itself against the wind, resolving even as he watched into the sought-after marker post.

The crossroads! the marquess concluded as he at last made out two other grooves just beyond which cut across their own lane at a neat right angle. Euphoric, he gusted a vaporous breath he had not known he had been holding and squeezed Serenity. With effort, he swallowed a triumphant shout.

"There it is!" he declared as softly as his excitement allowed, leaning down toward the rather large lump beneath his chin.

Serenity's head popped up immediately. "The c-crossroads?" she questioned tremulously.

"Yes, just ahead. It shall only be a bit longer, Miss Hoffenduffle," he told her, on impulse glancing back the way they had come. "Hold on, then. We shall soon be at Wald . . ."

Suddenly the marquess stilled.

"What is it?" Serenity breathed close to his ear, automatically parroting his turn.

"Blast! Blast it all!"

"Well, that w-was informative," she commented dryly.

Rand glanced down at her, his scold twisted at the corner of his mouth. "As it happens, I hear hoofbeats, Miss Hoffenduffle," he softly hissed into her ear's cold, shell-like curl. Again he slewed about to peer through one of the holes in the curricle hood. "Riders," he reported tersely. "Two of them. It doesn't appear that they have seen us, though."

"The highwaymen?"

"Undoubtedly."

Beneath his chin, Serenity swallowed. "What shall we do?"

"Change our plans," Rand replied, sucking at the new hole Miss Hoffenduffle had put in his tongue. "If there are but two of them behind us, it can only mean that the other two have gone on to Waldringfield as you suggested they might."

"Then we c-cannot go forward, nor can we go back," Serenity summarized. Slowly she once more faced front. "We are truly trapped this time, Chilton, are we not?"

"Not at all," Rand stated confidently.

"No?" she queried, turning about again.

The marquess smiled. "You are forgetting that our crossroads contains four conjoining paths, Miss Hoffenduffle. We and the highwaymen might be on one, Waldringfield and the other two blackguards at some point on another, but that leaves two others going in opposite directions."

"But Chilton, whichever road we choose, those jackanapes will simply follow us, will they not?" Serenity reasoned.

"I shouldn't think so," Rand disagreed.

"Why not?" Serenity asked suspiciously.

"Logic, madam," Rand stated firmly. "Since they have not as yet spotted us, and therefore do not know for sure that we even came this way, will they not assume that if we *had* done so, we would have taken the fork to Waldringfield?"

"I suppose so," Serenity responded.

"There is no 'suppose' about it, madam," the marquess stated confidently. "They shall reach this crossroads and be off in a trice along the lane toward Waldringfield. It is logical. Hah! I wish I could be there when they once again bump ignominiously into their compatriots. No madam, they shall never suspect that we have taken another road."

"They shall see our c-curricle tracks."

"Again, no. Look around you, madam. Within minutes of our passing, this storm shall have obliterated all sign of them."

"Yet we d-do not know what lies at the end of the other paths," Serenity pointed out.

"Fortuitous, is it not, Miss Hoffenduffle? . . ." Rand commented cheerfully, shoving Serenity back down inside the garrick. "As it happens, it has been long years since I have explored this neighborhood. I find I am quite in the mood for the adventure!"

Over Serenity's muffled gasp, the marquess swept the curricle into the crossroads at a spanking pace. Then, pausing only briefly to cast a final glance in the direction of Waldringham, he continued on along the lane a pause in the snowfall revealed as narrowing into infinity within the distant expanse of the bleak, frozen marsh.

The better part of an hour passed before Rand allowed himself the luxury of looking up from his rapt concentration upon the heavily drifted road to survey their environs.

They had come far from the crossroads, miles by his reckoning, far into the unknown isolation of the landscape. The whole world, he noticed, had become monochrome, layered in shifting shades of whiteness accented by shadows. Not a sound could be heard above the constant moan of the storm. Little could be seen but the narrowing groove beneath the bays' hooves and what short glimpses the fickle wind allowed of the unrelenting, snow-shackled grasslands spreading out and away for mile after countless mile.

Rand rubbed at his tired eyes, then, sensing that something had changed—was changing—he searched the sky. It was darker. Or was it? What . . . ? With exaggerated slowness, again he blinked once, twice.

What was the time? he wondered, his brain struggling sluggishly to hold onto the thought. He remembered . . . he had left Ipswich in the late morning. After all these hours . . . yes. The sun must be going down. That had to be it. The land was on the verge of night. The marquess huddled over Serenity, staring grimly ahead. Darkness hovered just beyond the horizon, and with it even colder temperatures. They had to find shelter. There was no more time.

Suddenly, one of the geldings stumbled slightly, then recovered, afterward glancing back toward its master almost apologetically. Rand clumsily rolled the ribbons over the bay's flank in forgiveness. Even his proud bloods were at their end, he knew. It would not be much longer for any of them. Soon they would have no choice but to stop where they were—the middle of nowhere. Cold would seep inside their clothing and steal away any remaining warmth. They would grow sleepy . . . lie down for a bit of a rest. And then, for all of them, it would be over.

Images of Serenity flooded his weary mind . . . the way she had looked the first time he had seen her sitting with Propriety amid lavender frills at that corner table at Gunter's . . . the color her eyes had become when she had said

she would marry him . . . how he would never have the
chance to touch what by rights should have belonged to
him, to taste the sweetness . . . of her body . . . her
mouth . . .

". . . Bloody hell," he suddenly muttered aloud, chas-
tising his vagrant thoughts. He was only a short time away
from death, was he not? . . . yet what was consuming him?
Deuce take it, that jade, Serenity Hoffenduffle!

"What did you s-say?" Serenity asked, again popping out
from inside the garrick.

"I said there was a muddy smell, Miss Hoffenduffle,"
Rand replied. "Must be the horses or . . . something.
Likely it is damp wool."

Serenity could only stare. "Indeed," she finally replied,
straightening in his lap once more. "D-Do you have any
idea yet where we are, Chilton?"

Rand drew in a deep breath. He would have to tell her,
he supposed. There were some things from which even a
gently bred lady could not be protected. She would, after
all, soon notice that his bays had begun to drop on their
feet. He would do his duty, therefore, as a man of his sta-
tion should . . . gently . . . though by no stretch of the
imagination was the benefactress of his thoughtfulness a
lady. But he would do his duty just the same. He was a
Torrent, after all . . . *"fort comme le chêne."* Let his final act
on this earth be a noble one.

"Ah, Miss Hoffenduffle . . ."

"Yes, Ch-Chilton?" Serenity asked, just barely loud
enough to be heard above the wind's wail.

"I-I have something I must tell you."

"G-Go on."

"It was a gamble, madam," the marquess bravely continued.

"A gamble?"

"I am afraid so. I could not know how far the road would
lead us, Miss Hoffenduffle, or even where. You have un-

derstood that from the start, have you not? I had, of course, hoped to find shelter . . ."

". . . And you have done so most admirably, I must concede, Chilton. I confess I did have my doubts . . ."

". . . Madam?" Rand interrupted, one brow stiffly rising as he stared at Serenity's snow-slubbed curls.

"Really, Chilton, I was quite within reason to think so. We neither of us knew where we were, after all. Oh, surely you do not expect an apology, sir?" Serenity questioned as, in her affront, she pressed herself even more stiffly into his legs' warm notch.

Slowly, with the greatest care, Rand touched Serenity's cold forehead with his warm wrist. And then his lips thinned with remorse. There could be no question, then. It had started. The cold had won its first bloody victory. Deuce take it, the jade's brain had already begun to cease functioning.

"Madam . . ." he began, again trying to shove her curls back within the garrick, unwilling to witness any more of her suffering.

". . . Oh, very well, Chilton, I apologize!" Serenity countered, popping back up to strike him smartly underneath his chin. "Now, will you please cease jabbing me down like a pocket handkerchief and drive us quickly to those buildings!"

"Buildings?" Rand echoed. And then he thundered, "What buildings?"

"Why, those, of course," Serenity explained, pointing a wiggling finger out of the garrick collar.

Instantaneously the marquess looked. Ahead, the river Deben lay like a frozen blue slash across the low marshland. More significantly, however, beside it, a tall, isolated tide mill rose up from the river's banks out of a fist of dark outbuildings which were thrusting like a defiant gesture up into the face of the maelstrom.

Fourteen

The tide mill seemed a reluctant hero. Planted on the quay adjacent to a huge, icebound millpond, it looked weathered and crotchety. One stair rail leading to the second floor entrance dangled by a single nail; its flaking, whitewashed clapboards creaked complaints to the wind.

The mill stood in four stories above the quay; scattered windows delineated them. At the fourth story two dormer windows peeked out from either side of the gambrel roof like rag-mannered children; another smutted window at the roof's peak revealed the presence of an attic. Attached to the side of the building closest to the long earthen causeway that had been built to capture and contain the river's tide, a weary lean-to clung to the mill's clapboards like a dependent wife, its sagging demeanor a resigned sigh to bearing the burden of the towering waterwheel.

From a distance, Serenity heard the boom and crack of the pond's frozen surface as it yielded to the vagaries of the contained tide behind its sturdy sluice gates. As the curricle approached, she tensed slightly while she searched for the source of the sounds. Finding it, for a few moments she watched the newly forming rafts of ice uplift and sag as they rode the water's motion only to join again in frozen union a short time later.

Her gaze shifted forward as the marquess drove his bays around the pond and out onto the quay. Within the narrow passage between the lean-to and the causeway, the waterwheel rocked continually in the wind, creaking like an aching joint before the sluice gates in its bed of slushy brine. Extending almost to the third story, the wheel seemed monstrous to Serenity. She wondered why the massive paddles were not frozen solid in such a narrow space.

"The wheel's constant movement is most likely preventing the water from freezing," the marquess uttered low into her ear.

Serenity started. "I had not realized that I h-had spoken aloud," she managed to comment.

"You had," he responded, rounding the quay and then quickly directing the team toward a rude rectangular building close to the tide mill. "But fortuitously. I am reminded that we both would benefit from the same thing. As soon as we get my bloods into that granary just ahead, you, Miss Hoffenduffle, shall help me rub them down."

"Of c-course," Serenity replied, her eagerness to help evident in the alignment of her spine.

"Devil take it . . ." the marquess muttered, again sucking upon his tongue. Taking a deep breath, he continued, "A man's life may depend upon his cattle, Miss Hoffenduffle."

"Without question," she readily responded.

"They must above all else be maintained in good health. Why, had my bloods not been in tip-top condition, just imagine where we would now be. Besides, a well-matched team costs the moon to replace."

"I am c-certain of it," Serenity agreed, once more blinking away snow as the granary came closer.

Rand glanced down at her with one wary eye. "I suppose you think I should sweep you into the tide mill first and find some way to warm you."

"Not at all," Serenity told him.

"I am no nipfarthing, you understand," he asserted, bringing the bays to a halt before the granary door. "I merely feel that the exertion would benefit you."

"I am already feeling more warm," she stated, patting his thigh.

"Well, then," he said, drawing in his cheeks, "I shall unfasten the garrick and open the doors. Take the ribbons, Miss Hoffenduffle."

"Take them, Chilton?" Serenity asked, turning toward him with owlish eyes. "You would just g-give them to a dog-cart driver such as I? Oh, I think not, sir! Only consider . . . a man's life may depend upon his ribbons. They must be well t-taken care of, I should think. I am persuaded that a matched set of ribbons must cost the m-moon to replace."

"Take the ribbons, Miss Hoffenduffle," Rand repeated from the recesses of his throat.

"Yes, sir," Serenity replied, complying. "Give the matter no further thought. It shall be just as you wish, of course."

Growling, the marquess quickly unfastened the straps of the garrick, shifted out from under Serenity, then dropped down into the nearly hip-high drifts. After carefully securing Serenity back inside the voluminous garment, he began to trudge toward the granary, using his body as a plow to make a path through the accumulation until at last he gained the building's wide double doors.

Taking both handles into his hands, he tugged against the resistance of the packed drifts, at last shouldering them aside before returning to the curricle and leading his team forward into the protection of the dark, musty space. He turned at once, then, releasing the traces to hold out his hands for Serenity, easily lifting her down onto the floor's thick covering of soft, stale hay.

"I shall unhitch the team, Miss Hoffenduffle," he told her, still having to shout over the frenzy of the storm. "See if you can find a lantern, and then close those doors."

"Yes, of course," Serenity replied, quickly crossing to the granary entrance, then gingerly running her fingers over the rough planks near the doorframe, soon locating a lantern and a box of lucifers hanging in the customary place on a nail driven into the wall just alongside. Moments later, a feeble light wobbled, then began to infiltrate the granary's gloom. That accomplished, Serenity next turned her attention toward latching the doors against the sucking wind.

"Much better," commented the marquess as he tossed the loose harnesses over a large stack of full grain sacks. "Now see if you can find a bucket or two. We shall need to start a small fire to melt some snow for water, and the bloods must be fed."

Serenity wasted no time. In truth, she was glad for the activity. It was warming, and, of a certainty, she reveled in that; but it was also more. In her occupation, she could hold her rather troubling thoughts at bay. What was she to do when *this* scandal broth broke? It was one thing to have been caught in a brothel with him—though to her knowledge no one had as yet discovered that particular breach of etiquette—one thing, too, to have through no fault of her own been locked in an abandoned building with him; quite another, however, to expect the *ton* to again believe that she had, quite beyond her control, once more become innocently stranded in the Marquess of Chilton's company. What in the world was to be this occasion's excuse?

Shaking her head, Serenity glanced about, then spotted several wooden pails near another large edifice of grain. Taking one of them, she placed it beneath the end of one of the bags, and with a tug on the stitching, parted the seam to pour nut-scented, whole oats down into the rope-handled container. She struggled with the weight of it, but soon several bucketsful supported the bays' steadily working jaws.

Rand, meanwhile, had cleared the area around the granary's small brazier and had started a small fire with a bit of coal he had found in a bin nearby. When Serenity placed the last of her buckets before the remaining bay, he straightened and motioned to her.

"Feed the fire while the snow melts," he said, taking a

moment to assess her. "Then you may give me a hand with the rubdown."

Still fighting her disquiet, Serenity nodded, then complied. Outside, the wind roared its omnipresence. Time dripped in slow seconds . . . minutes . . . and she warmed herself before the brazier, unaware of Rand's regard as, drying his bays with a handful of burlap, he monitored her, watching for signs of the return of her usual animation, for the renewal of healthy color; unaware, too, of how the sodden burlap in his hand had slowed almost to a stop along its rhythmic traverse.

Beautiful . . . she was so deuced beautiful, Rand thought as several coals collapsed into a shower of sparks which, for a moment, illumined her eyes' shadowed hollows. A small sigh eased between his lips. He turned again toward his cattle.

Full dark fell over the marshland.

"The water is melting nicely," Serenity stated moments later as she joined him. "How shall I help next?"

"Use some of that straw in the trough to rub the snow off Baby," Rand directed, gesturing with his drying cloth. "Afterward, you may dry him with a piece of this burlap."

"Baby?" Serenity repeated, not very handily biting back a smile.

"Never mind," the marquess growled, turning again to his task.

Chuckling softly, Serenity shoved the garrick's sleeves up past her elbows, imprisoning them against her ribs as, next, in a darting movement, she awkwardly bent to seize two large handfuls of straw, trying to accomplish the task before the sleeves could once more slide down to engulf her arms. Uncooperatively, however, the garrick sleeves slipped free. Vexed, Serenity again raised her arms high and shook the sleeves back into place, scattering straw as she kicked several cumbersome folds of the garrick out of the way, spun about, then planted her two handfuls against Baby's shoulder and, with an ungainly sweep, scraped her makeshift brushes down over the great horse's entire length.

The weary bay shivered with pleasure.

Serenity, however, quickly ran out of flank. Suddenly reaching the end of the animal, she tottered over open air, tripped over a length of thick wool, then collapsed with a solid thump against several stacked bags of grain. Almost as a gesture of comfort, the massive garrick settled over her with a soft wheeze.

The marquess's eyes danced. He thought for a moment, then was sure of it. Completely overwhelmed by the huge garrick, bits of straw riding her clothing and curls, the jade looked like a fledgling bird that had accidentally fallen from its nest. He regarded her from head to toe, biting back a burgeoning laugh.

"Don't you d-dare," Serenity warned, suddenly ducking to avoid the impatient swish of Baby's tail.

"Dare what, madam?" Rand asked, masking his mirth by taking blankets from the boot of his curricle and throwing them over the bays he had already rubbed down. "I have no idea what you are talking about." Sucking in his cheeks, he turned away judiciously, then crossed the granary to peer out through the slit that still remained between the weathered double doors.

He scanned as far as his vision allowed. Nothing living stirred on the quay aside from wind-tossed flotsam. Satisfied, he next sharpened his hearing. No suspicious sounds separated themselves from the constant whistle of the wind. Cautiously, he pushed one door slightly open. Again he looked about, afterward returning to douse the dying fire in the brazier.

"There doesn't look to be anyone about. Come, Miss Hoffenduffle," he said, quickly finishing Baby's rubdown before taking his valise from the curricle boot and stabilizing Serenity's stance upon the hay-strewn floor. "We have done what is needful here. Do what you can to get that garrick under control and let us make our way over to the mill."

Serenity needed no urging. Drawing as much of the woolen fabric as she could into her hands, she submitted as the marquess drew her without, then, after latching the granary doors, began to plow a path for them across the quay. Serenity struggled to keep up with him, stumbling over the garrick's length, wiping what she could of the snow from her face, using every pause to plan her steps before the next obliterating downdraft.

Not far from the granary, a rare patch of moonshine broke through the fury of the storm to reflect off the drifts with a bluish glow, giving them another glimpse of the mill's facade. Serenity quickly noted that the side of the mill facing them contained three entrances, one just above the other on the first three stories, each of the entrances' narrow doors accessed by an external stair whose risers crisscrossed the facade, pausing before each of them at little square landings. She quickly saw, too, that already the first level of the building, along with its stair and entrance, stood buried beneath the quay's building drift.

And then, once again the moonlight disappeared.

Rand resumed his battle against the wind shrieking off the frozen Deben. Tucking in his chin, he once more put his shoulder to the onslaught, at different times slipping and sliding, plunging thigh deep into the drifts, half-pushing, half-carrying Serenity until at last his fingertips touched, curved around weathered wood. With all his strength, he pulled, drawing both of them up out of the swallowing snow and onto the second landing.

"Are you all right, Miss Hoffenduffle?" he shouted close to her ear after he had helped her to establish her footing.

"Yes, quite," she cried out in return, reaching over to rattle the door handle. "Odd, though . . . the door appears to be l-locked, Chilton."

"Hardly odd at all, madam," he told her. "Most buildings are."

"In Town, certainly," Serenity agreed. "But not in the c-country, and not an isolated building such as this. Why, who even knows of this establishment, sir?"

"Its owners, of course," Rand replied, setting down his valise so that he might swing his shoulder toward the weathered planks. "And, as I think about it, I once did. I remember this place from my explorations that summer I spoke to you of earlier. By my recollection, we should be about five miles from Woodbridge."

"Five miles!" Serenity cried. "Oh, Chilton, that is all that is wonderful! I am persuaded that we should l-leave for the manse immediately!

"Oh, I say, sir, what are you doing?"

Rand slammed his shoulder against the door again. "Breaking in," he gritted out as his musculature connected and the wood trembled against its latch.

"Oh, but you c-cannot do that!" Serenity stated, grabbing hold of his forearm.

"Of . . . course, I can," Rand grunted, throwing himself against the wood again.

"But it is against the law!" Serenity insisted.

The marquess burst into laughter. "When did that become a concern, madam?"

"It has always been," she vowed hotly. "If you do not know that about me, sir, then you do not know me very well."

"Madam, I know you . . . too well," Rand stated, at last shattering the latch's hold on the door. As he stumbled into the mill's interior, he continued, "It was that which ended what was between us, if you recall."

"I don't understand," Serenity questioned. "I never understand when you s-speak in such riddles."

"Don't you?" Rand said, retrieving his valise from the landing. "Then perhaps you will understand this, Miss

Hoffenduffle. In the past, I was willing to let your previous misbehavior go unpunished, so certain was I that, once caught, you would never have the audacity to revert to crime again. But now I see that I was wrong. Here you are, yet in the thick of it again. In my mercy I have not helped you, have I? . . . only aided in your scurrilous schemes. Therefore, I warn you, when we do reach the manse, madam, I will speak with the vicar about what you have done. It is not merely treason now, as you are well aware. It is now an attempt to murder me."

"Revert to crime? Treason? *Murder?* Chilton, this is insanity!" Serenity cried, stamping her foot. "Very well, sir, let us by all means go to the m-manse. Accuse me before my father of all you think I have done, if that is your wish. I shall take great pleasure in watching him toss you out of St. Mary's parish on your ignorant, overbearing . . ."

". . . Unfortunately, that will have to wait," the marquess interrupted coldly. "My bloods cannot go farther without rest, nor can we."

Serenity's eyes widened. "What are you saying? It is only five miles . . ."

". . . An interminable distance, madam, given the severity of this storm. No, we have no choice but to remain here until it stops snowing. Even then, it may be days before enough of it melts for us to make our way past the drifts."

"But we shall be stranded here . . . t-together . . ." and then she moaned, ". . . *again!*"

". . . See here, Miss Hoffenduffle!" the marquess again interjected. "I wish to make it very clear to you that I will not allow you to use our situation to your advantage. No matter what Society expects of a man and a woman who find themselves in compromising circumstances, I will not allow you to have the safety of my name in which to cloak your nefarious activities. In case I still have failed to make myself clear, madam, let me repeat: there is no way under heaven that you are going to use this situation to force me into matrimony!"

"Matrimony!" Serenity gasped. "Whyever would I wish to marry you?"

"Why, indeed, since you and your cohorts are set upon murdering me?"

"I have told you," Serenity shouted most improperly, "it is not *you* they wish to m-murder, but *me!*"

"So you keep tediously repeating," Rand said, seizing her elbow to pull her into the deep shadows of the room. As soon as her form had cleared the door, he shut it behind her, then leaned against it, securing it against the buffeting wind until his eyes could adjust to the dark and he might spot something to prop beneath the handle.

"And will do so until you believe me!" Serenity vowed, brushing at the snow that was failing to melt from her cheeks.

"Which means that you shall grow very hoarse, very soon," Rand concluded.

Serenity's gloved hands fisted with frustration. "Chilton, I heard them say so themselves," she told him more moderately.

Rand's attention snagged against his will.

"Oh?"

"I have been trying to tell you as much. It was the two in the post chaise who said so, before you arrived on the s-scene. And . . . I must confess to you, too, Chilton, that today's attempt was not the first for them, either."

"Is that so?" the marquess asked, a tic startling the corner of his mouth as his gaze suddenly lanced into hers. "You have been threatened before, Miss Hoffenduffle?" he continued, his voice deceptively mild.

"Yes, twice."

Rand pushed away from the door, his glare keen.

"When?"

"Toward the end of the Season last year . . . not long after we ended our betrothal. The first occurrence was when I was almost run down by that dray outside of Budd and Calkins in Pall Mall. You must recall it, Chilton. You were there."

"What I recall, madam," Rand stated, one brow rising skeptically, "is that as I was exiting the bookshop, you leaped directly into my arms."

"At that particular moment, sir," Serenity frowned, "I would have c-collided quite smartly with anyone who had been standing in the way. I was trying to escape with my life, Chilton. The fact that you happened to be in my path was mere coincidence. I do thank you for your aid in pulling me to safety, however. I do not seem to recall doing so at the time."

Pursing his lips, Rand paused. "I gave you no opportunity," he at last confessed. "As soon as I determined that you were unharmed, I left immediately."

"Yes, I know. Where did you go?"

The marquess scrubbed at his jaw. "To ring a peal over James."

"Whyever w-would you do that?" Serenity asked with a tip of her head.

"Because I thought it was another of his schemes, of course," the marquess admitted. "I thought he had hired the dray to frighten us into each other's arms. He swore he had not, but, I confess, I did not believe him."

"Oh, dear," Serenity said, her gaze dropping to her clasped hands. She looked up then. "I suppose you assumed he was at the b-bottom of the other incident, too."

"Probably. What was it?" And then the marquess's gaze hardened. "Never say it was last June's boating expedition on the Thames?"

Serenity nodded, and then she averted her gaze. "You were escorting Susan Etheridge, as I recall," she softly accused.

Rand stiffened. "You were in young Pickering's craft."

"Yes," Serenity responded with a slight smile. "He had been making calf's eyes at me since the *Post* announced the ending of our engagement. I had discouraged his suit as best I could, but he was most p-persistent. I thought that I might use the occasion of the boating party to tell him quite plainly that I did not welcome his advances."

"Madam, that is hardly to the point, or any of my affair," the marquess snarled.

Serenity's eyes flickered. "Yes . . . well, we f-fell behind the others . . . Mr. Pickering is quite young, of course, and not as . . . able . . . as others who are older seem to be. He had been paddling quite strenuously, trying to catch up, when from out of nowhere another boat came up behind us, turned sharply in our direction and quite soundly rammed our craft. Poor Mr. Pickering!" she continued, shaking her head. "He was already exhausted, and then to have to d-deal with something like that . . . ! He tried very hard to row us to safety, but could not, poor dear. Those horrid men in the other boat were able to hit us again and again. As you might expect, our boat began to take on water. Quite naturally, I looked to the other b-boats to solicit help as soon as I saw what was happening. Everyone was so far ahead, however. No one turned back so that I might gain their attention, except . . ."

". . . For me," Rand murmured, knowing he was confessing more than he wished. "You were already in the water by the time I saw you . . . fighting to keep your head clear."

"My clothing quickly became impossibly heavy," Serenity explained. And then she chuckled. "Imagine a lady's predicament in that kind of situation, Chilton. If I were to s-save myself it would have been necessary for me to doff all my clothing. Yet if I had done that, my reputation would never have recovered. You saved me from both f-fates, did you not? And I did not thank you after that occasion either, did I?"

"Again, I had taken myself off to see James."

"To cut up nasty with him?"

"To cut him off," Rand told her flatly. "It had been the last straw, madam. I had warned him repeatedly not to interfere between the two of us, but he and your sister would not be swayed. I had no choice but to follow through with my threats."

"But he did not plan the attacks," Serenity said softly.

"How can you be sure?" Rand asked.

"Because the men who d-drove the dray and the ones who were rowing the boat were the same ones who tried to pull me from the post chaise."

Rand's gaze searched in the dark shadows, studied the woman before him.

"Do you believe me?" Serenity quietly asked, hoping for a sign of relenting so that she might at last tell him about the man hanging at the crossroads.

The marquess allowed a moment of silence to pass. "It does not signify whether I believe you or not," he finally stated. "All that your explanation has convinced me of is that I was right about you all along. You have indeed never stopped your involvement with criminals, Miss Hoffenduffle, and now have most certainly had a falling-out with your comrades in deceit. It may be as you say, and the bastards are not after me, but that changes nothing of what you have proven yourself to be."

"Ch-Chilton . . . !"

". . . No more now, madam," he interjected, holding up an arresting palm. "We must find a place to build a fire and rest for the night. You are tired and cold."

Fifteen

"What I am is v-vexed, Chilton," Serenity asserted over a shiver as the marquess propped her against the door and crossed to fetch one of several long-handled wooden paddles that had just become visible hanging upon the adjoining wall. Her gloved hands rose to rub a tremor from her upper arms. "It is very lowering to not be b-believed. No one *is* after you . . . except perhaps the relatives of your other jilts whom you have sh-shocked to the core with your perversity."

Returning, the marquess again deftly seized Serenity's shoulders and set her aside, then braced the paddle firmly under the door handle.

"Back to that are we?" he inquired levelly. "Madam, what I was doing that night was altogether normal and natural, *not* engaging, as you well know, in perversity." Quite suddenly then, he grasped Serenity's hand and began to lead her forward into what had only just before resolved into a single large room embracing the whole of the mill's first story. His glance was acute as it skated over each newly revealed object and surface. "And, for your information," he continued, "there are no other jilts. There has never been anyone else in my life *to* jilt except you. And you were not jilted. We agreed to part mutually."

Serenity's eyes widened. "There has been no one else?" she queried, swerving around a large bin that smelled of the acridness of rank wheat, afterward employing her remaining hand to clutch at even more of the sodden garrick. Somewhat off-balance, she clumped along behind, stumbling to keep pace.

"Of course not," Rand told her. "Do you think that after what I experienced during my first brush with the parson's mousetrap I would be eager to seize the bait again? Madam, I am not so foolish."

"I concede the p-point, sir," Serenity said pleasantly. "You are not foolish . . . you are insane."

The marquess yielded to a soft chuckle, his gaze still keenly searching their environs. And then quite suddenly, he paused. Serenity peeked around him. Just ahead, near the row of windows facing the Deben, a huge, inverted cone-shaped silhouette materialized from the edge of the darkness.

"Ah, just as I suspected," the marquess murmured mostly to himself. Then, smiling, he once more advanced, abruptly skirting a small table and two dark-stained chairs that stood in his path.

"What?" Serenity asked, just before, on a gasp, the table collided with her thigh.

Smarting, yet still sensible enough to swing her hips wide, she only brushed the adjacent chair, yet before she could recover to straighten properly, the toe of her boot caught against a slight, square-sided protrusion in the floor. On a startled cry, she dropped her handful of garrick, trod upon its hem, then pitched forward into a downward arc like one of the more poorly charged rounds recently leveled at them by the highwaymen.

Rand countered instantly. Pulling upward on her hand, he drew her toward him. In reaction, Serenity's body dipped low, bobbed about, then immediately swung back upward in a sweeping reversal, coming to an abrupt halt within the nest of the marquess's arms, her mouth only inches from his, every one of her personal protrusions crushed against his length.

"G-Goodness!" Serenity uttered as, with noses almost touching, her breath danced with his. Inner shudders slowed as the marquess's warmth began to seep into her wet clothing; her sputter trickled away into a shaky sigh. Quite remarkably, her toes completely thawed, and the room, the storm . . . dear heaven, the world seemed to fade away.

Adrift in deep sapphire, Rand's arms tightened about Serenity's shoulders and trim waist.

"Get away from me," he husked against her moist lips. A thick, sweet languor arose to thud through his veins; his hand slid slowly downward to flirt with the rising of one soft slope. He drew her nearer; he could not help it. His fingers spasmed. "Dear God, you are right, madam. I am insane."

"N-Nonsense," Serenity stammered, slowly mounting a defense. "I am persuaded that it has merely been a d-difficult day."

The marquess clutched at the reprieve.

"Yes, of course . . . you are right," he replied, somehow scraping together the will slowly, agonizingly, to unclench his arms. Several deeply drawn breaths stabilized his equilibrium. "It has indeed."

Serenity quickly increased the distance between them. She cleared her throat; fidgeted with the garrick's fastenings. "I-I regret that our former association might have in any way prevented you from fulfilling your obligation to your t-title, Chilton," she said suddenly.

Rand's glance touched her, then flicked away. Clasping his hands behind his back, he stooped to look more closely at what Serenity had tripped over. "Then you wish me leg-shackled, Miss Hoffenduffle?" he asked evenly. "What an odd desire . . . given that you are, in your own words, I believe, 'top over tails in love' with me."

Serenity's lips twisted slightly. "I was v-very angry when I said that, Ch-Chilton."

Rand's mouth quirked. "Madam, you were perverse."

Serenity flushed in the darkness. "I had been p-pushed to the very limit of my p-patience," she justified.

"Actually, you had been pushed between my l . . ."

". . . Chilton, if you please!" Serenity interjected. "Besides, I have not stopped being tired and c-cold, you know."

"Nor vexed, either, I see."

"Indeed not, sir," Serenity vowed warmly. "Owing to your lack of concern, I most likely have suffered a broken toe. Move aside, Chilton," she ordered, stepping forward. "I wish to see what you led me to trip over. We shall move it into a corner so it does not happen again."

Rand cast Serenity an amused glance. "You are certainly welcome to try," he offered politely.

Serenity bent before the low structure, placed her hands upon the rim and lifted. The square did not move in the slightest. She tried again. Once more nothing happened.

"By the saints!" she allowed herself to vow, trying to wiggle the box from side to side. "It won't budge. What is this thing, Chilton?"

"A grain chute," he told her, again bending over the square. "It extends from this story down into the one below. We seem to have entered the mill on the crown-wheel floor, Miss Hoffenduffle. That was what I was doing before you . . . er, *I* became remiss in my care of you," he told her, flourishing a pretty leg in mock apology. "I have never before been inside a mill. I was most curious to see the crown wheel."

"The crown wheel," Serenity parroted, following the marquess's gaze.

"Yes," Rand said, grabbing her hand again and quickly completing his journey. "See here, Miss Hoffenduffle . . ." he continued, stretching his hand toward the wide top of the cone-shaped structure, "can you feel these crenellations along the top of the wheel?"

Serenity stretched her hand alongside his. "Yes, I feel them."

The marquess immediately dragged Serenity around to the opposite side of the large, shadowed wheel. "The grooves are constructed to mesh perfectly with the ones on this wheel," he responded, placing his hand upon another flat, rounded structure set at a right angle to the crown wheel. "Feel this," he commanded, again taking her hand and stretching it toward the conjoining. "The shape of it is rather like the tiny cog inside a watch, is it not? And do you see this?" he again queried, running her fingers along a thick, horizontal shaft which extended from the flat wheel out through the wall of the lean-to. "This shaft joins this smaller wheel to the great waterwheel outside. When the waterwheel revolves, it turns the smaller wheel which, in turn, rotates the crown wheel."

"And the crown wheel . . . ?" Serenity asked, now genuinely interested.

". . . Turns another shaft which extends from its base down into the floor below," Rand told her. "At the end of that shaft is the millstone."

"Which receives grain through the chute on this floor," Serenity concluded thoughtfully.

"Just so," Rand confirmed.

"Most interesting," Serenity said, tapping her chin. "But what keeps the waterwheel from turning all the time?"

Rand again took Serenity's hand and crossed to the windows overlooking the millpond. "Look down there, Miss Hoffenduffle," he directed, pointing toward the small channel between the mill and the causeway.

Within a small portion of the channel, the portion closest to the mill, the huge waterwheel nestled. As Serenity watched, the wheel swayed slightly, its mass resisting the wind's erratic whim and the slow sloshing of its skirting of water. After a moment, the marquess lifted a finger and tapped the window's wavy crown glass.

"Do you see? Just to the rear of the waterwheel are the sluice gates. They are of the flap-valve type."

"What does that mean?" Serenity asked, pressing her forehead against the frosted pane.

"Just what it seems. The tide may flow into the millpond through the gates, but when the process reverses, the flap valves are automatically pulled shut by the water, trapping the tide inside and channeling it toward the waterwheel. The trapped water then flows through the channel when the miller releases it, passes over the wheel's lower paddles in the undershot manner and, *voilà,* on the floor below, the millstone begins to revolve."

Serenity ran her gloved hand over the simple lever. "A narrowed sluice opening would, of course, increase the water's pressure," she murmured consideringly.

"Yes, exactly," Rand responded, masking his surprise.

Serenity glanced up at him, then, and a sudden smile formed in her eyes. "Lower your brows, Chilton," she said, allowing herself a short laugh. "I may not have attended Cambridge, sir, but there is more in my woman's mind than just watercolors, the pianoforte, and the optimum fertilizer for daffodil bulbs."

"Reason enough for a man to emigrate, if you ask me," the marquess countered in rumbled tones. "Well, come on then," he continued, again seizing her hand. "Since you have mastered the workings on this floor, let us see what lies above."

With Rand leading the way, the two carefully retraced their steps, then reentered the narrow hall leading away from the door and extending the length of the building. At the hall's opposite end, an interior set of worn planks, hugged against the adjacent staircase by a smoothly rounded railing, cut through the tide mill's various stories in a steep, dizzying zigzag. Rand and Serenity took a moment's time to glance up and down the web-garnished stairwell, then entered and began to climb upward as quickly as the complaining planks would allow.

The steps debouched into what was obviously the living quarters of the mill. From the hallway, at whose opposite end stood the last of the mill's external doors, a much shorter passage led away to the left. Rand took Serenity's hand and started down it, but stopped abruptly when his shoulder collided with a lantern hung just beyond the corner.

"Ah, the very thing we need," he murmured, quickly lighting it with one of the granary lucifers he had placed in his vest pocket. Instantly a soft, golden globe of light surrounded them.

"Look, Chilton," Serenity whispered when the lantern light had spread beyond their immediate environs.

Rand glanced up to see her pointing toward the dark rectangle of a nearby door. Quickly Serenity seized the lamp from him and started forward.

"Have a care, madam," he warned, following after. "Deuce take it, you could be dashing into the miller's chamber."

"Nothing of the s-sort." Serenity chuckled when he had joined her. "See? It is only the scullery." With a wide sweep of her arm, Serenity shone the lanternlight into each dismal corner. "Not a very pleasant place, is it?"

"It does not have to be," the marquess murmured. "It merely needs to be utilitarian." He turned slowly, then, taking in the room's contents, nodding at the truth of their observation.

Against the far wall a stone sink and adjacent slop sink stood bolted by iron brackets to the wall's hidden frame. Just above, a wooden rack clung to the stuccoed surface, supporting a row of pewter cups and plates. In one of the corners, several tin buckets nested haphazardly in the company of a lolling mop and broom; in another, a coal bin stood dull, dented, and black-smeared. Serenity turned slightly, letting the light play upon other surfaces. At opposite ends of the scullery, two darkened doorways were suddenly revealed.

"The kitchen?" the marquess offered, pointing at one of the doors.

Serenity shook her head. "No, the space is too small," she said, stepping lightly toward the opening. "It is the larder and pantry, I should think."

As she spoke, she thrust the lantern through the door. A tiny passageway was instantly illuminated. On either side, even tinier rooms resolved, each of them surprisingly well stocked. In one, the pantry, roots such as potatoes, turnips, parsnips, and carrots reclined in sagging muslin bags upon the straw-covered floor. Other bags of flour, sugar, spices, and a great deal of salt sat upon a low counter beside a tin of biscuits and a rack of fresh-smelling eggs; twisted ropes of garlic and onions hung from rows of sturdy shelves, each of which supported a variety of preserved fruits and vegetables.

In the larder, several smoked, salted hams hung from huge, iron meat hooks. Beneath, great slabs of bacon and something undecipherable rested on a small marble slab. Serenity took a moment to study the object, her nose wrinkling slightly as her gaze rested upon the large pearly knob of bone protruding awkwardly from its center. Some sort of meat, she supposed, again letting her gaze wander over it. A joint of . . . something. Who knew what?

"Well, we shan't go hungry," commented the marquess, his own eyes skipping gratefully between one room and the other.

"None of this b-belongs to us, Chilton," Serenity scolded as she turned, crossed the scullery, and entered the kitchen through the opposite side.

She paused then, glancing at the large range dominating the spacious room and the several other furnishings lining the room's walls: a built-in dresser with hooks at the front of the upper set of shelves for hanging a collection of blackened pots, a coal hod, a bottle jack and meat screen which could be attached at the front of the stove's open fire to roast joints of mutton or beef, and, in the center of the room, a long kitchen table of thick oak planks, whitened with use, into half of which was inlaid a heavy square of black-veined marble.

"And when did that particular concept begin bothering you?" Rand asked.

Serenity sighed. "It has always done so."

"Only when it was convenient."

"You cannot leave it alone, can you?" Serenity suddenly asked, stepping out of the kitchen into the hallway they had first entered upon gaining the second story. "You are like a d-dog worrying a bone. It has been a year since we parted. Why will you not let it rest?"

"Because you made a complete gull of me!" the marquess exploded. "And because I loved you!"

After several moments of appalled silence, Serenity's features softened. Very slowly, she began to shake her head. And then she turned abruptly away.

"No," she replied evenly, starting forward into the hall again, glancing into both the parlor and dining rooms as she passed them by on her way back to the stairs.

"No?" the marquess parroted after he had caught up to her, seized her shoulders, and spun her around.

"No," Serenity repeated, staring bravely up into his blazing eyes. "It is my opinion that you love me still. Now come," she said, again turning away from him and starting up the stairs. "We must find the miller. It is only right that we should f-formally request his hospitality."

Stunned, Rand clumped up the stairs to the third story behind Serenity on leaden legs. His lips were white with obstinacy, with disbelief. His fists knotted at the ends of rigidly corded forearms. His nostrils flared; great gusts of vapor clouded the stairwell.

"I do not love you," he uttered tautly.

"You must," asserted Serenity in a low whisper, attaining the floor above. Without pausing, she started forward down the hall, leaving the marquess in quickly diminishing light. "Why else would you c-constantly bring the matter up?"

"Because it is very difficult to be around you and not think of it, madam," he responded, hurrying to catch up to her rapid stride.

"You have just p-proved my point," she stated, poking the lantern into each of the two smaller passages just long enough to determine that they only led to several small, rank-smelling, and quite empty, bedchambers. "Ch-Chilton," she said, suddenly wheeling around to face him. "This is most odd. The mill is deserted. Where are the proprietor and his f-family?"

His rebuttal thwarted by the change of subject, the marquess testily tucked his scathing reply away. "They could be any number of places, madam," he answered instead. "Perhaps they were in Martlesham getting supplies when the storm hit. In that case, it could be days before they return."

"There was hardly any need, sir. The pantry is well stocked," Serenity commented mostly to herself. "I must say, I d-do find that odd."

"What is odd, madam, is that we are standing in the freezing cold of a dark, airless hallway wondering about it at all when we could be downstairs emptying the larder before a warming fire."

At that moment, a heavy shudder wracked Serenity, quelling her tart response.

"P-Perhaps you have a p-point," she managed to say when she had recovered. "V-Very well, let us go below."

"Excellent!" exclaimed Rand, appropriating Serenity's elbow and steering her quite energetically toward the stairs. "I shall contrive to start a fire in the stove. Then you, madam, shall cook us a hearty meal."

"That should be interesting," Serenity muttered in reply, gathering the garrick close about her knees, "since I have n-never cooked a thing before in my l-life."

Sixteen

"Absolutely not!" Serenity cried somewhat later after Rand had finally managed to ignite a bit of the coal in the cold range using most of the straw from the broom in the scullery as kindling and every single one of his lucifers. "I will *not* take off my c-clothing!"

"Madam, you are soaked to the skin, and freezing with it," Rand argued, rubbing a streak of coal dust into the side of his nose as he blew gently on the resistant flames. "You must put on dry clothing. You shall die, else."

"It is not p-proper," Serenity stated, tightening the garrick collar about her throat. Slowly, steadily, ribbons of warmth began to infiltrate the kitchen's frigid cold. She held out her hands to it; her fingertips began to ache.

"You are more stubborn than these flames!" Rand flared, looking up at her. "We crossed the line hours ago, madam. What does it matter what is proper at this point? Who is there to see?"

A flash of remembrance, of what she herself had seen but a year past, suddenly skittered across Serenity's mind. He and that . . . that hussy! had been completely *déshabillé!* . . . rolling on the storeroom floor . . . his fingers moving over the woman's contours, probing . . . his body pressed . . .

Clutching at the garrick, Serenity swallowed, her eyes growing huge. There could be no doubt that she must retain her clothing no matter what her circumstances. Had she not seen the consequences of not doing so with her own two eyes? . . . of what happens when one is bare in the company of a gentleman? Of a certainty, it was indeed a worrisome condition, Serenity had long ago decided; of a certainty, too, it was one which by any stretch of the imagination could not be proper.

And yet, she pondered . . . how under heaven might such a wonder feel?

Suddenly, chiding herself, she shook the forbidden thoughts from her head.

"One c-cannot desert one's p-principles at the whim of circumstance," she at last countered breathlessly. "B-Besides, all my valises were stolen, if you recall. I have no clothing in which to change."

"It does not signify, madam. I have plenty," Rand argued, crossing to the table and opening his valise. "Here," he said, taking some articles from the bag after a time of rummaging around inside. "Put on one of my shirts and a pair of pantaloons. Then, for heaven's sake, get over here by the fire."

Serenity recoiled from the offered garments. Again, the image of writhing, grappling nakedness touched against the back of her mind. She stiffened, her eyes growing larger still. Within her thoughts, again the battle lines formed . . . the saintly women of her father's parish in their layers of neck-encircling muslins, gauzes, and bombazines; and across from them, a sea of naked harlots, gabbling, scrabbling, slavering in their wickedness. Oh, yes, without question, she again determined, clothing had to be the key to keeping this newest dish of suds within the realm of propriety.

She shook her head with resolve.

"Oh, for the love of . . ." Rand finally muttered, the shirt and pantaloons still extended. "What is it now?" he asked, his arm collapsing.

"I c-cannot wear your clothing," Serenity stated.

"Why not?" the marquess cried. "It is the only dry clothing available."

"A-A woman does not wear a man's sh-shirt," the lady alibied. "And she certainly does n-not wear a pair of his p-pantaloons."

"Of course not," Rand responded, throwing the clothing down upon the oak table. "Instead, she quite properly freezes. Well, do as you like, madam," he said, his countenance stony. "As for me, *I* shall change." Turning his back, he began to peel away his sodden redingote.

"Wh-What are you doing?" Serenity asked when he had also slipped off his buff cutaway.

"Exactly what it seems," the marquess responded, beginning to unfasten the pearl studs riding his forest green silk waistcoat.

Serenity's eyes grew monstrous; blinked rapidly. In the dimness, they shone a deep bottle blue. "B-But you cannot disrobe in my p-presence," she cried. "It is unseemly, sir!"

Rand peeled off his waistcoat and spun about to face her.

"Watch me," he said as, moments later, he divested himself of his snowy white shirt.

Serenity gaped. Even in the dim firelight, the marquess was magnificent. Slowly she closed her eyes; opened them . . . did so again. Acres of skin, smooth and brown in the light of the fire, rose and fell before her astonished eyes with each movement of his toilette, muscle rolling beneath it, surging and subsiding in practiced waves as if the total had been choreographed. Taut cords stretched and loosened, commanding the swells, teasing them into playful shapes. Serenity's skin pebbled even as her face throbbed with heat.

Rand glanced at her then. One brow cocked slightly at the strange look upon her face, at the sudden stillness that had come over her; one corner of his mouth curved into a smile. Yet his reaction unsettled him. It was an emotional response he found mirrored in the jolting chills that at the same time were coursing through her.

He frowned, then, as he drew the inside of his cheek between his teeth. She was beyond cold now. Why was she making excuses to keep from disrobing in front of him? He had no idea. Undoubtedly she had done so many times before in the presence of other men . . . he *had* discovered her in *déshabillé* in a brothel, after all. Yet still she resisted. Whyever? . . .

And what was he to do about it? Cajole her into it he supposed . . . which, devil a bit, meant that he would once more probably have to act the gentleman. Deuce take the jade. Deuce take her beautiful eyes. Deuce take the whole!

With a will the marquess smoothed the scowl lines from his brow. "There," he said soothingly as he slipped on another shirt followed by a thick, flowing robe of soft gold cashmere. "See how easy it is?" Smiling slightly, he belted the robe about his waist, then turned away again. In the next moment, sodden Blüchers thumped down to join his discarded shirt; in a moment more, his wet pantaloons slopped to the floor. "Ah, that's better," he sighed after he had fastened dry inexpressibles about his waist, put on dry stockings, and pivoted to warm his hands again over the open-range fire. Aware of Serenity's avid regard, he asked, quite solicitously, he thought, "Are you absolutely certain you would not like to change?"

"I will not wear a gentleman's pantaloons," Serenity stated emphatically.

."The robe then," Rand offered. "Wear it until your own clothes have dried. I am persuaded that it is not unlike your own, you know."

Another tremor shook Serenity's shoulders. "I simply c-cannot . . ."

". . . And it is quite as large as that deuced garrick you are clutching to your throat," the marquess continued, feeling renewed vexation dam behind his throat. "You shall be completely covered, head to toe."

"It is completely beyond the pale . . ."

". . . Deuce take it, change in the scullery if you like! . . ." Rand interjected, now quite provoked that the chit seemed to have no appreciation for his kindness, "or in the parlor. Jove, madam, change in the attic for all I care!"

"You needn't be so impatient, Chilton," Serenity replied.

"No? You are mottled, my dear," Rand countered, finally giving up any pretext of gentlemanly solicitude.

"Mottled?" Serenity replied.

"With the cold . . . with exposure to the damnable elements, madam! You look like a bowl of mulligatawny soup."

Serenity blinked. "I do?"

"Exactly so, Miss Hoffenduffle," the marquess replied. "You are perilously close to the beyond, and I do not intend to ruin my supper having to deal with your body."

"Nor is it my intention that you ever deal with it either, sir . . . in this life or the next!"

"Then choose, madam," Rand demanded, his eyes gleaming.

"Choose, sir?"

"Yes, Miss Hoffenduffle, choose. The robe or the pantaloons."

Serenity marched off to the parlor with a roll of soft gold cashmere tightly clutched to her mottled, mulligatawny breast.

By the time Serenity returned, the marquess was already beginning the preparations for their dinner, having placed the joint of meat on the marble end of the large kitchen table and brought in several sacks of various items from the pantry. Serenity eyed the collection curiously, then gathered up handfuls of the trailing robe and gingerly hurried to stand close to the range, as the kitchen was still quite cold away from the radiant fire.

"What is that thing?" she asked, motioning toward the grayish mass oozing slightly upon the marble.

The marquess glanced at her with a half smile.

And then his smile faded. Slowly, completely beyond his volition, and with the utmost care, his eyes traveled the length of her. He swallowed audibly, then again turned away. To his chagrin, only the intervention of his inner cheek preventing his teeth from fusing one to the other.

"You would call it 'mutton got up as lamb,' I misdoubt," he at last muttered. "Egad, madam, you really don't know anything about cooking, do you?"

"Unhappily, I do not," Serenity replied, moving to stand beside him. "What do you intend to do with it?"

"We shall cook it, Miss Hoffenduffle," Rand replied, perversely compelled by some inner demon to glance down into the deep vee of the robe's closing as she neared, into the seductive breach which widened and then narrowed in a sensuous rhythm with each of the jade's inhalations, teasing his nerve endings with only the suggestion of her breasts' shadowed cleft. Struggling with an urge to suck in a very deep breath, he instead cleared his throat. "I have brought onions, carrots, turnips, and potatoes in from the pantry. My plan is to contrive a peasant's stew."

"Excellent!" the lady cried, clasping her hands together. "How shall we go about it?"

"Regrettably, I thought you knew."

"Oh. Well, it would require a large pot, I expect," Serenity offered, glancing about.

"There is quite a nice one hanging on the cupboard. Would one put everything in the pot together, do you think?"

"It does seem likely," Serenity concurred, placing a finger aside her chin. "But everything is in little pieces, is it not?"

"Just so," Rand agreed, nodding. "Well, let us go about it then. I shall find us some knives." Turning, he began a visual search.

"One moment, Chilton," Serenity said, placing restraining fingers upon his arm. "What of the sauce?"

"Sauce?" the marquess replied.

"Yes, you know . . . that brownish liquor in which everything floats about. Is there a jar of it about, do you imagine?" she asked, starting toward the pantry.

"How should I know, Miss Hoffenduffle?" Rand groused, his stomach complaining noisily as he followed closely in her wake.

Together they crowded into the pantry and began to scan the rows of shelves, arms touching as they turned to search, bodies brushing only to leap apart, afterwards of their persons . . .

The marquess stalked from the room.

"The deuce!" he muttered when they had both returned. "We shall just have to roast the blasted thing instead. Come along, Miss Hoffenduffle. I saw a bottle jack in the kitchen. We shall hang the joint over the fire."

"What do we do then?" Serenity asked, following him back into the kitchen.

Rand stopped in his tracks. "You really *don't* know anything about cooking, do you?" he asked with a tinge of scorn.

"I have never tried to say otherwise," Serenity responded, drawing herself up. "And I cannot comprehend why you are so surprised. After all, cooking has never been the occupation of a lady."

"The very reason you should be a master," the marquess replied with distaste.

"Is that so?" Serenity asked, driving her fists into her hips.

The action pulled at the robe's restraints. Rand's provoked gaze dropped like a shattered expectation to the shadow suddenly revealed, to the gentle, round slopes, fire-kissed; then down again to the narrow slit of the skirt exposing a darkened silhouette of thigh above one delicate, light-dimpled knee. His jaw rolled aside the snag in his breathing. He captured a moan and glanced downward again. There, peeking out from beneath the puddled cashmere hem, were six toes, three from each soft, pink foot.

"Deuce take it, madam, you have bare feet again!" Rand shouted, relieving at least a part of his body's response.

"What does that have to do with anything?" Serenity shouted right back.

"*Ladies* do not constantly expose themselves," he sneered, ramming his own knuckles against his hips.

"How dare you, sir!" Serenity cried. "I am not exposing myself," she asserted, glancing down. And then she squeaked.

"I see that my point has been taken," he observed awfully. "And it is all the more blatant since I know for a fact that you have slippers in your reticule."

"I am well aware of that fact as well," Serenity stated, quickly clutching the robe tightly about herself again.

"Then, deuce take it, madam, why do you not put them on?"

"Because they are in my reticule!" Serenity shot back.

The marquess lanced her with his astonishment. "I *know* that, Miss Hoffenduffle. I just said so, if you recall. Blast it all, why does nothing you say ever make sense? No, madam . . ." he interjected, holding up an arresting palm, "that question does not require a response. Instead, please, do me the simple kindness of focusing your energies upon properly covering yourself!"

"I cannot," Serenity cried in a most unladylike volume.

"You cannot?" Rand bellowed in perplexity.

"No, I cannot!" the lady returned equally.

The marquess scrubbed his face with his hand. Gathering each frayed nerve ending one by one he finally, and quite reasonably, asked, "For God's sake, why?"

Drawing herself up to her loftiest attitude, Serenity replied, "Because."

The marquess stalked off to the pantry. Only the twentieth part of a moment later, however, he stormed his return. "Deuce take it, Miss Hoffenduffle, you are going to give me a straight answer or I shall do something drastic. Why can you not put your slippers on?"

"Because they are in my reticule," Serenity informed him, distinctly separating each syllable.

Seconds passed. The marquess's jaw dropped in utter frustration. "And . . . ?" he finally managed to blast.

". . . *And,*" Serenity continued, her spine quite rigid, "you still have it about your neck, if you recall."

Stopped cold in mid-tirade, the marquess glanced down. "Good Lord." He sighed, his shoulders sagging. "For the love of . . ." he muttered, tugging at the string-drawn bag. "Deuce take it, madam, come over here and get this thing off of me!"

Serenity stalked forward. "Pompous, self-righteous . . ."

"Never mind. Just take back your property," he interrupted, leaning down, "and put the deuced slippers on."

"Overbearing, arrogant . . ."

"And, devil take it, keep your toes away from me!"

"Gladly!" Serenity responded, taking out her slippers and steadying herself on the table edge while, bending down, she worked one after the other onto her feet.

Rand sucked in his breath at the sheer volume of uncharted flesh her unthinking action exposed. Slowly, he let his heavy lids slide closed; his fingers curved, and then clenched into tight fists of lust-control.

"I trust this meets with your approval," Serenity finally, tersely, said through the fog of his desire.

Slumberously, Rand opened his eyes again.

Serenity stood before him as rigid as a governess, her

hands clasped before her abdomen, his robe fastened so securely about her form that he was persuaded no circulation could possibly be squeezing its way past the constriction about her slender waist. He glanced at her face. Her eyes were huge in the flickering firelight, sparkling with challenge; her lips shone pink, lustrous, and full. She was adorable. There was no other word for it. A swell of desire inundated him like a storm tide.

She was a jade of the worst kind. God, why did she have to be so damnably beautiful?

"Well, sir?" the lady asked again.

The marquess forced an arrogant gaze to peruse her. "Much more the thing," he rumbled with as much hauteur as his thrumming body could muster.

Suddenly Serenity relaxed, letting her hands fall to her sides. "Very well then, sir. Let us continue with what we were doing. What do you suppose we do now?" she asked, her voice, to the marquess's amazement, bordering on the plaintive.

To his chagrin, the sound plucked several of Rand's deep inner strings. Unable to help it, he relaxed as well, a deep sigh its avenue of return.

"We put this roast over the fire," he answered softly. "Come, Miss Hoffenduffle, bring the bottle jack. I shall carry the roast over to the grate."

Surprisingly, it did not take the marquess and Serenity long to hook the reflective screen to the range around the grate and then attach the bottle jack to it. As soon as the device was in place, Rand hung the joint of mutton from the hook beneath it, then wound its inner clock spring. When he released the key, the meat began turning round and round over the open flames.

"Wonderful!" Serenity cried, quickly abandoning her pique. "Now all we must do is cook the vegetables," she added, hurrying to begin emptying the nearby sacks.

"Any ideas on how?" Rand questioned.

"Well . . . I suppose we must put them over the fire as well," she offered.

"That seems logical," the marquess agreed, taking handfuls of the carrots and turnips and scattering them near the coals.

"That looks good," Serenity added, tossing several potatoes into the center of it all. "There. Oh, Chilton, I am persuaded this shall make a wonderful meal," she said with an appreciative smile.

"And when this is hot," added Rand as he set a kettle of water on the nearby stove, "we shall even have tea."

"Oh, how splendid!" Serenity cried. "I should love a cup right now, wouldn't you? It has been a long time since the several I had at the inn this morning."

"Or those I had with my uncle in Ipswich," Rand agreed. "By this time I have usually consumed five pots of the brew."

"With lemon," Serenity added.

And then, quite suddenly, her expression changed oddly. A very small groove dug a path between her brows.

"Milk for me," the marquess commented, glancing toward her as he took a tin of tea down from a cupboard shelf, insensible of her alteration.

Serenity's eyes met his, instantly skittered away.

"Chilton . . ." she said quite suddenly, "I . . . I am afraid you shall have to excuse me." Not even waiting for a response, she abruptly dashed toward the hallway.

A short time later, however, she returned.

"Miss Hoffenduffle, whatever is the matter?" the marquess asked, regarding the look of urgency on her face.

"Chilton," she asked him in a tiny voice, "I-I don't suppose that in your explorations of this mill you have come upon a convenience?"

"Why, no," he replied, unsuccessfully containing the gleam invading his eyes. "Perhaps there is an outbuilding near the granary," he suggested, making a show of peering out the window.

"Of course," Serenity declared, spinning about. "I shall be back in a trice."

"No, you shall not," Rand countered mildly, poking the joint of mutton with a long-tined fork. "You are still freezing with the cold. You cannot go back out into the elements."

"But . . . that is, you see . . . Chilton, I really must . . ." Serenity insisted, at last reduced to wringing her hands. "Chilton, for heaven's sake, this is an emergency!"

At the confession, the gleam in the marquess's eyes became positively unholy. "Very well, follow me," he suggested helpfully, striding toward the scullery. Upon her arrival at his side, he placed one of the room's buckets in the center of the floor, and added, "There. This will do, I should think."

"I should think not!" Serenity stated, her countenance appalled. "At the very least I require a small room or closet with a door."

"The rest of the mill is freezing, Miss Hoffenduffle," the marquess reasoned. "Even if the mill had such an amenity, we could not use it. Whatever facility we devise must be kept close to the range's fire."

"Then you shall just have to devise a partition of some sort," Serenity told him, crossing her arms beneath her breasts.

"Between what and what?" Rand asked, feeling his brows soar.

"Between our two buckets, of course," Serenity answered.

"Two?" Rand replied, also crossing his arms. "What makes you think I shall set up two buckets?" he asked with deceptive calm.

"For the reason that it is proper," Serenity responded with a nod.

"Madam, it is wasted effort," Rand countered with a slow shake of his head.

"Why?"

"Obviously, because I am not planning to be in here at the same time you are," he told her very quietly, leaning forward into his verbal thrust.

Stymied, Serenity's exasperation huffed up to waffle several of her brown curls. "Very well," she finally stated loftily, "since I cannot convince you to do the gentlemanly thing, kindly remove yourself, sir."

"Posthaste," the marquess replied with suspicious sobriety, turning on his heel after sweeping into a low bow.

"And do not dare to look back in this direction," Serenity requested.

"Heaven forfend," the marquess replied, busying himself again with prodding and probing the roast, then removing it to a large platter.

"And sing," Serenity commanded.

"Sing?" Rand repeated, one brow arching back in the scullery's direction. "Whatever for?"

"For the reason, Chilton," Serenity told him, "that I do not wish you to . . . hear."

"Ah," the marquess nodded, quickly turning away again to scoop vegetables onto the plate, sucking a solemn countenance onto his face. "Say no more, Miss Hoffenduffle . . . and, by all means, er . . . carry on," he at last managed to tell her. "I shall do my best to drown you out."

"So kind of you, Chilton."

Moments later, from the kitchen, "Flow Gently Sweet Afton" began to waft about the tide mill in the marquess's booming baritone.

Hearing it, back in the scullery Serenity rolled her eyes and dropped her face into her palms.

"Was that particular selection altogether necessary?" she asked, returning to the kitchen a bit later after she had again adjusted the cashmere robe about her form.

"Did you not care for it?" the marquess queried as he

lay rude stoneware and silver upon the table, his gaze innocent. "I thought it the perfect choice . . . far better than the other selection that came to mind."

"Allow me to guess, sir," Serenity said flatly. ". . . 'God Save the King'?"

"The very one," the marquess nodded. "Lud, only imagine if I had chosen that anthem, Miss Hoffenduffle."

"In truth, sir, I'd rather not," Serenity stated.

"Why, if I had chosen 'God Save the King,' Miss Hoffenduffle . . ."

". . . Chilton!" Serenity warned.

". . . Through the whole of it," he happily ground into her discomposure, "you would have been compelled to stand."

Seventeen

Dinner passed a bit later in relative peace, owing to a lifetime of training in the proper social etiquette, of course, which required that each antagonist politely gnaw their way through slices of bloody mutton and sere, blackened vegetables, and quite properly ignore the explosions of their charred potatoes which to their amazement became altogether dangerous when pierced with a knife or fork.

At the meal's completion, Serenity retired to the scullery with a pail of hot water to scrub what needed to be washed. When she again returned to the kitchen, she found that the marquess had stoked the range with coal and, more, was in the midst of fashioning a thick, nest-resembling collection of blankets upon the floor in front of it.

"Whatever is that?" she asked, standing before the fire to refresh her warmth.

"A pallet," Rand replied, throwing two more blankets over the whole, slipping out of his shirt, then sliding into the bed's midst. "Hurry and help me warm it before the fire dies down."

"Help you warm it?" Serenity gasped, blinking twice. "What do you mean?"

"I mean get in," the marquess explained, glowering up at her, affirming the invitation by lifting up a corner of the blankets.

"I shall not!" Serenity vowed, completely unable to hold

her gaze above the vast, bulging expanse of the marquess's chest.

"Be reasonable, Miss Hoffenduffle," Rand offered next. "We both of us need to share each other's warmth. When the fire dies, it shall soon return to freezing in here."

"Nevertheless, I am quite sensible, sir, of what a man like you can get up to with a woman, in *déshabillé,* on the floor," Serenity told him, sitting down upon one of the kitchen chairs instead, then tightening the robe about her neck.

On a sigh, the marquess let the corner of the blankets drop. "Is that what this is all about?" he asked, his lips curled with pique. "You are jealous because of what you saw at Charity's Place?"

"I am not jealous in the least!" Serenity tossed back at him. "It is merely that it is not proper for a man and a woman to . . . to lie about disrobed in each other's presence."

"This from a woman I discovered in a brothel," Rand muttered, dropping the corner of the blankets to scrub his face. "Madam, considering what *I* saw that night, your objection makes little sense, but if it will get you into the pallet, very well . . ." he conceded, bounding up lithely again and once more donning his shirt, "is this more to your liking? I am now no longer *déshabillé!*"

"It *is* better," Serenity allowed with a tremble, "however *I* am still disrobed," she concluded, both hands clutching cashmere tightly against her throat.

"As far as I can tell, Miss Hoffenduffle," the marquess responded, niggling memories of what bulged beneath the cashmere insinuating into prominence just behind his forehead, spinning about as a result to dig a silver hip flask from out of his valise, "you are about as robed as it is possible for a woman to be." Having spat out that evaluation, he then flipped the lid on the flask and dosed himself with a hearty swig. "Here," he finished, wiping his lips on the back of his hand, then extending the flask. "Have some if you like."

"What is it?" Serenity asked, a shiver jostling her shoulders.

"Brandy."

"I do not drink strong spirits," she stated, the elevation of her nose moderated somewhat by another series of tiny chills.

"It will warm you, deuce take it!" Rand exclaimed. "If you are determined not to lie down on the pallet, at least take some of this."

Chewing upon her lip, Serenity thought for a moment. "Well, I suppose there are certain occasions when physicians do prescribe a bit of brandy for medicinal purposes," she allowed. "Very well," she at last agreed, standing, releasing her grip upon the cashmere, then slowly starting forward.

Delicate knees evaded the robe's edges with rhythmic revelations as she approached; the collar gaped. The marquess swallowed thickly at the sight of it, then tipped up another hearty measure from his flask.

Arriving at the pallet bed, Serenity took a tiny sip. And swallowed

A holocaust began at the back of her throat and slid all the way down into her stomach.

"Goodness!" she gasped, feeling each muscle in her body weaken and give way, sinking down onto the blankets. "Goodness!" she repeated, sipping again. "This certainly . . . works!"

"It certainly does," Rand agreed with elevated brows, marveling at the almost immediate change sweeping over her, leaning his hip against the table and crossing his arms over his chest.

"This is really rather tasty, too," Serenity evaluated with a giggle she immediately stopped behind her fingertips, sighing back against the piled blankets as she sipped again, one slim bare leg again peeking out.

"Lud, yes," the marquess agreed, his gaze repeatedly riding the curve.

"Does that mean that you would care for more, Chilton?" Serenity asked with a smile, throwing an arm back over her head as she stretched.

Dragging his gaze away, the marquess ran several fingers through his hair. "No, I do not!" he growled, bending down to throw the blankets over her. "And if you have any goodness in your heart at all, Miss Hoffenduffle, be so good as to get under the covers!"

"What? . . . Oh, good heavens!" she gasped after a downward glance, balancing the flask while she adjusted the robe beneath the blankets. "There, now I have been put to rights again." She smiled up into his vexation, her focus several seconds behind her gaze. "That sounds ridiculous, does it not?" She next giggled. "Put to rights, right and tights. Oh, and I am *wondrously* warm," she cooed, feeling her spine release its grip on her vertebrae, raising the flask high above her head. "And I am most grateful, Chilton. Have I said that I am most grateful? I am. I am altogether grateful for your kindnesses. And so wondrously warm."

"Well, at least one of us is," the marquess groused, shaking his head.

"Are you not, too, then?" Serenity asked, struggling to sit back up. "Why, of course you are not! You are now out there, and I am in the pallet," she giggled again. "I, within, and you, without. How did that state come about? Hah! I made a poem." She chuckled once more. Suddenly, her expressive brows dropped into a frown. "Chilton . . ." she asked warily, "are you still trying to get me down onto the floor?"

"No need, madam," the marquess responded tightly. "If you will notice, you already are."

"Why, so I am!" Serenity exclaimed. "Goodness, I must get up!"

"No, you must not. And be reasonable, Miss Hoffenduffle," the marquess argued. "You shall perish if you do not stay covered."

"Yet it is not at all proper, Chilton." Serenity sighed, flopping back down upon the piled blankets.

"No one questions that, madam, nor the fact that neither of us wishes to be in this improper situation, but in it we are. And while in the midst of it, we must endeavor to do what we must to stay alive. And if your objection is still that we are in *déshabillé*, I would suggest to you that although, granted, our clothing is a bit out of the ordinary for social congress, we are both covered head to toe. And best give that back to me, I think," he commanded, stretching out beside her, commandeering the flask.

"Very well." Serenity placidly smiled, next passing several moments in which she stared at the ceiling and played with a series of curls. "Do you know, Chilton? . . ." she at last added, suddenly rolling over to face him, one breast sliding almost all the way into the robe's firelit gape, "what you say makes sense."

"Oh?" he managed to choke.

Staring deeply into his eyes, Serenity nodded. "Now that I am thinking more clearly, I am convinced of it," she whispered. "You can barely stand to be in the same room with me," she told him, absently drawing up a bare knee. "Why should I be concerned that you would want to touch me in the ways Propriety warned me men might wish to but should not?"

While the question hung between them, an age passed. Then, "Perhaps because I do, blast it all to the devil," Rand finally, quietly, admitted, afterward clenching his jaw against the confession, knowing that it had only been squeezed out because he had been mesmerized by that . . . that misbegotten dimple just aside her knee and her unblinking perusal of his own gaze with hers of sparkling cobalt blue.

Slowly, however, and with a soft smile, Serenity denied the claim. "No, you do not. That would be too great a contradiction," she whispered, her gaze still flowing into his, tucking one hand beneath her cheek.

Across from her, the marquess huffed. "No greater a contradiction than a woman named Propriety who once punched me in the nose, or another named Serenity who has, since the day I met her, cut up my peace," he complained with a slow smile, growing languorous as he studied the play of firelight upon her gray-flecked irises. "Why the deuce did the vicar name you that, anyway?"

"For the same reason he named my sister Propriety," Serenity told him, her gentle laugh a tickle worrying each of the marquess's nerve endings. "Papa always said it was wishful thinking."

For long moments after Serenity's explanation, the marquess chuckled softly. Then, tucking his hand, too, beneath his cheek, he gave in to the compelling need simply to look at the woman lying so close beside him, to fill his being with the scent of her, to search for the flaw in her skin that he knew he would never find.

"You drive me daft," he at last whispered, his dark gaze bleeding into hers.

"I know," Serenity breathed. "You do the same to me."

"I know that, too," the marquess responded, slowly, ever so slowly, closing the distance between their whispers.

At last, as softly as the touch of fairy wings, their lips touched.

The twentieth part of a moment later, however, Serenity's cheeks ballooned out with a captured belch.

"Oh!" she gasped, jerking away, quickly pressing her fingertips to her lips. "Oh, goodness, Chilton!" she exclaimed, sitting bolt upright. "I . . . I think I am about to be sick!"

As quickly as the warning was out, Serenity found herself snatched up, dashed away, then ignominiously suspended over the makeshift convenience.

"Better?" the marquess asked sometime later when Serenity emerged from the dark scullery holding a cold cloth to her forehead.

"Frankly, I am not altogether certain I ever shall be again," Serenity replied, shakily lowering herself onto one of the kitchen chairs. "Chilton, I . . . I must apologize," she said, looking up at him meekly. "I vow I have never been quite so mortified." And then she paused. "Well, actually, that is not true. I was certainly more so . . . that night."

"Understandable. You had at last been discovered," Rand stated softly, putting tea leaves and hot water into a pot, then pouring them both a cup.

"On the contrary, sir," Serenity countered, looking up at him as her anger prickled. "My mortification came from the fact that *you* had been."

"*Me?* I was doing nothing wrong!" Rand insisted on a surge of vexation, taking up his cup and throwing the scalding liquid down his throat.

"Nor was I!" Serenity insisted, lending him no sympathy at all while he cursed, spun about, and choked.

"You simply will not admit it, will you?" he bellowed after he had downed a chaser of cool water.

"Admit what?"

"Your part in the whole affair! Oh, never mind, deuce take it!" he loudly dismissed, slashing his hand through the air, then climbing back beneath the blankets. "It does no good to rehearse this again and again," he declared, tucking the covers beneath his chin. "Come to bed!"

"When England tunnels beneath the Channel," Serenity vowed, folding her arms beneath her breasts.

"Deuce take it, Miss Hoffenduffle, you shall freeze," the marquess argued.

"Then I shall freeze."

"Very well, then, do so for all I care!" Rand shouted, turning his back to her pique.

"I shall!" she countered, deciding after a few moments of his complete disinterest that he would not notice it if she snuggled her toes beneath the robe's hem. Glancing toward his still form one more time, she did so. "I certainly shall never join *you* in *there.*"

Much later, however, when only a weak amber glow struggled within the range's ash-covered coals, Rand felt the blankets move behind him, followed by a wash of frigid air creeping over his spine. And then, suddenly, Serenity was spooned about him, her breath moist against his neck and collar, her icy fingers burying themselves between his upper arms and sides.

"Good Lord," he husked when she squirmed even closer, pressing her soft breasts against his back.

"This is not in the least what you think," Serenity murmured, wriggling again.

"Indeed," he managed in a gentlemanly whisper, a complete contrast to the pandemonium taking place within his groin.

"Indeed not. I have been considering the matter, Chilton, and have concluded that in refusing your request, I am most likely being remiss in my Christian duty."

"Oh?" the marquess wheezed.

"Yes, indeed," Serenity said. "You see, in joining you I can alleviate some of *your* discomfort," she stated, shivering for a moment, then even more tightly cupping the afterward of his person within the forward portion of hers.

"You think so, do you?" he next growled, instantly losing every shred of self-righteousness as he jammed two knuckles into his mouth and battled the parade of impulses

marching through his abdomen that would have him rolling the jade over and dragging her into his arms.

"Of course, I do. And the least you could do, Chilton,
is to hold still," she added when, during another low
moan, the marquess halfheartedly attempted to extricate
himself. "You, sir, are no gentleman," she insisted, again
closing the slight distance between them and insinuating
her cold nose into the warm hollow behind his neck.

"Good Lord, woman, you have no idea how wrong you
are," the marquess groaned. "Now, for the love of God,
Serenity, hold still yourself!" he afterward managed.

"There, you see?" Serenity whispered, fitting her shins
precisely against his well-rounded calves. "You have just
proved my point. No gentleman would use my Christian
name absent my permission."

"As it happens, I am a gentleman of the highest stare,
madam," the marquess countered in an attempt to parry
the sensations driving him daft.

"How so?"

"It is a point of honor with me to call all the women I
take to bed by their Christian names," he told her. "Besides," he added over her appalled gasp, "I have tangled
my tongue over 'Miss Hoffenduffle' long enough. Each
time I manage it I feel as if I have expelled something
unspeakable from my airways."

That said, the marquess then fell asleep, content that
even if it were beyond him to control his physical reaction
to the chit, at least he had finally managed to wrest a small
measure of advantage in their verbal boxing match.

When Serenity awoke the following morning, she was
alone in the pallet bed. Slowly sitting up, looking about,
taking the moments in which she did so to recall where
she was and how she had come to be there, she at last rose
and tightened the loose folds of the marquess's cashmere

robe about her, then padded off on slippered feet to discover the dratted man's whereabouts.

A glance out of the parlor window looking down upon the quayside gave her the answer. Below, the marquess struggled against the steadily driving snow, dragging a thick coil of stout rope along behind him which he had tied to the railing of the second-story landing and was obviously intending to attach next to the handle on one of the doors of the granary.

Nodding, Serenity allowed that it was a sensible plan. The horses would have to be fed, after all, and a rope between the two buildings would give the marquess a guideline should he be forced to leave the mill during the heavier snowfalls, as well as give him something upon which to hang when the biting gusts threatened to blow him onto the unstable floes of the millpond.

Taking advantage of the marquess's being otherwise occupied, Serenity then returned to the kitchen, drew out a pan full of hot water from the range's cistern, then carried it to the scullery where she quickly performed her toilette. Afterward, grateful for the privacy, she again donned her now-dry traveling gown and blue pelisse, determined not to be too vexed that she was now no longer able to add the finishing touch to her ensemble, which had been her brand-new, and utterly charming, she thought, nesting blue bird hat.

As she was returning to the kitchen to chase away a new wave of chills before the range, however, she paused to glance back toward the marquess's improvised, and altogether public, convenience arrangement. It was the outside of enough, she exclaimed to herself with a thinning of her lips.

It was then when the thought occurred to her that with the marquess otherwise occupied, no one was about to naysay her devising her own arrangements. Breaking into a mischievous smile, Serenity hesitated not a whit in seizing

the second of the two scullery buckets and quickly beginning a search for the perfect place.

The site for her own private necessary did not present
itself until she had climbed all the way up to the tide mill's
attic—a dim, dusty room, she saw as she entered, that was
used principally for storage and lit only by what daylight
managed to filter through the soot-covered panes of the
steeply slanted roof's row of shallow dormers. There were,
however, aside from scattered pieces of furniture—chief
among them a huge clothespress—four trunks, a collection of odd-shaped pieces of wood most likely once part
of the waterwheel, and several neat stacks of unused grain
sacks stored against one of the room's low walls. Quickly
determining that the sacks were just what she needed to
build her private quarter's high, sound-absorbing walls,
she began to remove armfuls of them from the stacks and
arrange them in the stretch of standing room available
just beneath the roof's peak.

The activity took surprisingly few minutes, and warmed
her nicely. As she was completing the first side of her chamber, however, by accident she bumped against the clothes
press.

With a soft snick, the rusted latch on the doors gave.
Slowly, one door began to swing open with an aching creak
that would have felt perfectly at home within the pages of
a gothic by Mrs. Radcliffe.

A bit annoyed at the interruption, Serenity turned to
close it again.

At that exact moment, however, a cold, lifeless arm
dropped down out of the widening aperture to settle heavily against the notch of her neck.

Eighteen

The marquess had just enough time to turn himself about after Serenity's shriek of his name before she leapt from the second-story railing and landed squarely on top of his chest.

"What the deuce? . . ." he exclaimed after the two of them had stopped rolling across the drifted quay.

"Oh, Chilton," Serenity whispered, wriggling even closer, burying her face into his snow-covered neck. "It is him . . . u-upstairs," she gasped, clinging to his lapels as she raised her head. "The other one. Oh, do come! It is the other man," she cried, pointing toward the mill, "and I cannot conceive of what it means!"

"What are you talking about? Serenity, what has happened?" Rand asked, squeezing her tightly against him. "What other man?"

"Th-The one upstairs," she responded shakily, her gaze pouring fear into his, "in the attic."

"There is a man in the attic?" Rand repeated, pulling them both quickly to their feet.

"Yes!" Serenity exclaimed. "First it was the one on the gibbet, and now the other. Oh, do come, Chilton!" she pleaded, tugging on his arm.

Needing no further urging, the marquess took hold of Serenity's hand, dragged her back into the tide mill, and raced up the stairs. Moments later, the two stood before the gaping doors of the clothespress, staring into the frozen, blue-tongued visage of the man still hanging stiff and waxen by his coat collar from one of the hooks fastened at the rear of the press's interior.

"Do you see?" Serenity whispered, clinging to Rand's sleeve. "It is him. Just like the other . . . dead."

Glancing down at her, the marquess unclenched his jaw. "Serenity, I am sensible that it must be oversetting for you to encounter two of these corpses in the space of two days," he comforted, drawing her within the circle of his arms, "but . . ."

"Oh, Chilton, it is not that they are dead! . . ." Serenity exclaimed, pulling away from his grasp. "Dear heavens, what am I saying?" she cried, pressing fingers to her forehead. "Of course it is all that is horrible. Yet . . . the thing is, you see, I *know* them!"

At the confession, Rand stilled. "Two more of your partners, are they?" he concluded, staring down at her in distaste.

"No!" Serenity cried, gripping his waist, not allowing him to turn away from her frightened sapphire gaze. "Oh, please, Rand, do not start rowing over this same pond again. Do you not yet believe me? I have no partners. I have done nothing wrong!"

"Then how do you know this man?" he snapped.

"He is one of the men who abducted me that night, don't you see?"

"Abducted you?" Rand repeated as his jaw gaped.

"Yes! . . . and so I would have told you if you had ever given me the chance! I was not at the brothel willingly that night, Chilton," she told him. "I was only there because this man and the man on the gibbet forced me to Charity's Place!"

For long moments, Rand stared at Serenity. Then, closing the doors to the clothespress, he again faced her.

"Start at the beginning," he firmly commanded.

Inexplicably, all of Serenity's disquiet vanished in the face of the marquess's arrogance.

"It is true that when we were betrothed I was keeping a secret from you," Serenity told Chilton a bit later after he had removed her from the attic to the much warmer kitchen and had forced her into yet another clothing change.

"Go on," the marquess quietly urged, pouring boiling water from the range top over the handful of tea leaves he had tossed into the teapot.

"St. Mary's parish, you see, sponsors a school in London for workingmen's children," she confessed from the apex of the garrick's sixteen capes.

"I am aware of that, Serenity," Rand responded quietly, glancing toward her, "as well as the fact that upon occasion during our engagement, you visited there. Your sister said as much to James."

Momentarily, Serenity's brows knit, then settled. "Not surprising, I suppose," she allowed. "However, Proppie did keep one secret."

"Which was? . . ."

"That, because of the illness of Mrs. Burton, our school's headmistress, I took on her duties."

"It is hardly a hanging offense for a young woman of breeding occasionally to scribble a few numbers into a ledger, my dear," the marquess stated, pouring tea into two stoneware cups. "Why did you feel the need for such secrecy?"

"Because I took on *all* of her duties," Serenity explained. "I taught, I dealt with the contributions and ordered supplies, I saw to the school's maintenance . . ."

". . . Unorthodox, but hardly unacceptable," Rand allowed.

". . . I slept on the premises at night."

"Ah," the marquess evaluated, drawing in a deep breath which he was slow to release. "Serenity, do you realize what might have happened?"

"Of course, I do! I should have been scandalized, as well as you. Why do you think I kept it secret?" she asked, accepting his offer of a steaming cup. "Yet someone had to do it, Chilton, for the children's sake. And there was no one else."

"So you passed your days with the children, returned to your aunt and uncle's house each evening for dinner and social occasions, then—no doubt abetted by your sister—returned to your parish's school for the night," he concluded.

Serenity nodded. "That is the reason why, on the night that our betrothal ended," she confessed, "I was at the school. That is also why—quite by accident, I swear!—I was present when those two men came to the school long after everyone had retired."

After a moment in which the marquess evaluated her words, he slowly walked to the table and took the chair across from her. "Go on," he at last stated. "Why had the two come?"

"To deliver several sacks of grain," Serenity told him.

"Indeed?" he repeated, straightening a bit, his gaze sharpening.

"Yes. At first I thought the delivery to be merely a routine charitable contribution to the school. I soon found out, however, that they had made a significant mistake. Their real destination was the brothel."

"Serenity, there is a marked difference between a school and a brothel," Rand noted skeptically, leaning back in his chair.

"Ordinarily I would agree. Yet I am persuaded that this error was understandable," she countered, resting her forearms upon the table. "The two men said that the grain was bound for Charity's Place in Garrick Street," she explained, opening her hands. "Where they had mistakenly delivered it was to Charity's *Hands*, Chilton, our parish school, in Cloak Lane."

"Good God," the marquess uttered, finally beginning to realize the enormity of his own error, his broad shoulders sagging almost all the way down over his rib cage.

Serenity had not betrayed him, he suddenly understood. Never. Not once. She had not been involved in the smuggling ring. And now that he knew the truth of it, he could not fathom how he had failed to see it before. She knew nothing of men. Had he been more open-minded where she was concerned, any further doubt of that fact should have been quickly quelled long ago by simple observation. She had not been pretending. She had truly never seen before what had been going on that night between himself and that brothel light-skirt. Even more ludicrous, she had truly believed that he had been holding his pistol in his lap during the curricle chase. How had he not comprehended it? She was an innocent, protected all her life by Propriety and the vicar. Deuce take it, how had he thought she could be a jade of the first stare when she could not even bring herself to utter the word *arse?*

"I take it that when they realized their mistake, they took you along with them because they knew you could identify them," he tautly concluded, all the while wondering how the deuce he was ever going to apologize adequately.

Serenity nodded. "I cannot help but think so, Chilton. While we were still at the school, one of them said, 'She knows us now.' At the brothel, they put me into the care of the proprietress," Serenity added, "who then took me belowstairs to the room where you . . ."

". . . Watched you tumble top over tail," the marquess quietly interjected, muscle rolling beneath his cheeks, "then settle with a chalice on your lap which had spilled out from one of the grain sacks. Devil a bit, Serenity! I had a hunch when I entered that traveling chaise that I would find the solution to the whole theft ring bumble-broth, but I never guessed you would be the key."

"Rand," Serenity said plaintively, "I swear to you that I had nothing to do with any of it."

"Of course you did not," the marquess replied, waving his arm dismissively. "I know that now. But do you not see? One of the very two who were in possession of sacks taken to Charity's Place is *here* . . ." he explained, his tone growing tight. "Serenity, that can only mean that we must have stumbled onto the very mill! . . .

"Blast it all! . . ." he next burst out, exploding from his chair. "Do you see why I would have shaken you senseless had I known you were living all but alone at that school? Due to your own foolhardiness, that night you came very close to being killed!"

"Due to that same foolhardiness, my lord," Serenity hotly countered, swiftly rising to her own feet, "I came to know more than I ever wished about you!"

"I told you before . . . I was there for a reason!" the marquess shouted.

"Obviously!" Serenity cried just as loudly, planting her sleeve-swathed fists upon her hips.

Vexed almost beyond bearing, the marquess scraped ten calming fingers across his scalp.

"Serenity, I . . . oh, sit down again, deuce take it!"

Reluctantly, with great dignity, Serenity sank once more into her chair.

The marquess released a long gush of air. "Serenity, I . . . have my own confessions to make."

"What a surprise," she commented, using the four-teenth cape to buff her nails.

"You are not going to make this easy for me, are you?" Rand sighed. "Very well, fair's fair. I confess that during our betrothal, I, too, was keeping secrets from you."

"What secrets?" Serenity asked with a wary tilt of her head, curiosity quickly overwhelming her hauteur.

"For well over a year now I have been working for the Home Secretary," he told her, sitting, too, in his chair.

"For Sir Robert Peel?" Serenity asked. "Why?"

"It began with a request from my uncle Paul," the marquess explained.

"The bishop?"

"Yes. It was his wish that I become the church's liaison in the Home Office's investigation into who has been stealing church treasures all across England."

"I know of this, Chilton," Serenity stated, her blue eyes large. "St. Mary's lost several artifacts, including a beautiful gold cross."

"I am not surprised," he commented. "The thefts seem to be centered in Suffolk."

"And you have been investigating them," Serenity pondered aloud.

"With the aid of Bow Street. I have been working with a Runner named Ben Bradshaw, trying to discover who is involved in the thefts so that we might infiltrate their ring."

"This is all well and good, Chilton," she stated testily, "but it hardly explains why I found you rolling about on the floor . . ."

". . . It does," he interjected, holding up a silencing hand, "if you will kindly listen a moment longer. Shortly before the night we encountered one another at Charity's Place, Ben Bradshaw received a tip from an informant that some of the artifacts were due to arrive there that night in bags of grain."

"Grain! . . ." Serenity breathed, her eyes growing round.

"Yes. You see, we had already determined that, after they had been stolen, the artifacts must have been stored somewhere and then most likely brought to some place along the coast where they were then smuggled out of the country. The difficulty lay in the fact that we had no idea where the two sites were. That was what was so important about the tip."

"You now knew where the point of embarkation was," Serenity assessed.

"Yes, exactly." The marquess nodded; his excitement in the sharing was evident in his deep voice. "And not only that, but the shipping site's discovery gave us the opportunity to seize evidence from the brothel that might indicate where the storage site was."

"So you set a trap," Serenity concluded.

"Just so. That night, Ben Bradshaw positioned Runners all about the brothel."

"And you?"

"Because of my status as a gentleman about town, I was appointed to infiltrate the establishment," he told her quietly. "My plan was to await the grain delivery and then to signal the Runners when I determined there were treasures in the sacks."

"I see," Serenity commented mildly. "And with what did you intend to signal, Chilton? From what I could see, you had nothing in your possession at the time. Did you plan to heave that . . . that woman of questionable character out the window?"

"Nothing of the sort," the marquess chided. "Serenity . . . matters got out of hand."

"It appeared to me as if matters were altogether *in* hand," she replied, afterward drumming several fingertips.

"There was a reason for it, I tell you!" the marquess barked, tunneling even more fingers through his tousled hair. "Lud, Serenity, I was discovered almost immediately upon entering through a service door. Happily, it was assumed that I was merely a gentleman of quality who had not wished to be recognized in such a low establishment and among such rude clientele while I . . . indulged myself," he began to explain. "As a result, I was taken into a special room where I was allowed to choose from among the brothel's more exclusive . . . staff.''

"Which, it seems, you did," Serenity noted, averting her gaze.

"As a matter of fact," the marquess countered acidly, "I did not. After my introduction to the ladies, I said that none would do other than Hildegarde."

"Hildegarde?" Serenity repeated, facing him again as her brows rose.

"Yes, Hildegarde!" Rand groused. "It seemed a foreign-enough sounding name."

"Hildegarde."

"Well, who would have thought a woman named Hildegarde would be working clients on the *English* waterfront?" he bellowed, again surging to his feet and beginning to pace.

Quickly turning aside again, Serenity choked back a sudden urge to laugh.

"So it was *Hildegarde* I saw . . ."

". . . Yes, deuce take it!" the marquess stormed. "Now are you going to let me finish?"

"Why, of course, Chilton," Serenity airily waved.

"Very well then," the marquess harrumphed. "As I was saying, I chose Hildegarde. Happily, however, she was occupied at the time."

"Hildegarde," Serenity inserted. "Yet you object to *'Hoffenduffle.'* "

"If I might be allowed to finish? . . ." Rand growled.

"Go on, Chilton."

"I was left alone in the room to await her," he concluded.

"Which, obviously, you did not," Serenity added with another elevated brow.

"Well, of course not!" Rand rumbled. "I had not gone there to . . . oh, never mind! As soon as the hall had cleared, I left the room and began to explore. It seemed logical to me that any evidence would most likely be in a storeroom in the cellar, so I quickly made my way there. I was just about to open one of the grain bags in the room you saw me in when the door opened, and . . ."

". . . *Hildegarde?*" Serenity sweetly asked, fluttering her lashes.

"Hildegarde," the marquess concurred, his chin sagging down to his chest. "I swear to you, Serenity, my only consolation in the whole blasted bumblebroth was that the lady in question had more hair than wit. She readily accepted my explanation that I enjoyed unusual locations for my . . . diversions."

"And so you just . . . *proceeded?*" Serenity questioned, chewing on her inner cheek.

"Well, what was I to do?" Rand exclaimed, ceasing his pacing long enough to throw up his hands. "To do else would have made even one of the grain sacks suspicious! Besides, nothing really happened," he said, again subsiding. "The delivery came—I now know by way of the two men who abducted you—you screamed upon seeing me, and that quite satisfactorily alerted the Runners, who swarmed the building only to find that everyone inside had been forewarned by your scream as well and had escaped through a tunnel leading down to the wharf."

"Randall Torrent, are you saying that *I* am responsible for the failure of your scheme?"

"Yes, when you get right down to it," the marquess retorted.

The air huffed out of Serenity's chest. "Merciful heavens, I suppose that I am," she conceded with a sigh, dropping her face into her palms. "During every moment in your presence that night I must have appeared to be aiding and abetting the enemy, did I not? It is no wonder that you wished no further congress with me."

"Serenity . . ."

". . . Well, at least I now comprehend the chalice I

found lying upon my lap," Serenity noted, slightly nodding. "For all these months I have thought it was a gift you had brought for . . . *Hildegarde* . . and that you had instead thrown it at me."

"The deuce," the marquess remarked, unable to help chuckling as he shook his head. "I happen to be a gentleman, Serenity. Why would I throw something at you? . . . and, while we are on the subject, why did you toss that cricket ball at me, anyway?"

"I have no idea," Serenity softly confessed, granting him a rueful smile. "I do remember an image of the last time I had seen you crossing my mind at the time. Perhaps I was throwing it at . . . *Hildegarde.*" Suddenly, Serenity began lacing her fingers. "I don't suppose you would be inclined to forgive me," she wondered, peeking up at him as she chewed the bottom of her lip.

"Done"—he grinned—"and done, too, a good measure of the mystery I have been trying to unravel."

"Yes, happily."

"Serenity, it all fits," the marquess agreed with an excited nod. "We have always known that Suffolk has seen the worst of the thefts. Later, we discovered that the stolen artifacts were being taken to the embarkation point in grain sacks."

"So you truly do think it no coincidence that one of the men who was involved in the artifacts' delivery was hung on a gibbet not far from here, or that the other man was found dead in this very mill?"

"No, indeed."

"Then we *have* somehow managed to find ourselves at the thieves' storage site, have we not?" Serenity breathed, her eyes growing huge.

"The conclusion seems inescapable, Serenity," the marquess responded, his features firming beneath a hardening gaze.

"But that would mean we are still in grave danger," Serenity concluded, tightening the garrick collar about her neck. "What shall we do?"

"First, I think we must assume that the thieves will return when the weather clears, if not before," Rand told her. "Next, I believe we must take precautions against the event."

"And then?"

"Search for evidence," he stated, "in every corner . . . in every deuced grain sack."

"But what of the man upstairs?" Serenity questioned on a soft breath.

Pulled back from his planning by her voice's worried tone, the marquess glanced toward her.

"I am persuaded it would be best to leave him as he is for now," he replied, kneeling down before her, taking her two cold hands into his. "If the thieves do return, they will expect to find him there," he counseled, "as well as everything else in the mill just as they left it. For that reason, from now on, to the extent we can, we must take care ourselves to leave no mark on the scene so that it will not appear as if anyone has been here should we be caught by surprise before the storm lets up enough for us to leave. I believe that this will give us our best chance for escape."

Gripping his hands, Serenity nodded. "Where shall I start?" she whispered bravely.

"With forgiving me," he murmured in return, dragging her up from the chair and into his embrace.

Nineteen

"Serenity . . ." Rand whispered, his fingers cradling her soft brown curls as he covered her with kisses, his breath hot against her flushed cheeks and neck.

". . . Rand . . ." Serenity sighed, clinging to him, riding each successive surge of sensation with marveling, feeling her knees begin to tremble and weaken.

"I have been a damned fool," he murmured, his lips laying claim to her ear's soft, pink shell.

"Yes, you have," Serenity agreed, pushing up to tiptoe, daring to scatter light kisses along the line of his jaw.

"And so have you," the marquess completed, one hand sliding down to flirt with her . . . her . . . well, you know.

Her nose nestling into his neck, Serenity began to chuckle.

"Oh!" she then exclaimed when his fingers suddenly began to probe. "Whatever are you doing, Chilton?"

"Everything I can manage of what I have been wanting to do for a solid year," he growled, next setting a course for his eager lips across the bridge of her nose. "Given our history, it might be a long time before I get another chance."

"Yet I am persuaded it must be highly improper, sir." Serenity sighed, her head falling weakly against his shoulder when he began to nibble at her neck.

"Hang propriety," the marquess husked, suddenly brack-

eting her head between both his palms as he stabbed her gaze with his, "and hang your feminine sensibilities which have always kept me from doing this before. And, deuce take it, Serenity . . . kiss me back!" he commanded, his breath warm and sweet against her lips.

"Like this?" Serenity asked, boldly stretching up to brush her softness across his.

"No . . . like this," Rand growled.

Afterward, of course, he proceeded to teach her exactly what he meant.

"Chilton . . ." Serenity softly sighed when at last he settled his mobile mouth over hers and lay claim to it, his touch at times tender, at times demanding; pouring into their joining all that had bedeviled him over the past year, all that he had dreamed of, all that he had missed.

And Serenity fed his giving with her own building desire. "Rand . . ." she breathed, opening completely for his tongue's entrance, arching into his eager caresses, helplessly yielding; at last understanding the rightness, the beauty, in loving another. "I love you . . . I love you," she gasped between each consuming kiss.

In response, on a ragged indrawn breath, the marquess molded Serenity's body tightly against his.

"Serenity . . ."

"You love me, too," she told him after a time, her small fingers rising to stroke the back of his neck.

Still clutching her to him as if she were a part of his own skin, the marquess drew back a bit and began to laugh against her lips.

"I do, do I?" he at last murmured, smiling down into her twinkling blue eyes.

"I have always told you so, Chilton," Serenity loftily replied.

"Then, I suppose," he said, fingering a curl away from her forehead, "as you are now such a pattern card of respectability, I must believe you. It must be true."

"It is," she responded, planting a quick peck upon his chin. "It is also true that I should like to hear it from you."

"Hmm, how is it that I did not notice before how demanding you are?" he asked, leaning down to kiss her nose.

"Because you were too busy being stubborn," Serenity told him.

"Stubborn!"

"And irascible."

"Iras . . . !"

". . . And you still have not said it, sir," Serenity reminded him.

Slowly, the marquess swallowed the walnut in his throat. "Very well, I love you," he tersely allowed.

"Yes, you do," Serenity concurred. "Now come along, Chilton," she ordered, willing solidity back into her knees, "we must be about the business of preparing for the worst. And," she added, glancing back at him with excitement playing about her features, "we must search for loot!

"Unless . . ." she questioned as an afterthought under hopefully raised brows, "you had something else you wished to contribute to our current activity? . . ."

"Lud, I am in love with a lusty adventuress," Rand groaned, allowing himself to be tugged. "What? You are not going to take me to task for that comment?" he asked when they had reached the stairs.

"Why, no, dear," Serenity responded, starting down the risers. "I shall never take you to task for such a statement. It is quite true, after all. And you did admit that you love me all by yourself."

"Goodness, Chilton, just listen to the wind!" Serenity exclaimed some moments later in the midst of her treasure hunt through one of the grain bins located not far from the huge millstone resting silently upon its base on the tide mill's ground floor.

The marquess paused and tipped his head. Far above him, clapboards moaned; weary windows rattled objections to the continued assault.

"Yet I am persuaded that the storm *is* abating slightly," Rand offered as he continued in his rearrangement of several stacked grain sacks into a small, low chamber just beneath one of the story's snow-covered windows. "And that is all the more reason to finish this hideaway quickly, I think. Have you found anything?"

"Not yet," Serenity told him, swirling her arm through the dusty grains of rye, as she did so struggling to hold the garrick sleeve up and out of the way. "Chilton, several matters still trouble me about this whole bumblebroth," she then shared.

"Oh? . . . What?" Rand asked, stepping back a bit to assess whether or not his construction duplicated the appearance of the rest of the stacks.

"Well . . . I am sensible of why Ned and Ollie might wish to see me eliminated from the scene . . ." she responded, moving to the adjacent grain bin.

". . . Ned and Ollie?"

"Yes, the two men who brought the grain to Charity's Hands," she explained. "As I was saying, I can understand that they had reason to fear that I might at some point have identified them as my abductors, if not participants in the theft ring. But who are the highwaymen, Chilton? . . . and why have *they* been so persistent in trying to harm me?"

"No doubt for the same reason, my love," he gently suggested, responding to her quiet distress. "I think it likely that the highwaymen are also numbered among the thieves."

"But until they tried to run me over with the dray, I had no idea of their identities," Serenity countered.

"No, but you could identify Ned and Ollie," Rand argued.

"Who are now dead," Serenity softly stated, placing fingertips to her lips when understanding came. "Ned and Ollie were hunted down by the highwaymen, too, were they not, Chilton? . . . because they had failed in their mission, and because if captured they, in turn, might be forced by the authorities to identify the others?"

"Most likely," the marquess replied. "No doubt the others in the ring saw Ned and Ollie as unraveled threads that needed to be clipped."

For several moments, Serenity stood quietly, staring at her wringing hands.

"These are very bad men, aren't they, Chilton?" she finally whispered, looking at him, anxiety darkening her sapphire gaze.

"Yes . . . but so am I, Serenity," he told her firmly, seizing a final sack from off the top of a rudely constructed box that had been hidden beneath the lot of them, then positioning it to mask the hideaway's entry.

Suddenly he straightened.

Not noticing, Serenity began to chuckle. "Are you indeed, my hero? *Fort comme le chêne,* eh?" she teased.

"Exactly so," Rand replied, still peering down into the box as he shifted into an arrogant stance. "Now come here."

"Whyever should I?" she grinned. "Is there a dragon behind me?"

Challenged, the marquess slowly shifted his hooded, gleaming gaze. "No," he murmured softly. "I wish for you to come here, Serenity, because I have a sudden desire to kiss you cockle-brained."

A short time later, he had done so to his satisfaction. Serenity, however, was still trying to climb inside his skin. As a kindness, therefore, he added, "I also wish to show you the treasure."

". . . What?" Serenity questioned, drawing back a bit from her dreamy daze.

"The treasure," he repeated after a smile, nibbling upon her lower lip. "There," he elaborated, gesturing toward the wooden box as his mouth next toyed with the point of her chin.

"The treasure?" Serenity asked, really not caring whether or not she received an answer one whit.

"Um-hmm," Chilton responded, nipping at her neck. "I uncovered it when I moved that last grain sack."

"You did?" Serenity breathed. Then, pushing away a bit, she looked.

And then gawked. Just at her feet, dozens of jewel-encrusted plates, candlesticks, cups, and crosses caught the dim light of the room, even within the box's dark interior gleaming like the hoard in a pirate's chest.

"Chilton!" Serenity cried, kneeling down to peer inside. "Good heavens!"

"Remarkable, is it not? Serenity, this is all the proof we need that we have found the thieves' storage site," he concluded, dropping down beside her. "If only Ben Bradshaw were here to share the moment."

"The Runner you have been assisting?"

"Yes," he replied, tucking her against his warmth. "He gave a good portion of the past two years to see this moment come about. Regrettably, however, I have not set eyes on him since that night at the brothel."

"What happened to him?" Serenity asked. "Oh, Rand, was he killed?"

"I cannot think so," Rand replied, shaking his head as he pulled them both to their feet. "Had that happened, his body would have been found somewhere about Charity's Place. Of a certainty, the thieves would have had no reason to carry him off."

"Then where might he be?"

"My guess is that he was somehow able to infiltrate the

ring," he told her. "Either that, or he found himself in the position of being able to follow and observe the thieves, but to let anyone know of it would have risked compromising his situation. At any rate, with matters breaking now as they seem to be, I misdoubt he shall show up to take a good deal of the credit"—he smiled—"or at the very least to get in on the action."

"And when will that happen?" Serenity warily asked.

"Not until I have you safely in Woodbridge if I have anything to say about it," he responded with a warm smile, leaning down to kiss the curls atop her head, "nor before we put the mill back to rights. Certainly not before you have cooked my supper."

"I thought you wished to get me *safely* to Woodbridge," Serenity groused with a roll of her eyes as he slipped his arm about her waist and started her toward the stairs.

"Now, now, my dear," the marquess dismissed as they began to ascend, waving one hand, "a man's needs must be met if he is to rise to the occasion."

"Indeed," Serenity responded, peering up at him beneath one raised brow. "Now, why does that strike me as something you might have said to *Hildegarde*?"

"I have already explained about that," Rand replied, a bit smug in the face of her obvious display of jealousy. "I had to go through with what I had inadvertently started, and well you know it. If the raid were to be a success, I had to maintain the front that I was a customer."

"From what I could see," Serenity stated testily, "you were certainly holding up your end of it, milord *Fort comme la chêne!*"

Reaching the kitchen, the marquess broke into a wide grin. "So it bothers you that I had my fingers on the woman, does it?"

Hearing that, Serenity broke from his embrace and whirled about to face him. "What do you mean, 'on her?'

Your fingers were *in* that . . . that woman of questionable character!"

"They slipped," he shrugged after a wicked smile.

Not for a moment, however, did Serenity believe that plumper.

The marquess was spooning up the last of a collapsed turnip when distant rattling sounds began to insinuate themselves above the storm's moan and the door suddenly burst open one story below the kitchen on the crown wheel floor.

"Chilton? Is it . . . ?" Serenity breathed, pausing in the crunching of her potato, her eyes round with apprehension.

"I am afraid so," he whispered evenly, reaching over to squeeze her hand. "Come, love. Gather up the food and dishes in the cloth as quietly as you can and bring them with us. I shall put out the fire."

"Thank goodness you prepared a hideaway for us," Serenity murmured, hurrying to do as she had been told, rough voices now filtering up through the tide mill's rudely planked floors.

"Unfortunately, we shall not be able to get to it," Rand told her softly, emptying the hot water remaining in the teapot into the stone scullery sink. "Because of the banked snow, the thieves can only have entered on the floor between us and the millstone story."

"What shall we do then?" Serenity asked *sotto voce*, tying a secure knot into the cloth.

"The attic will give us our best chance to hide from them until nightfall, I think," Rand responded, seizing her elbow, then propelling her gingerly out onto the hall's loose planking, hastening them both toward the stairs. "After all, there *is* plenty of room for three in the clothespress," he added, glancing down at her with a quick grin.

"Randall Torrent, if you think that I shall . . . !" Serenity managed to scold before the two of them gained the first of the risers and the marquess firmly clamped a silencing hand across her lips.

Twenty

"There, that should do it," Rand murmured, lying down beside Serenity in the deep nest he had just fashioned out of the empty grain sacks she had used earlier as walls for her convenience. "If we are very quiet, we should be able to evade detection up here. Later on, after the thieves have settled for the night, we shall attempt our escape," he added, pulling a thick layer of sacks over the top of them, then arranging a tiny viewing hole so that, should he need to, he could spy upon anyone entering the cramped, frigid room. "Are you comfortable, my dear?"

"Chilton, there is a dead man hanging in a clothespress not three feet away from me, and I am lying in the arms of a man who is not my husband amid a pile of grain sacks in a tide mill in the middle of nowhere," Serenity whispered.

"Hmm. Point taken." The marquess grinned.

"How am I to be comfortable when it seems lying about with you is all I have done over the past two days?" she continued more plaintively. "My reputation is ruined, you know."

"Quite thoroughly," the marquess agreed.

"It was one thing to escape censure over the incident with the cricket ball," she added on a tiny sigh, "another to rationalize to everyone how I might have emerged unscathed from being locked in an abandoned building with you by my well-meaning sister and future brother-in-law . . . but how shall I ever be able to explain all *this* to Proppie and Papa?"

In the musty darkness beneath the heavy burlap, the marquess tucked Serenity closer to his warmth. "You shan't have to," he comforted, kissing her temple. "I shall do it."

"By which method? . . ." Serenity asked, brushing bits of the chaff filtering down out of the burlap from her brow, "with one of Papa's pistol rounds in your forehead or his sword embedded in your heart?"

"Oh, ye of little faith . . ." Chilton softly intoned, shaking his head. "You must learn to trust me, Serenity. I tell you, I shall explain everything to your father," he repeated, kissing her again, "and all shall be perfectly in order when I do."

"You are anything but a man of the cloth, Chilton," Serenity noted. "How do you intend to perform this miracle?"

"With you at my side," he blithely explained.

"As your shield?" she questioned.

"Not a bit of it," he countered. "As my marchioness."

Barely able to be seen by the light entering by way of the viewing hole, Serenity gaped. "But that would mean we would have to be married!"

"Very good, Serenity," the marquess calmly replied. "We would need a special license, of course. Yet Uncle Paul should be able to use his considerable influence to gain us one quickly from the Archbishop. I am persuaded we could have the deed done before we ever returned to Woodbridge."

"But you do not wish to marry me!" Serenity breathed.

"Whatever gave you that idea?" he asked, peering down into her wide cobalt eyes.

"Whatev . . . ? Well, let me see . . ." Serenity whispered,

one brow frowning, the other elevating, all at the same time. "Might it be because you said so?"

"A paltry argument," the marquess dismissed. "I thought you a thief and a woman of questionable character at the time."

"We argue continually," she continued to enumerate.

"Undeniably, we do. Of course, that only means that for every argument we must also hold one another and kiss one another, and, mmm . . . *apologize,*" Rand countered, leaning over to nuzzle her neck's soft curve.

Stopped short, Serenity thought again. "You think me illogical," she stated, poking him in the chest.

"True."

"And hopelessly impulsive . . ."

". . . Hopelessly."

"And slow in coming to the point."

"Vexingly. Yet you think me stubborn, demanding, and irascible," he reminded her.

"Which shall only cause us to argue all the more." Serenity sighed, turning to rub her forehead against his shoulder.

"Shall it?" The marquess grinned, raising her face to his with one finger, then nibbling upon one corner of her lips. "Jove, what a fate! I shall be compelled to make even more apologies."

"Not at all," Serenity whispered, swallowing twice before shaking her head. "I think it only fair to share in such expressions. I assure you, Chilton, I shall not be remiss in making my own apologies."

"Shall you not?" Rand murmured with a gleam rising in his eyes. "I give you my promise, then, my love, if you will do the same for me, I shall always hold myself open to receive your offerings."

For a moment, Serenity quieted.

"I shall cut up your peace," she at last whispered into his mouth.

"Yes," he murmured, "and I shall drive you daft. Which only proves that we are neither of us perfect, Serenity. The point is, can we accept these things in the other?"

"Yes. I always have done."

"Then will you marry me?" Rand asked her, his hand moving to cup her chin.

"Oh, Rand, do you truly want this?" Serenity sighed, sliding her arm around his waist.

"The question is, what do you want, Serenity?" he asked in return, his gaze somehow softening and intensifying all at the same time.

"I . . . I want you," Serenity breathed.

"Done," Chilton growled beneath the grain sacks. "Now for the love of God, Serenity, take possession of what you have claimed! . . ."

Unhappily, Rand had not even managed to work the cumbersome garrick up above Serenity's knee before heavy footsteps began to rhythmically scrape up the approaching stair treads.

"Chilton, they are coming!" Serenity whispered, breaking off the suction between their mouths as the footsteps neared, drawing back from his embrace.

"Blast it all, I shall never get l . . . !" the marquess mumbled, drawing in several very deep breaths.

". . . Rand?"

"Never mind," he groused, checking their covering layer of grain sacks as he rolled toward the viewing hole. "Just lie very still, my love, and do not make the slightest noise."

"As if I could!" his lady whispered around the clot that was forming in her throat, unthinkingly snuggling her fists between her personal protrusions and the marquess's back. "As if I could utter anything with murderers set to enter this very room."

". . . Serenity!" Rand hissed in exasperation.

The footsteps paused.

Suddenly, the door slammed open. Stifling a cry, Serenity buried her face in the wool of Rand's redingote.

Through the viewing hole, however, the marquess watched as a single man cautiously followed his drawn pistol into the attic, then, after peering about as if to determine whether or not he was alone, began to make his way toward the dominant feature in the tiny room, the clothespress, the most likely place, of course, to yet conceal an ambush. With Rand still observing him, he slowly stalked toward it, paused, then reached out to turn one of the ornate handles decorating the front. That accomplished, his chest expanded with a deep inhalation; on its release, he flung aside the impediment.

The twentieth part of a moment later, the pistol ball he fired in his alarm at discovering the other thief's body shattered one of the attic dormer panes, creating an icy stir in the dust motes riding the room's lazy currents. Seconds later, he had already thundered down to join his comrades.

"Dear heaven, Chilton, what happened?" Serenity whooshed out against the back of his neck after the sound of the report had faded.

"For some reason," the marquess whispered back in her direction, his ear attuned to the muffled shouts taking place below them, "the thief seemed startled to see the dead man. Hush now," he urged when the rude floor planks beneath them began to tremble once more under the weight of several running footsteps again climbing the attic risers. "I shall tell you all later."

Even as the marquess finished speaking, more than half a dozen rough-looking men gained the landing just outside, then spilled into the small space. Beneath the layers of sacks, Rand and Serenity froze. Through the tiny viewing hole, the marquess struggled to see what he could through a thick forest of shifting, crowding legs.

"You see?" the man who had discovered the body cried,

spinning back and forth toward one or the other of his cohorts. "It be just as I told you. It be Ned!"

"Wot's it mean? . . . 'im being here, an' all?" another asked, his voice awestruck, tautly gruff.

"Be at ease, lads," a third voice calmed from the doorway before the legs belonging to it began to stroll down the corridor made by quickly parting bodies. "Most likely all it means is that Tyson couldn't think of a better place to stash 'im."

Deep within the darkness of the grain sacks, Rand's body suddenly tensed.

Blast it! . . . no! It cannot be! he thought, rejecting what his own ears had revealed to him even as he strained to prove the truth of it through the viewing hole's limited range.

"Then it weren't a warning like Ollie were?" Ned's discoverer asked. "Tyson don't suspect we know about this place?"

"I shouldn't think so," the newcomer concluded. "If that'd been the case, Tyson would've hung the bastard on one of the outside stair landings so's we couldn't've missed 'im. No, lads, for now we're safe. Come on then," he said, beginning to herd the group toward the door, "we've the stash to find and ship while the bad weather holds."

"Wot abou' Ned?" the second deeper voice asked.

"Leave 'im," the leader commanded, pausing long enough to give the corpse a backward glance. " 'E'll keep. After all, the poor bugger's froze through."

It was the pause, the turn in his direction, that confirmed what Rand had known from the beginning but been loath to admit. As the marquess looked on, framed by the viewing hole, the leader of the thieves revealed himself to be none other than the Bow Street Runner, Ben Bradshaw . . . his friend.

Twenty-one

"But I thought you said he was helping you," Serenity murmured sometime later in the midst of the marquess's whispered explanation.

"So we all thought," Rand bit out, watching the night deepen against the horizon through the viewing hole and the nearest of the dormer windows. "Blast it all, Serenity, I trusted him! Now to find out he is the leader of the ring . . ."

". . . Well, I for one do not understand how that could be the case, Chilton," Serenity interrupted. "If he were involved, why would he lead a raid against his own ring's embarkation site? . . . more, why would he put his men—his whole operation, for that matter—in jeopardy?"

"Damned if I know," Rand responded, tucking her closer to his side.

"Chilton!" Serenity chided.

"Well, it makes no sense to me either. Rest assured, however, that I shall find out," he ground out, his eyes full of purpose, "just as soon as we are shed of this blasted mill."

After a pause, Serenity deeply inhaled. "On the bright side, Chilton," she noted, "you do now know where Mr. Bradshaw has been all this time."

"Yes, stealing more of the diocese's treasures," the marquess muttered. "Nice try, however," he allowed, granting her a brief smile which she could not see and a soft peck upon her temple.

"What about this, then?" she offered as an alternative cheer. "Unless I miss my guess, the wind seems to be far less fierce."

"Yes, it does," Rand conceded. "And that shall make it all the easier for us to hear when the others have settled down for the night."

"So that we can make our escape," Serenity concluded with a smile and a nod.

"Au contraire," the marquess growled. "So that I can hunt that mongrel down and drive my fist . . ."

". . . Chilton," Serenity warned.

Glancing in her direction, the marquess paused. And sighed.

"Very well, so that we can make our escape," he finally grumped.

Yet in his heart of hearts, the marquess knew that had his impulsive betrothed not been in need of his level head, he would have . . .

Well, by God, he *would* have!

"Serenity," Rand whispered some hours later into the thick, cold darkness of the following morning. "Wake up, love."

". . . What?" Serenity murmured at the gentle jostling of her shoulder. "Oh! . . . Rand, is it time to go?"

"Yes," he responded, carefully laying back the covering sacks, allowing the frigid night air to spill over them. "I have heard nothing stirring below for almost an hour now," he told her, stiffly rising, then helping her to her feet. "Even the wind has grown silent."

In the midst of securing the garrick and slipping her reticule about her arm, Serenity paused. "Goodness, so it has. How odd it seems after so many days of blowing," she whispered, feeling the complete silence almost as a pressure against her ears. "And look, Rand," she added, gesturing toward the windows, "it has stopped snowing!"

"So I see. Come on, then," he whispered, taking her hand. "We shall never have a better opportunity." Slowly, testing each step against the unstable planks, the marquess led Serenity across the attic, then, feeling his way along the wall, to the door. "Step down upon each riser at the same time I do," he mouthed into her ear just before moving to stand next to the stair railing just beyond the exit. "Balancing our weight at the ends of the boards should minimize their creaking."

Serenity nodded. "On the count of three," she mouthed, positioning herself across from him next to the wall.

After providing the whispered numbers, with the utmost care, step by cautious step, she began a studied descent to the third floor. Touching down, she glanced at Rand and smiled; the sounds of snoring rattled from several of the distant rooms.

"No, I do not," the marquess loftily vowed.

"We shall see, shall we not?" Serenity softly commented, gingerly rounding the landing.

"Jove, what a fate," Chilton said easily, grinning. "Yes, we *shall* see, my love."

In the darkness, Serenity frowned. "Just once, Chilton," she softly scolded, "I would appreciate it if you could attempt to keep a civil thought in your head."

Again they descended, measured steps taking them down to the empty parlor and kitchen level and past. At last, their leg muscles aching from their slow, controlled descent, they reached the first story. Once more the marquess glanced about, his gaze penetrating into the darkness stretching out across the vast chamber; listening. Far across the expanse of the room, the huge crown wheel stood in silent silhouette against the lightening sky.

"Just a bit more, my love," Rand murmured when he had judged them safe. "That way," he pointed. "If you recall, the door we first entered is just at the end of the hall."

Serenity nodded and started forward. She had taken only a few cautious steps, however, when, from out of the darkness, the butt of a pistol flashed to clip quite soundly against the back of the marquess's neck.

"Rand!" Serenity cried out as, stunned, he dropped with a noisy thud to his knees.

"Grab 'er, mate," someone behind her growled.

Suddenly, Serenity's arms were pinioned behind her. Crying out again, she began to twist and squirm against the imprisonment. "Let me go, you . . . you bounders! Let me go! Chilton, now would be a very good time to get us out of this!"

"Go on and take 'er to 'im," the one with the pistol ordered patiently, watching as the marquess shifted his feet beneath his body, then staggered upright, all the while trying to shake sensibility back into his head. "I'll be right behind wi' this one," he finished, poking the pistol barrel several times into Rand's ribs.

At the prodding, the marquess rounded threateningly on the man. "Keep your pistol . . . !"

". . . Keep my pistol where, milord?" the thief responded, instantly shifting his aim toward Serenity. "Keep it there, sir?" he sneered.

Efficiently countered, Rand abruptly halted, then stood glaring at the man with his fists bailed at his sides, rage billowing from his nostrils with each vaporous breath.

"I warn you, you will pay," he ground out after a time, "if you so much as harm one hair on my lady's head."

"Well, that remains to be seen, don't it, yer lordship? . . ." the man replied, "as I be the one wi' the weapon? Now, go on an' follow 'er," he commanded with a jerk of his head toward the floor's interior. "You be expected."

Slowly, his jaw muscles rolling, the marquess turned toward the vast yawn of darkness opening out beyond the hall into which Serenity had only seconds before altogether disappeared. For long moments, he stood staring—glaring—into it. Finally, he ended the stifling silence.

"How did you know I was here, Ben?" he asked the blackness. "I made sure to erase all sign of our presence."

In response, in the distance a light flared, then touched a lantern wick atop the table with which Serenity had almost collided when they had first come to the mill on their way to inspect the crown wheel. As Rand watched, a glass globe settled over the flame, disbursing it, creating a circle of gold which washed over the tall, spare form of the man who had lit it. Near the crown wheel, the dragging hem of the huge garrick warped and twisted with Serenity's struggles just at the circle's rim.

"That you did, lad," Bradshaw at last replied, blowing out the lucifer burning close to his fingertips, glancing toward the marquess with a quick smile. "Unfortunately, you forgot the warm water remaining in the range cistern."

In the hall, in vexation, the marquess's jaw bulged.

"Careless," Bradshaw continued, gesturing for the man with the pistol to bring Chilton forward. "Gave you away right off, lad. Had my men search, of course, but coming up empty weren't of no moment. I knew whoever were here would try an escape. Didn't know it were you, however, lad . . . nor that you'd bring the woman from Charity's Place. She an operative, too, lad?"

"Cut line, Ben," Rand ordered. "Miss Hoffenduffle is my *fiancée,* as you well know. Only yesterday I rescued her from one of your attacks upon her, if you recall."

"Did you now?" the leader murmured, an odd gleam

of understanding glinting within the depths of his shadowed eyes.

In his disquiet, however, the marquess did not notice. Instead, unable to bear his ignorance any longer, he asked, "Why, Ben? Why?"

"Why, what, lad?" Bradshaw responded.

"Why have you taken part in this?"

Slowly, the smugness fell from the leader's face. "Because I be Catholic, yer lordship," he replied tautly, his gaunt frame becoming ramrod straight, "as are all the lads."

Drawing in a deep breath, the marquess relaxed the fists bailed at his side. "Do you mean to say that all this has to do with the emancipation issue?" he asked, his brows joining above his surprise.

"Can't understand it, can ye, *milord?*" the man holding Serenity sneered.

"I am beginning to," Rand stated, staring deeply into the eyes of his partner. "This is all about revenge, is it not? . . . about taking what is precious to Anglicans in payment for what you perceive they have withheld from you?"

"It be only right, lad," Bradshaw confirmed, "to my way of thinkin'."

"We be British citizens just the same as you, milord," someone called from the room's deep shadows.

"What be fair . . . what be just! . . . about takin' a man's taxes, but denying 'im the vote or public office?" another added to the others' mumbled assent.

"Yet there were other avenues open to you," Rand countered acidly. "Parliament . . ."

". . . Has done nothing! . . ." Bradshaw bit out. "Nor will they until British Catholics gain the power to force 'em to it. And we won't get that power without blunt, lad."

"And so you steal," the marquess said flatly.

"From our oppressors." Bradshaw nodded. "We take

your treasures, sell 'em abroad, then see that the cash fills Catholic coffers."

"Allow me to guess," Rand offered. "You see the money into Daniel O'Connell's hands."

"Aye."

"In spite of the fact that the man is known to be unscrupulous in his dealings? . . ." the marquess argued. "That he is strongly suspected of using his Catholic Rent fund, and the cause that you hold so dear, to his own personal gain?"

"What does that matter, lad," Bradshaw softly asked, "as long as he gets th' job done?"

After a moment's pause, the marquess removed his beaver and raked several fingers through his hair. "Ben," he stated at last, resting his knuckles upon the table, "I believe you to be a good man . . ."

". . . Yet time comes, does it not, milord? . . ." Ben softly countered, "when even a good man comes to the end of his tether? We've all of us"—he gestured toward the darkened room—"all the lads, seen the issue of emancipation raised and defeated time and again since the beginning of the century. What other recourse was left to us, I ask you, but to do whatever was needful to force it to be dealt with?"

"But, to kill, Ben? . . ." the marquess rasped, leaning even further forward, "to *kill*?"

At the accusation, the leader straightened. "You mean him what's upstairs, o' course." Bradshaw nodded. "We didn't do that, lad."

"I gathered that from your man's reaction upon Ned's discovery."

"So you saw that, did you? Meaning you and Miss Hoffenduffle were in the attic all this time, eh?" His partner chuckled.

"I rather think that is beside the point, don't you?" Chilton tersely replied. "What I was referring to was your attempt upon my lady and me."

Instantly, the leader's laughter died. "We didn't do that either, lad," he softly asserted.

"Who, then?" the marquess demanded.

"Well, as to that . . . it be a long story," Bradshaw tiredly replied.

"Deuce take it, Bradshaw, *who*?"

Suddenly, across the room the door to the outside landing clicked. Instantly, Rand and the others slewed toward the sound.

"Why, that'd be me, I suppose," confessed another deep, echoing voice from the darkness of the hall. "Take 'em, lads!" the intruder then shouted.

The twentieth part of a moment later, in a darting movement, Ben Bradshaw blew out the lanternlight.

Blinded by the abrupt, drenching darkness, Serenity cried out. Only seconds later, the man who had been holding her prisoner was wrenched away and thrown to the ground at the same time that she was forcefully shoved toward the room's outer wall. Deciding for the first time in her life that this was not the occasion to argue, she obeyed the unspoken command, spinning away to press herself against the security of the coarse planks, then sliding along them until at last her ribs sharply contacted the sluice gate lever.

All around her, the room seemed to explode.

"Oh, Rand . . ." she whispered, as fists slapped in random ricochets against grizzled flesh and bodies thudded against unseen impediments.

Suddenly, again the lantern bloomed. Quickly Serenity blinked and acclimated, then sent her gaze on a wild swerve to take the measure of what had changed. She immediately ascertained that the room was filled with new faces; distressingly, however, each was holding one of Ben Bradshaw's ring members at pistol point. Even more alarming, near the table, Bradshaw himself was struggling to lever himself to his feet, his eyes burning points of hatred in the story's gloom, his temple sporting an angry, rising welt.

But worse yet was the fact that in the center of it all stood the marquess, one fist filled with a complete stranger's crumpled shirt, the other cocked and obviously itching to bloody other portions of the grinning man's mouth.

"Chilton!" She tried very hard not to screech.

"I wouldn't hit me again if I was you, sir," warned the marquess's prisoner in the same deep voice as Serenity pressed knuckles against her lips. "Tell 'im, Bradshaw. Tell th' nob wot 'appens to them wot don't follow my orders."

"Let 'im go, lad," the leader said softly, flatly, glaring at the man, supporting himself unsteadily upon the table. "He won't just threaten to kill your lady . . . he will."

"Who is he?" Rand rasped, still panting with frustration and exertion, drawing the man up by his shirt to within inches of his face, after a moment shoving him away.

"Tyson," Bradshaw spat.

"That's right, me name's Tyson," the man concurred with an oily smile, adjusting his clothing, then wiping blood from his mouth on the back of his coat sleeve. "Not that it signifies, ye understand."

"Oh, I assure you," Rand ground out with soft menace, "it does."

"Nay, y'poor bastard, it don't," Tyson disagreed, disinterestedly drawing out a pistol from somewhere inside his clothing. "After all, nothing signifies, do it? . . . to them wot's already dead?"

Twenty-two

"No doubt your compatriot upstairs would agree," Rand stated levelly, staring hard at the man, peripherally searching for an avenue of escape.

"Ned? Aye." Tyson chuckled, checking his pistol's prime. "Both 'im and Ollie. They both disobeyed."

"They made a mistake," the marquess countered.

Tyson shrugged. "It comes to the same thing. They got themselves seen. By *her,*" he then accused, swinging the pistol barrel toward Serenity who was still papered to the opposite wall. "Had to be taken care of, don't y' see? At any time, she could've named 'em. And the two of 'em in the Runners' 'ands? . . . well, soon we'd all be in the suds."

"Why did you not simply send them into hiding?" Rand asked, using the question and his idle stroll in Serenity's direction to deflect Tyson's attention away from her.

"Didn't 'ave to," the thief responded. "Hid themselves, they did. An' stayed hid, too, until recently. 'Course, they wasn't hiding from the likes o' the Runners."

"Oh?" the marquess questioned, using his body to block Serenity from the thief's line of fire.

At the invitation to continue, Tyson grinned malevolently. "Oh, no, milord. They was hiding from me. Found 'em, however. Did wot needed to be done."

From behind Rand's shoulder, Serenity gasped, "What

needed to be done? You sentenced one of them to an unspeakable death on a gibbet!"

"Nice touch, weren't it?" Tyson remarked with pride as the marquess rounded on her intrusion and tried to silence it with a glare. "Aw, I ain't so hard, missy. Didn't I give ol' Ned a nice, clean send-off? Besides, I needed to give Ben here a warning, ye ken, an' Ollie were it."

"A warning of what?" the marquess asked, again blocking Serenity's view.

"Of wot were planned for 'im and the others when we took over the operation, o' course," Tyson responded. "A warning, too, to stay away from here. We knew he'd been looking for us since 'is scheme to have the Runners put a period to us come a cropper. Knew exactly when he'd found the mill, too. It were easy to figure that 'e were only waitin' for us to be gone afore 'e went for wot we stole. So we thought we'd turn the tables. We left the mill deserted, 'id ourselves, and set our own trap," Tyson chuckled. "Sure enough, as certain as sunset, 'e showed."

"But why?" Serenity badgered, again shifting to peek out from behind Chilton's broad shoulder, annoyingly tangling the drawstrings of her reticule on the sluice-gate lever. "What are you in all this?"

"A rogue," Ben Bradshaw suddenly, venomously, spat.

"Why, Ben, how you cut me," Tyson pouted, his black eyes enlarging as he pressed his pistol flat against his chest.

"Deny it, then!" Bradshaw exclaimed, driving his knuckles into the tabletop. "Deny that you and your followers be traitorous dogs who plundered to your *own* gain what the rest of us secured for the Emancipation cause."

"Under the present circumstances, Ben, lad," Tyson replied, glancing about at his confident troops, "I hardly see the need." Once more he grinned. "O' course me an the lads set up our own business. Who wouldn't with all o' that blunt there for the taking?"

"How did you begin?" the marquess interjected to continue the thief's narration.

"Bit by bit at first," Tyson confessed, strolling over to lean against the huge crenellations of the crown wheel, "so's Ben here wouldn't notice the things gone missing before 'is contacts in Ireland transported our takings off to th' Continent to be melted down into bullion, then put into O'Connell's 'ands. It were easy for me an' the lads to snaffle a piece or two here an' there. Then, after me da died an' left the mill to me, it only made sense to increase the operation an' use this place as a base. It weren't long afore we'd collected enough for a run, ye ken. When we had, we carried 'em in grain sacks to my sister."

"Charity is your sister?" Serenity blinked, peeking again, the action tightening the reticule strings even further.

"Aye. Right away the dearie said she'd fence 'em for us, she did. Sold most to one o' her regulars . . . a sea captain, I believe she told me. Said he had 'is own concern going in Bengal and along the Ivory Coast."

"How did you find him out?" Rand asked, turning toward the Runner.

"It were only but a few months before the raid that I began to notice discrepancies in Bow Street's records between what were reported missing and what I were shipping out to my contacts in the Continent," Bradshaw inserted tautly, taking the few steps around the grain chute. "I knew someone were siphoning off the artifacts. It were a small matter to find out who."

"A bit more complicated, however, to devise a scheme to use British law-enforcement forces for your revenge against him, wouldn't you say? . . ." Rand snapped testily, "to use me?"

Pausing not far from him, Bradshaw's lower lip twisted against his teeth. "I used what I knew would do the job," he stated, his voice taking on an edge. "I had to, milord. I needed the manpower. By the time I learned of the bastard's scheme, he had already lured enough of my men over to his side to put a period to the rest of us whenever he wanted. I had to put a stop to it however I could or risk not only the cause, but our own lives."

"What you risked," the marquess leveled, "was my lady."

"In fairness, Chilton," Serenity interjected, stepping forward a bit more, touching his sleeve, "that was an accident. Had it not been for Ned and Ollie's mistake, I never would have been involved."

"True, missy . . . yet you are involved now, are y'not?" Tyson pointed out. "And, you'll notice," he added, waving his pistol back toward the room at large, "thanks to several long nights' surveillance of the mill from th' granary loft, we *have* taken over the operation."

"The loft? Then you knew we were here all this time?" Serenity scowled, stretching her strings even tighter.

"Why, o' course," Tyson gleefully admitted. "And you dasn't be able to imagine how glad we was to see you, too, dearie. Why, wi' you showing up, all we 'ad to do were to sit back an' wait for Ben and the lads to get word o' the bodies by your post chaise an' hie theirselves back 'ere to the mill to see if we was involved, then tie up all the ends at once in a nice, neat bow. A happy prospect, don't y'think?"

"I *think* . . ." Serenity scolded, "that it is a travesty, sir! . . . against all that this country stands for . . . against every right we claim as British citizens! . . . against *God*, sir!" she cried, thrusting one finger high into the air, ". . . against his lordship! . . . against every personal portion of my . . . of my personhood!"

"Serenity, for the love of . . ." the marquess pleaded.

". . . I shall not be stopped, Chilton!" Serenity vowed.

"You shall," Tyson countered evenly, "when you see wot we 'ave planned for his lordship. Take 'im, then, lads," he suddenly gestured even as Rand was instantly seized by three burly thieves.

"Rand!" Serenity gasped.

"Serenity, will you kindly stay out of this?" the marquess requested with exasperation, the pause required for the exercise allowing his captors to become even more entrenched.

Tyson, however, unexpectedly hesitated. "On second thought," he reconsidered, "it be my opinion that mayhap we should delay our plans for 'is lordship," he decided, slowly raising his pistol to point it directly at several—well, two at least—of the nicer personal protrusions of Serenity's personhood. "It might be best to begin with you, dearie."

"Tyson! . . . no!" Chilton shouted toward Serenity's rounding eyes, the veins in his neck bulging with his strain against the imprisoning arms.

"Now, now, only think about it for a moment, milord," the thief continued, thumbing back the hammer and sighting one open eye down the length of the barrel, altogether ignoring the marquess's gathering musculature. "It be only right, ye ken. After all, over the past year the lass's been devilish hard for my men to kill. Best not to take a chance on it 'appening again," he added.

The twentieth part of a moment later, with stunning suddenness, he pulled the trigger.

"Tyson!" Rand roared as choking smoke from the explosion swept over him. "Good God, *no!*"

Yet when the air had again cleared, it was Ben Bradshaw who lay sprawled and bleeding from his shoulder upon the dust-covered floor.

Taking advantage of the diversion, instantly Rand burst into motion. With one sudden jerk he broke free of his captors, spun about, then slammed his fives into two of their grizzled faces just before his knee did painful damage to the nether portions of the third.

Seizing their opportunity as well, Ben Bradshaw's men rounded on Tyson's followers. Immediately after, gunshots peppered the startled atmosphere, unheard of profanities

rent Serenity's tattered sensibilities; in short, the whole of
the crown-wheel story erupted into the veriest bare-knuck-
led mill. Before Serenity could even think to object, however, the marquess appeared out of the clouds of dust
being raised by the scuffle to seize her fiercely and snatch
her into his arms, the movement finally adding all the
tension needed upon the reticule strings to slowly force
the sluice-gate lever upward.

"Serenity!" he breathed into her tangled curls as outside, with a groaning, the sluice gates began to creakingly
swing open and icy, pent-up water began to trickle into
the adjacent narrow channel and down toward the Deben.
"Dear God, I thought you had been shot."

"As did I, if truth be told," she exclaimed, abandoning
the impeding reticule to dangle from the lever so that she
might cling fiercely to the marquess's lapels. "Oh, but Chilton, it was Mr. Bradshaw who prevented it from happening!" she cried, at last looking up at him. "He jumped in
front of me just at the last moment. Rand, he took the
round!"

"Aye, for all the good it did him," Tyson suddenly
growled not far distant from them, instantly dropping
down to seize a pistol abandoned by one of Chilton's captors, then rising again to steady his arm within one of the
crown-wheel crenellations, determined not to miss the second time as he again took aim.

"Serenity, get behind me!" Chilton cried out, spinning
her away as, outside, the sluice gate opened fully and the
millpond began to spill into the narrow channel.

"Rand!"

"Why so taken aback, dearie?" Tyson smiled, quickly
cocking the pistol, sighting down the barrel again. "Did
you think you could escape my reach?"

It was a question the thief could not know, however, that
fate had already answered.

Even as he was speaking, with startling suddenness, the

thin skin of ice imprisoning the wide paddles dipping into the channel just outside crumbled, freeing the huge waterwheel to begin to turn. With its movement, almost unheard above the sounds of the melee, the shaft entering the building creaked to life and began to rotate its smaller wheel within the crenellations of the crown wheel just adjacent to the outlaw. Seeing it, knowing he could do nothing to stop what would happen, immediately Rand folded Serenity's face against his redingote.

"Tyson!" he then cried out in warning as the encroaching meshwork of wheel upon wheel began to advance. "Move your arm, man! *Move your arm!"*

And yet, already it was too late. As the marquess looked on aghast, the startled thief's coat sleeve caught within the crenellations, held fast against his horrified struggles to extricate it, then disappeared beneath the smaller wheel's crushing teeth.

The man's scream of agony was enough to flay souls.

"My God," Chilton breathed.

"Oh, Rand!" Serenity barely responded, her fists crushing her lips to her teeth.

"Quickly, we must get out of here," he commanded, shaking movement into Serenity's immobility.

"But, surely we must try to help . . ." she hesitated.

"Serenity, the man tried to kill us!" the marquess exclaimed, supporting her stumbling progress toward the outer landing.

"But what of Mr. Bradshaw?" Serenity asked, stumbling over the garrick hem, then hiking it up most improperly.

"He has a chance," Rand evaluated, throwing open the outer door and muscling her out onto the stairs, "and, owing to his bravery, so do we. This one. And we cannot waste it, Serenity, nor his act of valor. We have to escape this nest of vipers and go for help."

"But . . . oh, Rand!" she finally capitulated into his redingote when they had reached solid footing upon the quay.

"I know, love," he comforted, hurrying her along the path in the snow, then opening the granary doors, again kissing her curls. "Try not to think of it now. Here, let me help you up on Baby's back," he offered, boosting her up with his interlocked hands. "I am persuaded it shall be faster going without the curricle."

"Obviously, you have not seen me ride," Serenity noted. "Chilton, I cannot help but feel badly that we are doing nothing for Mr. Bradshaw," she objected one last time while Rand took his pistols from their case, secured them within his redingote pockets, then mounted another of his bloods. "He did try to protect me. Can we not . . . ?"

". . . Serenity, the best I can promise at the moment is to return for him," the marquess tightly vowed, filling one hand with horsehair. "My first duty, however, must be to see you safely to your father. Now kindly cease your questioning of my carefully considered plans and hang on to Baby's mane," he instructed with a backward glance just as he dug his heels into his mount's side. "And, deuce take it, stay close!"

" 'Stay close,' he tells me," Serenity repeated with a sigh.

Moments later, the two of them had already gained the road to Woodbridge.

They had not gone far at their headlong pace, however, before Serenity began to wish with all her heart that she and Propriety had not rubbed honey upon the saddle of their riding instructor quite so many times, nor salted the underside of his mount's blanket quite so frequently with chestnut burrs, sending him away with avowals never to return while they hied off to the woods to spy upon the altogether fascinating play of the neighboring Billingsgate brothers. For, try as she might, she was only achieving limited success in her attempt to straddle, much less progress down the road, on the back of the bouncing Baby.

How do gentlemen do it? she wondered, desperately clutching at her mount's thrusting neck, freeing one hand to tug violently at the impeding garrick as she again struggled to square the afterward of her person atop Baby's rolling rump. *And how under heaven do they do whatever it is they do astride?* she groaned, feeling her muscles cramp, wincing from the repeated sharp contact of a furry spinal column against portions of her personhood only old nanny Clements had the right to slap.

Worse, she was falling farther and farther behind. Ahead. the marquess's mount easily plowed a path for her through the storm's aftermath. Serenity bent low and tried to spur her mount faster—no small accomplishment, it must be said, in slippers—yet, suddenly, one of the garrick capes took flight on a remnant of the storm wind and flipped forward, startling Baby before momentarily obscuring her vision. Shying, the horse reared slightly, veered, and stumbled. Taken by surprise, Serenity slipped sideways again, righted, then rolled over the top of her mount's ears to land, comfortably, but quite mortifyingly, in a soft, virgin snowbank.

"Chilton!" she immediately shouted, less in warning than in vexation.

Instantly, the marquess halted, then galloped back in her direction.

"Serenity, are you all right?" he asked, jumping from his mount and dropping down beside her.

"Yes, quite," she replied, taking the offer of his hand and rising to her feet, "though I cannot say that I care for this exercise," she added, brushing snow from the garrick. "How is it you gentlemen manage to straddle these beasts?"

"Quite easily, actually," Rand replied, scraping ice crystals from her curls. "Are you truly hurt, love?"

"No, not really," she told him, emptying one glove. "I am merely embarrassed."

"You merely cannot ride," he evaluated.

"Let me put it this way, Chilton," Serenity testily insisted.

"I am persuaded that after the past two days in your protection, the afterward of my person shall never be the same again."

"Alas," he remarked with a grin, waggling one brow. And then he cleared his throat. "You *would* seem to benefit from a course of lessons, my dear. Shall I see to the chore?" he asked, a wicked gleam rising above his smile.

"That would be most kind in you, Chilton," Serenity allowed.

"Then consider it done," the marquess responded, leaning over to nibble at the corner of her mouth. "We shall begin just as soon as we are leg-shackled, I think . . . and, of course, in consideration of your sensibilities, we shall certainly wish to begin your straddling lessons upon something of much less width than a horse."

"Most thoughtful, Chilton. Now . . ." she said, reaching toward him and raising her sodden slippered foot, "if you will but help me back up onto Baby . . . oh, but Chilton, look!" she cried as she was boosted up, glancing over her mount back in the direction they had come.

"Tyson's men," Rand murmured tensely as he again lowered Serenity, concentrating upon the dozen or so specks bearing down upon them from the direction of the tide mill, specks that were steadily growing larger against the Deben's cold blue slash and the field of pure white snow. "The deuce."

"Could they not be Mr. Bradshaw's?" Serenity tautly inquired.

Rand shook his head. "Unlikely, I should think. Bradshaw's men were outnumbered at the mill."

"Then we must go, and quickly," Serenity directed, once more facing her mount.

"Serenity . . ." Rand murmured, the hesitancy in his tone arresting her, causing her to turn back toward him again.

"Yes, Chilton?" she responded, her pure sapphire eyes huge in the morning light.

"My love, you must go on ahead," he told her.

"What? No!" she cried, suddenly throwing her arms about him, then framing his face with her hands. "What nonsense! What can you be thinking to do?"

"Hold them off," he told her gently, stroking more snow from her curls. "Give you the time you need to reach Woodbridge."

"No! I shan't leave you here alone!"

". . . Serenity, only consider it, my love," he pleaded, wrapping his arms about her waist. "You cannot ride fast enough to escape them. You know you cannot."

Faced again with her childhood negligence, Serenity could only clap both trembling hands to her lips. Peering into the marquess's face once more, she tenderly touched him. Her eyes flooding with tears, she next traced one finger along the dear, deep groove marring his forehead. Within, her heart stuttered, then began to flail against her ribs.

"But how shall you manage it?" she at last whispered, tears beginning to spill down her wind-reddened cheeks. "You have only your two pistols against so many. Wait!" she suddenly exclaimed with a sniff. "I shall give you my uncle's weapon!" And then her shoulders sagged. "Oh! . . . but I cannot, can I? Oh, Chilton!" she wailed, this time burying her face in his neck cloth. "My pistol is in my reticule!"

After a moment, the marquess sighed and prompted, "And . . . ?"

"And . . ." she sobbed, "and . . . oh, Chilton, I have f-forgotten it again!"

"Never mind, love," Rand murmured into her curls, squeezing her tightly against him as he softly grinned. "I shall return for it later."

"Sh-Shall you?"

"I give you my word," he told her.

"I shall hold you to it, you know," she gruffly vowed.

"Your pardon, if you please!" the marquess exclaimed in offended tones. "I am a gentleman!"

Slowly, gathering herself, Serenity looked up at him. "*My* gentleman," she informed him, attempting a smile. "I love you, Rand," she then breathed. "Please come to me."

"Nothing could prevent it," he whispered. Then, with the greatest of tenderness, he set his lips to the business of sealing his pledge. "Now go, my love . . . and be safe," he ordered, boosting her up again onto Baby's back.

Tears spilling over her lids once more, Serenity hesitated.

"Oh, Rand, I cannot! . . ." she at last breathed, seizing her lower lip to still its trembling. "Please do not ask me . . . !"

"Ah, but I do," he told her. "Now, go," he commanded, slapping the horse's flank.

Carried along with her mount, Serenity traveled a few yards. Suddenly, however, she managed a cow-handed halt.

"Chilton," she stated in a watery voice, not turning back toward him so as to prevent his witnessing her strengthening sobs, "you love me."

Unable to help himself, the marquess grinned. "I love you," he gruffly allowed. "And I shall come to you, Serenity," he told her, his tone softening. "I shall always come to you."

Her back still toward him, she nodded.

Yet as she rode away, Serenity was very much afraid that, against so many, it was unlikely that this proud, strong man she loved with all her heart would ever be able to keep his vow.

Twenty-three

The sun shone on James and Propriety's wedding day. Thinking of it in her room at the manse as she dressed for the ceremony, slipping a soft yellow merino gown over the shivers playing over her skin, Serenity smiled faintly. Surely the sign boded well for her sister and future brother-in-law. Certainly something should after the fortnight that had just passed.

It had taken Serenity several hours after she had left the marquess to slip and slide her way to Woodbridge, yet she had done it, drawing the exhausted Baby to a halt in front of the manse only to topple from her back, still swathed in the impossible garrick, into her family's arms. Moments later, a cup of tea in hand, she had quickly spilled her tale.

Even before she had finished, James had gathered what bows had already arrived for the wedding festivities and had ridden off to his brother's aid.

Four days later, however, he had returned to report that although they had found the place where the marquess had made his stand against the outlaws and had searched the surrounding area judiciously, there had been no sign of him. No sign either, moreover, of any fallen. Only "evidence of wounds," James had murmured dejectedly to his uncle Paul and her father when he had thought she could not hear. An altogether odd situation, the vicar had then pronounced, afterward declaring that it now was, of course, quite out of the question for the wedding to proceed.

As a result, given no alternative but the necessary proprieties, after expressions of their deepest sympathy, the guests had taken up their gifts to the bride and groom and had returned to their various piles.

Serenity had taken up riding lessons while she awaited the marquess's coming, much to the family's scandal. How could the chit countenance such a disrespectful activity? they wondered in family huddle after family huddle, given that full mourning was certainly called for, not to mention a period of calm retirement after such an oversetting Ordeal. The apothecary was sent for, therefore, even over her steadfast objections that Chilton would, of course, come soon.

However? they all wondered, staring at her warily.

Serenity's response was even more worrisome: because, you see, he had promised her.

More parties were sent in search of his body. The days had lengthened.

Until Propriety at last had dashed a perfectly good Limoges tea service against the drawing room fireplace's Italian tile and screeched, "I want to be married!"

Appalled, her father had recalled to her the proper etiquette for such situations, how it was simply the outside of enough to undertake a marriage during the requisite year of mourning; James had comforted.

"I want to be married!" Propriety had reprised, dispensing with two matching Sèvres vases.

Serenity had been given one hour to get ready.

Suddenly the door to her chamber swung open, putting an abrupt period to her recollections.

"Have you finished dressing, Rennie?" Propriety asked, gliding into the room in a gown of green Barege wool and matching silk bonnet fetchingly filled with her dark brown chignon, a bouquet of forced daffodils bouncing about in her green-gloved hand.

"Just," Serenity replied with a soft smile, tying a confection more closely resembling a display of fruit from Gunter's window than a bonnet upon her own brown curls. "Has the dogcart been brought round?"

"Only a moment ago. Oh, Rennie, I am so very happy!" Propriety sighed, flopping down altogether indelicately upon one of the fireside chairs.

"So I see." Serenity softly smiled, crossing to her clothespress to find the perfect shawl to wear with her merino, pausing to finger the clean, neatly folded garrick instead. "And so you should be on your wedding day."

"Oh, dearest," her sister remarked, at last sensing her sister's mood, "am I terribly callous to feel as I do? James is quite overset, yet he wishes to please me."

"I am persuaded he is just as anxious as you are, Proppie," Serenity consoled, taking the garrick into her arms. "Besides, his world shall right itself again just as soon as Chilton returns."

Rising slowly from her chair, Propriety's eyes brightened with concern. "Rennie," she said softly, gently, "I spoke with Father this morning . . ."

"Did you?" Serenity asked, stroking the garrick sleeve. "Concerning my irrational behavior of late, of course," she concluded, "which, as it happens, shall soon be proven to be not at all irrational. Chilton shall come, Proppie."

Near the fire, Propriety's jaw set. "It seems Chilton's passing has affected you more deeply than any of us believed," she tautly noted. "Darling . . ."

". . . He shall come, Proppie."

Seeing the familiar obstinacy flare in her sister's eyes, Propriety approached from a different direction. "I vow that I cannot comprehend all this, Rennie. Why such sudden loyalty to the marquess? James and I became persuaded that your feelings for the curmudgeon had ended long ago. If you recall, you were the one who convinced us of the fact. Did something happen while the two of you were together to change that?"

"The simplest of things," Serenity admitted with a soft smile, slipping the garrick about her shoulders. "We at last took the time to talk about what happened that night . . . to uncover the secrets. Oh, Proppie, the entire bumble-broth was no more than a horrid mistake! . . . and both of us too stubborn and proud to allow the possibility!" She laughed. "In the end, however, we were able to accept that our feelings for one another had really never altered."

"After all this time," Propriety sighed, her gaze bleeding compassion, shaking her head, "and after all James's and my attempts to force the two of you into one another's company. La, why did it not occur to us to lock you in a tide mill?"

"Hopefully, because good sense prevailed." Serenity chuckled. "Some things must simply be worked out on their own terms."

"And . . . were they?" Propriety asked, her gaze intensifying.

"I have just told you so," Serenity replied, slipping her arms into the garrick sleeves. "Why do you ask again?"

"Because . . . oh, darling, even James has concluded that Chilton cannot have gone missing this long and still have survived. And you were alone in his company for so long. Rennie, did you and he . . . ? Dearest, did he leave you with . . . ?"

". . . No." Serenity smiled. "Nor would it matter if he had. He shall come back to me, Proppie."

"Oh, darling . . ." her sister whispered, crossing to draw her into her arms.

". . . Not a bit of it," Serenity stated, firmly pushing Propriety away. "He will. I cannot know why he is taking so long, of course, but he shall come soon. He promised."

"Rennie . . ." Propriety breathed, her eyes filling with tears. "Dearest, you must try to accept . . ."

". . . No, *you* must accept, Proppie, that I shall not," Serenity countered. "Now, goodness, I am persuaded that we must be putting everyone below out of countenance with our dawdling," she stated, busily securing her fruit platter with a hatpin. "Mama must already be in the dog-cart waiting for me to take the ribbons. Do you know, Prop-pie, I became quite the whip during my adventure," she remarked, taking her sister's arm, then striding quickly toward the door. "Chilton was altogether impressed. Why, with no hesitation at all, he gave me complete charge over his curricle and four."

"Did he indeed, dearest?" Propriety asked, swiping at tears.

"Oh, yes! Did you ask Devlin to harness Baby to the cart as I requested, Proppie?" Serenity asked.

"I did, darling."

"Well, come along then," she responded, ushering Pro-priety into the hall. "Mama must be altogether exhausted from standing so long, and I am quite looking forward to giving all of you a demonstration of my newly acquired skill."

The wedding ceremony began not long after the party from the crowded dog cart had entered St. Mary's narthex and again adjusted their clothing—the gentlemen to sort out their various beavers; the ladies to return proper shawls to their assorted owners and to tuck order back into their *à la Tites* and *à la grêque's*. Four of them proceeded, then, to stand before the altar: James and Propriety, of course, as the bride and groom; Serenity and the Right Reverend Paul Torrent as their attendants—the bishop called into service, as was only proper, of course, in the place of his absent nephew, the marquess.

In compensation for the complete shattering of mourn-ing taboos, what audience was in attendance consisted only of close family, those worthy souls who had remained behind to lend their support, unsolicited opinions, and appetites during the trying time following Serenity's Ordeal: Lady Mary Torrent, Marchioness of Chilton; Mrs. Augustus Hoffenduffle, wife of the vicar; and the earl and Countess of Swinburne, come all the way from London to witness their niece's wedding in that devilish snowstorm, and damned if, after all that effort, they would turn right around and go home again so soon.

In addition there was in attendance Miss Sarah Tilburn, the church's thin, transparent-tissued organist, who, after a spate of powerful piping as the principals had marched down the aisle, had been duly nodded toward by the vicar, an accustomed banishment to an unobtrusive post several rows behind the carved screen constructed to mask the choir.

At the head of them all, however, resplendent in his vestments, stood the Reverend Augustus Hoffenduffle, who peered down at his daughters over his glasses, then, after harrumphing and loudly reaming out his vocal chords, at last flourished the Book of Common Prayer.

"Dear friends . . ." he intoned in a voice rolling with deep vibrato, raking his gaze across his audience as if the heavens had opened and all below had just heard the Archangel, "we have gathered today . . ." he thundered, "to join this man and this woman in holy matrimony . . ."

"Without me?" came a sudden voice from the narthex. "How very inconsiderate. I am hurt . . . highly offended . . . pierced, I vow, to the core."

Instantly all eyes turned toward the sound.

"And make that *men* and *women* who are to be joined together, if you please, sir," the intruder continued, starting forward. "I've a mind for a double ceremony."

"Rand!" James cried, racing forward to meet his brother's rapid approach in a crushing embrace. "Thank God!"

"And a few others," the marquess allowed, clapping James upon his shoulder.

"Randall, my boy!" the bishop exclaimed upon his arrival at the reunion, imposing an exuberant hug upon his nephew before being displaced by the marchioness. "Whatever in the world? . . ."

"Chilton!" Propriety whispered, appearing below his nose with eyes awash in tears, to his everlasting astonishment, throwing her arms about his waist. "We thought . . . we thought you were . . ."

"Did you?" he asked with a wry smile, dropping a kiss upon her cheek before disengaging from her cling. At last, over the tops of each of their heads, he let his gaze rest upon Serenity still standing immobile before the altar. "Did you *all?* . . .

"Well? . . ." he repeated after a time, cocking his head to the side, slowly spreading his arms.

"No, we did not," Serenity stated tersely, her huge blue eyes swimming with tears. "We never doubted for a moment that you would return. And you are quite late, Chilton," she accused.

"Unconscionably."

"It is also my opinion that you have a great deal of explaining to do," she groused, afterward biting her lip to still an annoying quiver.

"And so I shall," the marquess whispered. "But, first, my love, come here. My arms are getting deucedly tired suspended here as they are, and I need to hold you."

"And well you might, given the fright you subjected me to," she chided, dashing a lengthening runnel from her flushed skin. "Hieing me here and there about the countryside in a terrible snowstorm . . . subjecting me to mortal danger and then altogether abandoning me . . ."

"Serenity, love, *mercy!* . . ." Chilton laughed.

". . . Making far too free with personal portions of my personhood, Randall Torrent!" she indicted, fists now balled at her sides.

"Serenity, for the love of . . ." the marquess growled, glancing about the room.

". . . What's this?" the vicar bellowed from far above them. "Making free with what?"

"I suppose you think you may simply stroll down the aisle and find me more than willing to beg at your feet for the honor of becoming your wife," she scolded, her fists rising to take root upon her hips.

"Serenity . . ." the marquess repeated, adjusting his expression to perplexity.

". . . Where have you been, sir?" she finally shouted. "And why did you send no word of your circumstance?"

"Dearest . . . your *tone!*" Mrs. Hoffenduffle shrieked softly, glancing toward the marchioness, hiding her mortification behind a waffling of painted chicken skin.

"Serenity, I was in no position to send word," Rand stated quietly. "I was being held captive."

Instantly, Serenity's pique ended.

"By Tyson?" she breathed, fingers rising to her lips.

"As a matter of fact, by Bradshaw," the marquess ruefully shrugged.

"Mr. Bradshaw!" Serenity exclaimed, her jaw prettily dropping. "But he . . ."

". . . Somehow survived," Rand completed with a smile, "then managed to put a period to those of the rogue group Tyson had ordered to remain behind to guard him while he and the rest of his cutthroats pursued us. That done, he next went after Tyson himself."

"Which would have led him straight to you," Serenity concluded.

"Just in the nick of time," Chilton nodded. "I was at the point of throwing snowballs when Bradshaw and his men arrived."

"Dear heaven!" Serenity whispered, tears again flooding her eyes. "Chilton . . . !"

"It was most unsettling, I can tell you." The marquess

sighed, widening his arms' invitation while he cast Serenity a doleful glance. "Of a certainty, a man could benefit from a hug after such an ordeal."

Nearby, Serenity's lips pursed. "A woman would benefit more from a continuation of your explanation," she quelled.

Disgruntlement played over the marquess's brow. "Bradshaw had the element of surprise," he at last replied, his voice no longer coaxing. "The fighting was furious, but in the end, he overcame."

"And this man Tyson?" James asked.

"Killed," Rand told him, "along with the rest of his men."

"Yet . . . you were spared," Serenity realized, letting her shoulders relax.

"Yes, because Bradshaw was never motivated by self-gain in what he did, my dear," the marquess responded softly. "His sole aim was the furthering of the Catholic Emancipation cause. Murdering innocent people was never a part of his political aim. Besides, we had been partners, he and I . . . on a certain level, friends. Never once did he wish me actual harm, yet at the end he knew that if he let me go free after he had put a period to Tyson, I would have no choice but to bring the authorities down upon him. He and the others had, after all, committed treason. He knew that it would have been my duty as a member of Lords to see him brought to justice, and that there was no way under heaven that I could shirk the obligation."

"And so he took you captive?" Serenity concluded.

"For a time . . ." Rand nodded. "Until he could arrange passage to the Continent for himself and the others who survived." The marquess chuckled softly then. "Most likely by now they are already planning a way to smuggle themselves into Ireland to join with O'Connell."

"Do you truly think so?" Serenity asked.

"There is little doubt. He is a resourceful fellow, my

dear. He will be safe. Now," he stated, again widening his arms' stretch, "as you are finally in possession of the complete story of why I could not let you know where I was or what had happened to me after I sent you ahead to Woodbridge, will you please come here?"

"Now?" she breathed, still hesitating.

"Now."

"But . . . it would not be at all proper," she whispered, glancing about at their audience before releasing a tiny sigh.

"No, only terribly necessary," he husked. "Do you not understand, my dearest? I *need* to touch you again and hold you. Only then will I know for certain that you have come to no harm."

"Oh, Rand," Serenity finally sobbed, "I need to hold you, too."

"Well, come here then, deuce take it!" he implored.

Only the twentieth part of a moment later, the marquess was squeezing the very marrow from Serenity's bones.

"Here, now!" the vicar boomed from behind the altar.

"Yes, sir," Rand called up to him, his voice rough with emotion. "At last I *am* here, and ready to do my duty by this rackety hoyden."

"Hoyden!" Serenity sniffed, rearing back from his embrace.

"Rackety hoyden," the marquess repeated, "was my exact expression, I believe."

"Jove, milord, are you saying that there is a *need* for you to do a duty by my daughter?" the vicar roared.

"I am afraid that there is, sir," Chilton stated.

"Rackety!" Serenity reprised.

"Oh, I say!" the reverend heartily expelled, pounding upon the lectern. "We shall have words about this later, milord, I assure you. But for now, you had best stand before me, sir!"

"An excellent suggestion," Rand commented, stepping ahead.

"Beg pardon, my boy," the bishop suddenly called to his attention, "but you cannot be thinking to make your *amende honorable* today!"

"Oh? Why not, Uncle?" the marquess inquired, halting with a pleasant smile.

"I most certainly am *not* a hoyden!" Serenity insisted, tapping upon his chest. "Rackety or otherwise . . ."

". . . Because, barring three weeks of reading the banns, lad, you would need a special license from the Archbishop . . ." his uncle told him.

". . . And if anyone in this room is impossible, Chilton . . ."

". . . If you will notice, my boy, you do not have a special license," the bishop finished.

"*I* do," James then startlingly declared.

All eyes but Serenity's turned toward him.

". . . It is *you* who is impossible!" she muttered instead, giving his musculature another jab.

"James, never say that you and Propriety at some point intended to elope!" the marquess exclaimed with a bark of surprise.

"Of course not," James chided.

"You, after all, are irascible . . ." Serenity informed him.

"This license is for you . . . always has been," James continued, digging down into his waistcoat pocket to produce a piece of folded parchment. "See?" he said, opening the sheet. "Your own name is upon it."

"Whyever are you carrying around a special license for me?" the marquess asked with astonishment.

"Well . . ." James began rather sheepishly, "if you must know, so that on the odd chance one of Propriety's and my schemes should have actually worked, all would be ready."

"You devil!" Rand laughed, reaching over to slap his brother upon his back.

". . . And you never let me complete what you yourself have asked me to explain," Serenity added to the list.

"Deuce take it, let us begin then," the marquess commanded with enthusiasm, maneuvering Serenity toward the foot of the altar again, then taking his place beside her, James and Propriety positioning themselves just beyond. "Vicar, commence with the vows, if you please. I believe we all know why we are gathered here together."

"Why I should ever think that we could have a happy life together . . ." Serenity chastened, looking up at him, shaking her head. "You will be such a scold, Chilton, you know."

"Begin with the vows?" Reverend Hoffenduffle roared. "Most rag-mannered, to my way of thinking . . ."

". . . But expeditious," Rand interjected, dropping a kiss upon one of the grape clusters crowding Serenity's brim, then threading her hand through his arm.

"You will likely expect me to allow all manner of unseemly familiarities with portions of my person, will you not?" Serenity added. "Well I mean to tell you here and now, Chilton, I will not! . . ." she vowed.

". . . Consider, too, vicar, that such a shortcut *will* very quickly divest you of your happy responsibility for both Serenity and Propriety. For all time," the marquess added, smiling up at his future father-in-law.

Reminded of that, the vicar took only a moment for the semblance of thought.

"Will you, James Torrent, take Propriety Hoffenduffle for your lawfully wedded wife?" he suddenly boomed as, behind the choir screen, Miss Tilburn snorted into sentience and both proud mothers began to sniffle and sigh. "Will you promise to love, honor, and cherish her so long as you both shall live?"

"I will," James murmured.

"Will you, Propriety, take James for your lawfully wedded husband?" he then asked, shifting toward his daughter. "Will you promise . . ."

". . . No, I shan't," Propriety stated firmly, staring deeply into James's eyes. Just as quickly, then, her gaze softened. "But I *will* marry him," she whispered with a warm smile.

"Propriety!" Mrs. Hoffenduffle gasped.

"Never mind, madam," James laughed. "I shall happily take her however she comes."

"You will probably expect me to live the rest of my life never having a meaningful thought in my head," Serenity listed next, drawing in a deep breath and releasing it as a heavy sigh.

"Then by the authority vested in me . . ."

"Haste, vicar, haste," Rand reminded him.

"Oh, very well," Reverend Hoffenduffle harrumphed. "I now pronounce you man and wife. Now you, sir," he continued, swinging his gaze toward Rand. "Will you, Randall Torrent, Viscount Wallenford, Earl of Brumleigh, the Earl of Cranmoor, and the Marquess of Chilton, take Miss Serenity Hoffenduffle to be your lawfully wedded wife?"

"I will," Rand said with a wide grin.

"I *will,* however," Serenity insisted with a tiny stamp of her slippered foot. "I may not have attended Cambridge, Chilton, but there is not a thing lacking in my reasoning capabilities."

"And will you, Serenity, take Chilton to be your lawfully wedded husband?" her father asked.

"I *will* continue to read and learn!" she vowed.

"Well, daughter, will you?" her father bellowed down upon his second-born's rag-mannered inattention.

"Er . . . what did you say, Papa?" Serenity asked, at last aware that she had been addressed, looking up at him after blinking several times.

"Your father was merely wondering," the marquess interjected, "what it was you were saying, my love. Something about reading and learning? . . ."

"Indeed it was," she told him firmly. "I said that I *will,* Chilton."

"Would you mind repeating that?"

"I will," Serenity reprised.

"Excellent," he said, enfolding her in his arms. "Vicar? . . ."

"Then I pronounce you, too, man and wife," he stated with all finality, slapping his Book of Common Prayer shut.

"I am afraid you shan't think it is so wonderful, Chilton," Serenity continued, "when I tell you that for all the reasons I mentioned, I cannot marry you."

"Can you not?" the marquess asked, kissing the tip of her nose.

"No." Serenity sighed, patting him gently on the chest. "How shall we ever be happy, dear?"

"How shall we not?" the marquess laughed, squeezing her waist. "As I told you before, my love, we shall drive one another daft. Serenity, we shall never live a dull, tedious day for the rest of our lives. We shall have a marvelous time! Now, come along," he ordered, starting her down the aisle after his brother and his new wife. "We must return to London immediately. Parliament reconvenes in but three days for another vote on the Catholic Emancipation issue and I wish to be present in Lords to add my vote to Peel's."

"But . . ." Serenity objected, trying to balk at their steady forward progress, "but I cannot travel with you, Chilton. I would have to be married to you in order for that to be proper."

"Exactly so," he confirmed. "And so you are."

"What? *What?*"

"You shall have to sign the registry, of course," he told her, flourishing the parchment, "but you may do that after we return. James and Uncle Paul have already signed as witnesses."

"But . . . vows must be made, Chilton," she objected.

"And so they were."

"They were? . . . But, when? Oh, Chilton, never say so!

I cannot recall . . . Papa?" she called out, casting her father a bewildered look back down the length of the aisle.

"Have a pleasant trip, my child," he called back to her as he joined the bishop before the altar, waggling his fingers in her direction and giving her a benediction of a smile.

"But . . . I cannot be married!" Serenity gasped. "How could such a thing have happened without my knowing about it?"

"Well, you *are* rather forgetful," Rand suggested, struggling with a smile.

"Forgetful!" Serenity parroted, rounding on his poorly masked mirth. "Chilton, I vow . . . !"

". . . And you keep the deuce of a lot of nonsense in that 'ridicule' of yours," the marquess chided, finally reaching the narthex and opening the church's huge door, "which slowed my return considerably, I might mention. Once I had retrieved it from the tide mill and muscled it onto my curricle, my poor bloods were hard-pressed to haul the thing the five miles to Woodbridge. Do you know, I actually had to get down and walk beside the beasts to relieve them of some of their load?"

"Randall Torrent! . . ." Serenity warned.

"Yes, my love?" the marquess responded with a mischievous grin, pausing to sweep her against him and kiss her knees into aspic before stepping out into their wedding day's cold, crisp sunshine.

"You are a rag-mannered *Corinthian!* . . ."

"I am, am I not? And to think, my sweet, biddable Serenity . . . it shall only get worse."

". . . And you already *are* daft," she added, stepping toward the awaiting curricle.

"But you love me, Serenity," he teased, bending quickly to place an arm behind her knees, then hauling her up against his chest.

"Only half as much as you love me, Chilton," her father heard her counter with a laugh.

"Come along, then, wife," the marquess urged after again kissing her soundly. "London awaits, yet for some reason I have a rather powerful urge to pay one last visit to the tide mill."

"Powerful, eh?" Serenity commented, her sapphire eyes deepening with suspicion.

"Powerful," Rand growled with a waggling of his brows. " *Forte comme le chêne.*' "

"Randall Torrent!" Serenity exclaimed.

A moment later, the marquess's muscular bays surged forward down the road toward the Deben marsh, cutting short the marquess of Chilton's responding bark of laughter and, "If you think for one moment that I shall loll about for yet another evening on a pile of dusty grain sacks, you are to let in your attic!" . . . all that remained to drift to the villagers' ears on the winter air of his wife's serene, ladylike response.

After they had gone, gilded dust motes scattered silence over St. Mary's sanctuary.

"They shall be at each other like Bill Neate and the Gas-man, shan't they?" the vicar judged with a shake of his head.

"Like Shelton and Randall," the bishop nodded.

"Like two cocks at Westminster," the vicar concluded. "Yet what man is there in all England who could stand against her but Chilton?"

"None," the bishop responded. "But take heart, Augustus. What woman is there in all England who could make it a fair fight?"

"They do seem to love one another," Reverend Hoffenduffle nodded with a rumbling laugh, coming to stand beside his friend.

"They do, and it is a point in their favor, to be sure," the bishop agreed, putting his arm around the vicar and starting forward. "Now come, Augustus, let us trust that God knows what He is doing and go sample some of that roast I smelled earlier this morning. With two fewer mouths at the wedding breakfast, you know, there shall be all the more for us."

"You forget, sir," the vicar reminded him, opening the door for his superior, "Swinburne is here."

"Ah, yes, how remiss of me," the bishop responded with a boom of laughter that once more rattled Miss Tilburn from her snooze, vaulted her to her feet, then sent her scuttling again toward the organ.

"By the way, I meant to ask you, milord," the vicar inquired when they had navigated the length of the aisle and stepped outside. "Was I mistaken, or was my daughter wed in a garrick?"

"A garrick? Oh, I hardly think so, Augustus," the bishop judged. "That would have been most improper. But . . . did *you* notice . . . ?" he began, the usual assurance bolstering his voice oddly waning, ". . . was my nephew . . . ?"

"Was he what, milord?" the vicar kindly asked.

"Was my nephew . . . ? Oh, I am certain it is nothing, Augustus, but did you happen to notice . . . is it possible that my nephew was leg-shackled with a piece of blue wool stuck to his head?"

"Blue wool? Impossible," the vicar dismissed. "The man is a peer of the realm, sir."

"Indeed." The bishop nodded on a gushing sigh, smiling with relief. "Indeed he is, sir."

The heavy door closed behind the two men of God, then, and they started forward across the square.

All alone now within St. Mary's, Miss Tilburn began to pedal furiously. Soon a muffled recessional began to wheeze forth from the ancient organ to accompany them toward the manse.

ABOUT THE AUTHOR

Jenna Jones lives with her family in Phoenix, Arizona. She is the author of four Zebra regency romances: A MERRY ESCAPADE, A DELICATE DECEPTION, TIA'S VALENTINE, and SAVING SERENITY. Jenna is currently working on her next Zebra regency romance, THE CHRISTMAS BRIDE, which will be published in November 1998. She loves hearing from her readers and you may write to her c/o Zebra Books. Please include a self-addressed stamped envelope if you wish a response.

DANGEROUS GAMES   (0-7860-0270-0, $4.99)
by Amanda Scott

When Nicholas Barrington, eldest son of the Earl of Ulcombe, first met Melissa Seacort, the desperation he sensed beneath her well-bred beauty haunted him. He didn't realize how desperate Melissa really was . . . until he found her again at a Newmarket gambling club—being auctioned off by her father to the highest bidder. So, Nick bought himself a wife. With a villain hot on their heels, and a fortune and their lives at stake, they would gamble everything on the most dangerous game of all: love.

A TOUCH OF PARADISE   (0-7860-0271-9, $4.99)
by Alexa Smart

As a confidence man and scam runner in 1880s America, Malcolm Northrup has amassed a fortune. Now, posing as the eminent Sir John Abbot—scholar, and possible discoverer of the lost continent of Atlantis—he's taking his act on the road with a lecture tour, seeking funds for a scientific experiment he has no intention of making. But scholar Halia Davenport is determined to accompany Malcolm on his "expedition" . . . even if she must kidnap him!